Sarah's Education
Madeline Moore

This book is a work of fiction.
In real life, make sure you practise safe, sane and consensual sex.

First Published by Black Lace 2009

6 8 10 9 7

First published in Great Britain in 2009 by
Black Lace
Virgin Books
Random House, 20 Vauxhall Bridge Road,
London SW1V 2SA

www.blacklace.co.uk
www.virginbooks.com
www.randomhouse.co.uk

Addresses for companies within The Random House Group Limited can be found
at: www.randomhouse.co.uk/offices.htm

The Random House Group Limited Reg. No. 954009

A CIP catalogue record for this book is available from the British Library

ISBN 9780352345394

Typeset by TW Typesetting, Plymouth, Devon

The Random House Group Limited supports The Forest Stewardship
Council (FSC®), the leading international forest certification organisation.
Our books carrying the FSC label are printed on FSC® certified paper.
FSC is the only forest certification scheme endorsed by the leading
environmental organisations, including Greenpeace. Our
paper procurement policy can be found at
www.randomhouse.co.uk/environment

MIX
Paper from
responsible sources
FSC® C016897
www.fsc.org

Printed and bound in Great Britain by Clays Ltd, St Ives PLC

Sarah's Education

A thousand hummingbirds fluttered their tiny cold wings inside Sarah's tummy. Dragging her feet, and having no problem looking scared, she rounded the bed and bent over his left knee. His right knee clamped hers. He'd done this before. His hand pushed down between her shoulder blades.

What was she supposed to do with her hands? Veronica should have given her lessons.

Sarah felt her skirt being lifted. Christ, here it comes. Any moment now . . .

A hand smoothed over her bum, which might as well have been bare for all the protection her thong gave her. Maybe the thong had been a mistake. If there'd been some sort of fabric covering her cheeks, it might have helped.

'Very nice,' he said.

That was her bottom he was talking about. One cheek was compressed gently. Perhaps he wasn't actually going to spank her. Perhaps it would be pretend, not for real. He was stroking her skin now, as if he was admiring it, not at all as if he . . .

1

The pink marble wall was cool to the touch. Sarah trailed her fingertips along it as she ventured further into the brand-new Toledo Royal Avenue Hotel. Great glittering crystal chandeliers lit the huge space. Urns of fresh tropical flowers and exotic fleshy plants created a bright, welcoming look that softened the austerity of the marble and brass décor. If it hadn't been for the watchful eye of the concierge Sarah would've pressed her flushed cheek to the marble to soak up some of the cool. But he was watching, and she suspected she knew what he was thinking: *What's that cheeky little schoolgirl doing in my fancy new hotel?*

He couldn't be blamed. She'd just finished a shift as a tour guide for Seneca University, and the powers that be decreed that their guides wear old-fashioned uniforms of short tartan kilts, crisp white shirts, white bobby socks and black patent Mary Janes.

Her chestnut hair was caught up in two untidy bunches that approximated pigtails. She wore no make-up, not even a coat of mascara on her lashes or a gloss of colour on her lips. Sarah didn't think she needed make-up – her lashes were thick and her lips were lush and pink. Her eyes, which she considered her best feature, were wide set and such a dark blue that they'd been compared to sapphires (by her dad, true, but still . . .) and described as navy blue by her boyfriend, David. She'd never felt the need to colour her lids or her cheeks or her mouth – not until now, when she wished with all her heart she could suddenly look like a grown woman, not a little girl. A woman who belonged here.

It would pass. The awkwardness she always felt in new places would fade away as she got used to the hotel, if she lingered long enough. She was tempted to hoist up her knapsack, heavy with books, and turn tail, but she resisted the impulse. It was steamy hot outside, more like the middle of summer than the end. There was nowhere for her to go, nowhere but home to her room or to David's place, where he, a teaching assistant in the history department, was conscientiously marking the first papers of the fall semester and nursing the first of his winter colds. She flushed with anger. No way.

A loud whoop resounded in the cavernous lobby.

A lobby bar! Sarah's lucky day, and why not? It *was* her birthday, after all.

She glanced longingly at the exclusive shops that called to her, like sirens, from the right side of the lobby. It would only take ten minutes to pick up the clothes and make-up she needed to masquerade as a woman of means. Ten minutes and a credit card that wasn't already maxed out, as hers was. No.

Much as she might enjoy the feel of silk or suede against her skin, it wasn't to be. No more so than a room in this hotel, likely cool and understated, with fresh flowers and a spacious bed made up with luxurious linens and a pristine white duvet, waiting for her to enter and make it hers. No.

But a split of champagne, in the lobby bar? Yes. That she could *almost* afford. That was why she was here. She'd waited for this moment for a long, long while, never once succumbing to the urge to so much as slug back a beer or sip a margarita or a zombie or a screwdriver. She'd had a plan, ever since puberty had ripened her, and she'd kept to it: she'd lose her virginity on the very day she could legally drink, age twenty-one. Not old, but not too young, either. To sip champagne and lose herself in sexual delight – both for the very first time – it had seemed a perfect plan. Worth waiting for. But plans have a way of not working out.

That didn't stop her from making them. Sarah had a well-ordered mind; she was smart, conscientious and skilled at absorbing information and extrapolating possibilities. These skills should have helped her make sense of the world, which she desperately wanted to do. But people rarely behaved as expected; there were so many variables in the real world, too many, in her opinion. Sarah was beginning to think she'd never find her place in it. She would always be a weirdo, an outsider in a world that must make sense to some, but never would to her.

Bah. Just because stupid David had forgotten her birthday didn't mean she had to suffer all day. With a longing farewell glance at the enticing shops she veered to the left.

Before she could venture into the lobby bar and find a table for one, she was intercepted by the bartender. He held out his hand. For a moment she thought he expected a tip before serving her.

'ID?' he asked.

Right. Sarah let her knapsack drop and bent over to root for her wallet. She produced her driver's licence for inspection, and was gratified when he said, 'Happy birthday, Ms Meadows.'

'Thank you.'

'Your party is right over here.'

Sarah hoisted her knapsack back up and followed. Her party? She glanced around, half expecting to see David at a table, champagne in a bucket and a room key in hand. It would be so great to discover he hadn't forgotten her birthday, especially this particular one, and instead had arranged a magnificent . . .

The bartender led her to two thirty-ish men in business suits and three younger, vivacious women. All three were dressed in sexy, sophisticated party clothes; one in a very off-the-shoulder top, two with deep cleavages. Before Sarah could protest, she was greeted effusively by the two men and a chair was pulled out for her.

She sat.

'I'm Jack,' said a good-looking man, extending his hand, 'and this is my partner Bill. You are . . .?'

'I'm Sarah.'

'Glad you could make it – finally,' muttered one of the women.

3

'I got lost,' Sarah mumbled, not understanding how she could be late for an appointment she hadn't known she had. Still, in a way it was the truth. After her shift she'd headed into downtown Toledo to pick up the textbooks she'd ordered from Barnes and Noble, using a gift card she'd received for Christmas. It had seemed worth the extra effort to use it, rather than spend cash at the university book store. But, of course, she'd gotten lost trying to get back to campus from the City. She had zero sense of direction. Nothing short of a personal GPS would make it possible for her to go anywhere without winding up spinning in a confused circle, wondering where the hell she was. It always happened. It always made her mad.

Even worse, a young passer-by, a straw-haired, snub-nosed girl in a too-young too-short candy-striped poplin dress, had asked for directions to this very hotel. Sarah had said, in her best tour-guide voice, 'The Royal Avenue Hotel is about ten blocks south, I think.' The gum-smacking girl had not been pleased. Five minutes later Sarah had turned the corner to discover the new downtown Toledo Royal Avenue. Some tour guide she was!

'No problem, no problem,' said Jack. 'What are you drinking?'

'It's my birthday today. I was planning to order a split of champagne.'

'Your birthday! Marvellous! Bartender, a magnum of Dom Perignon, please.'

'I can't – I couldn't possibly –'

'Birthdays come but once a year. And we're celebrating, right, Bill? We just sold our dot-com company for ... well ... a great deal of money.'

'Congratulations.'

Bill piped up. 'It's a coup, no less. We set it up just in time to be a thorn in the side of the major web-based industries and, sure enough, one was forced to buy us out. Thanks to Jack, here, we're set for life.'

Set for life. What must that feel like? Pay off her student loan, her car loan, the repairs to her car ... Sarah had no time to further ponder the concept.

Frosted flutes were set in front of everyone. The bartender presented a large, elegant bottle. 'Dom Perignon, 1998, sir,' he murmured. Jack nodded, and the bartender twisted the cork free. Jack motioned to the glass in front of Sarah, so she was the first to be served.

'It's so pretty,' she whispered. She couldn't help it. The pale-yellow liquid bubbled to a white froth on top. Glasses were raised all around.

'To Sarah,' said Jack. 'Happy birthday!' His dark eyes travelled her body, from her face to her patent Mary Janes, and back. He seemed to like what he saw.

'And to you, Jack and Bill.' Sarah glanced from Jack to his bigger, balding partner, and back.

'And to Andrea and Silky and Me-Me,' said one of the women. She eyed Sarah suspiciously. 'To a good time.'

Everyone clinked glasses.

Sarah had her first ever sip of alcohol. Stunning. The champagne burnt her tongue and bubbled up to her brain and down her throat at the same time. 'Wow,' she blurted, 'How delicious.'

'One would think you'd never tasted champagne before,' said the dusky, exotic woman whose name, Sarah had gleaned, was Silky.

'I haven't,' she confessed. 'I've never had an alcoholic drink before. I wanted to wait until I could drink legally, and then start out with champagne. But I wasn't expecting Dom Perignon, nor was I anticipating such a big bottle!'

'Adorable!' Jack was clearly pleased with her, even if the young women seemed standoffish. 'Let me top up your glass.'

He refilled her flute. Expensive foam dribbled down the side. Sarah's tongue flicked out to catch it. She didn't want to waste a drop of the precious fluid. This time, she poured a healthy amount down her throat. It didn't burn her mouth at all, but rather glided down like liquid silk. She giggled.

'Let's get out of here,' Jack said in a low, throaty voice.

'But – the champagne!' Sarah couldn't imagine leaving half a magnum of champagne behind. The very thought of it was painful.

'We'll take it with us,' said Jack. 'Let's go.'

He stood, as did Bill. The other three women stood as one, and Sarah was left with no choice, really, but to rise as well, though she swallowed the last of the wine in her glass first.

'Whoop!' She tottered a bit. 'This stuff is powerful,' she squeaked.

'God, you're too good to be true,' said Jack.

'That's for sure,' muttered the woman Sarah knew only as 'Me-Me'.

Jack tucked the magnum under his arm, which surely wasn't allowed, yet the bartender did nothing to stop him. He threw a wad of cash on the table. The party of six made its merry way out of the lobby bar and into the elevator. On the way up, Silky pulled Bill's head down for a long deep kiss, which paused when an elderly couple entered on the fifth floor and resumed when they exited at the tenth.

There were only two doors at the top floor of the hotel. Jack slid his key card into one and ushered everyone inside. It was nothing like Sarah had imagined, but then she'd envisioned a room, not a penthouse suite. A row of windows along the far wall allowed sunlight to bathe the huge central room, which was tastefully decorated and accented by vases of fresh-cut flowers and colourful art that had to be just as real as the flowers.

'Wow.'

'What?' Bill was looking at her. The other women were getting comfortable on the massive cream leather sectional, but Sarah was rooted to the spot.

'I'm . . . I'm overwhelmed by the decadence,' she said.

Jack laughed. 'You're perfect. Come, sit.' He relieved her of her knapsack. 'What's in this thing, bricks?'

'Books,' she said.

'You really take what you do very seriously, don't you?'

'Of course.'

Bill dived onto the sofa amidst the three women. Andrea and Me-Me fell on him like vandals, one loosening his tie and nibbling his ear while the other expertly slipped his belt free and off.

Silky tilted her head, her lipstick smeared, a cool look of enquiry in her eyes.

'Is there something you need?' Jack asked Sarah, his voice kind.

'Yes. I'd like to – um – take in the view.' Sarah felt she could trust him, even if the others seemed odd.

He laughed. 'You're a funny one,' he said, tugging one of her pigtails playfully. 'Go ahead. Join us when you're ready.'

Sarah practically skipped to the windows. Toledo was laid out before her like a relief map. There was the university, not that far away after all, and there was the airport. A jumbo jet was just taking off. She watched as it rose steeply, defying logic, tucked up its wheels and disappeared into the stratosphere.

'Fantastic!' She tore her gaze away from the window. All five of her companions were making out madly on the sectional, obviously not at all interested in the spectacular view. 'Oh.' Once again she was overwhelmed with the decadence of the scene.

Bill was now naked except for his open white dress shirt. Andrea was sliding down between his parted legs with feline grace. Me-Me nibbled at his left nipple and caressed his chest. His eyes were closed and his head was thrown back.

Jack, who Sarah had begun to think of as 'hers', was proceeding more slowly. Although Silky had kissed Bill fervently in the elevator, now she was kissing Jack. One of his hands was inside the top of her dress. Silky slipped down the spaghetti straps and tugged the blue satin down so that her large breasts were bared. Jack groaned and buried his face in the valley between them, still toying with one, so that while Sarah watched an espresso-dark nipple stiffened at the centre of an areola like a perfectly round puddle of milk chocolate pudding.

It was shocking. It was sexy. She didn't know what to do. This view in the suite was even more enticing than the one outside the window. She edged closer, quietly, not wanting to interrupt.

Silky's hand dropped down to Jack's lap. The outline of his penis, straining against the crotch of his trousers, made it clear he was turned on.

Everyone was writhing, as if a sex switch had been thrown in the few minutes Sarah had spent watching a plane take flight.

She was used to foreplay. Endless foreplay that led nowhere. Control. Abstinence. Sobriety. This was the opposite of everything she knew.

Her cheeks were hot again, not from anger this time, but from – what? Embarrassment? No. Her private parts were tingling, as if she'd taken another sip of champagne and this time it had travelled, not dispersing throughout her body but flowing directly to her clitoris and nipples. Watching the uninhibited, amorous group at play was an incredible turn-on. The word stuck in her brain. Turn-on, like that sex switch she'd imagined, or any machine that hummed to life the moment you pressed the right button. Her clit begged to be that button. Touch me. Turn me. On.

Jack called to her. 'C'm'ere baby, come play with us.'

'I want to,' she said, 'really I do, but I'm scared.'

Me-Me clucked disapprovingly. Silky and Andrea ignored Sarah. Silky reached down and popped the buttons of Jack's fly while Andrea grasped Bill's hard-on by its thick base and started sucking him off, as cool as you please.

'Don't be afraid,' said Jack, his hips twitching against the squirming hand that Silky had slipped into his fly. 'We're not going to hurt you.'

'I've never done anything like this before.' Sarah edged closer to the leather sectional, closer to him, closer to the door.

Jack laughed. 'Right! Of course you haven't.' He rose, which sent Silky sprawling sideways on the couch. Jack tucked himself in as he came to where Sarah stood. 'Come with me,' he said, and took her hand.

The last thing Sarah saw before Jack closed the bedroom door was Silky, scrambling to join Andrea at Bill's feet.

'I'm sorry,' she mumbled. 'I didn't mean to break up the party.'

'No problem. Those girls are a dime a dozen. You're something special. This is your first time, right?'

'Right.'

'A sweet virgin who's never had a drink before, never been fucked. A schoolgirl who needs a man to teach her the joys of sex.'

Sarah nodded.

Jack picked her up and sat her on the bed. He knelt between her legs, so that she was higher than him, and kissed her.

It was nothing like David's kisses, which were always either tentative or sloppy. This kiss was commanding, its intention clear. She was being taken. She kissed him back, mouth open, tongue flitting, and it went on for some time. When it stopped, they stared at each other with mutually misty eyes.

'Take off your shirt,' he said. She did. 'Your bra, too.' She did.

'They're not as big as Silky's,' she apologised.

'They're perfect.' He covered each of her breasts with one of his hands. His fingers widened so that her pale-pink nipples poked between his knuckles. He nibbled one, then the other. A delicious thrill raced through Sarah. Obviously, she was in the hands of a consummate lover. Her nipples stiffened and darkened, so that when he raised his mouth from them it was as if he might've been wearing lipstick and had transferred the colour with his kisses.

He stood and stripped off. His penis was erect. It seemed huge.

Sarah's finger touched the tip, tentatively. He shuddered. She'd done that.

He reached under her kilt and stripped her of her white cotton panties. 'I should probably eat you,' he said, 'to make you good and wet. This being your first time and all.'

'I'd like that,' she replied, 'but I think I'm plenty wet already.' She touched herself and nodded. 'Yup,' she said.

Jack laughed. 'You kill me, kiddo,' he said. He stood between her legs so that his cock was wagging right under her nose. 'Make my cock wet, then,' he said.

Sarah circled it with her lips. It wasn't the first time she'd had a penis in her mouth. On a few occasions David had whined so piteously she'd topped off a handjob by sucking him for a few minutes until he spurted in her mouth. This was different, though. For one thing, Jack was in complete control of himself, and the situation. She felt sure he wouldn't come from a few flicks and twirls of her tongue.

And his cock, which was the right word for it, this thick warm thing that grew even bigger inside her mouth, his cock was much bigger than David's, and circumcised, so that the head was prominent, making it seem more naked, and so braver, somehow, than David's.

'So you've given head before?'

She nodded, his cock still in her mouth.

'That's nice,' he said. 'Do it again.'

She nodded again, kept her tongue moving, her lips soft but tight around him.

He didn't shove it down her throat as she feared he might. He just stood, making little approving noises, while she tickled and teased him to the very best of her ability.

'Lie down.' He withdrew. Pushed her back onto the bed. Slid a condom on. Bent over her. Raised her skirt up to her tummy. Put his cock to her pussy's tender lips. Plunged.

'Christ, you're tight,' he muttered. He pushed harder and gained another few inches.

Sarah didn't make a sound. It hurt, more than she'd anticipated. Perhaps there'd be blood after all, even though she'd spent her early summers at a riding camp. She'd hate to make a mess on the fluffy duvet but more than anything she'd hate to interrupt Jack from – ouch.

'I'm in,' said Jack. He was bent over her, supporting his weight on his hands. He shook his head, trying to get his floppy dark hair out of his eyes. 'Why didn't you tell me you were so tight?'

Sarah brushed his hair back for him. 'I don't think it's so much about me being so tight as you being so big.'

He laughed. 'You've got all the lines, Schoolgirl Sarah.'

Jack pulled back. She'd been so filled by him that she could feel his cock tugging at the slick lining of her pussy. He paused at the opening and rocked back and forth, teasing her labia and clit with the head of his cock.

Sarah yipped.

'What was that?' Jack grinned at her. He continued the little movements that kept the head just inside her.

'I don't know. Please –' She was mortified by the injured puppy noise she'd made but he was torturing her, admittedly in a most enjoyable way. She just had to get that cock deeper inside. She humped her hips at him, gaining an inch. She yipped again.

'Baby's cock-hungry, hmm?'

His words were coarse but she liked it. She nodded, jerked her hips, yipped again. It seemed she might come, given enough time, although she'd never had an orgasm without direct clitoral stimulation before. Sarah didn't want to wait to find out.

'May I?' She wiggled her fingers.

'Allow me,' he said. He pressed his thumb to her clit and rotated it in slow circles. At the same time he let her have another few inches, so that he was properly pumping into her once more.

'Oh my God, that's so good!' Sarah's blue eyes were wide with astonishment. 'I mean really, really good. Fantastic!'

'You like?' He seemed highly amused by her, but in a benevolent way. He'd be laughing with her, not at her, if she were laughing.

But she wasn't laughing, she was making that strange yipping noise. It embarrassed her half to death but she couldn't stop, especially not when he was fucking her long and slow, filling a part of her that had never seemed empty before, but clearly had been.

'You like to fuck?'

She nodded. Her eyes were locked on to his. She wanted to do something, to stroke his back or his balls or something to show she could give as well as take. But he was in charge and he seemed pleased to fuck her like this. To make that odd little sound escape her lips again, and again, until she truly was yipping like a wild thing, a horny wild she-beast that needed just a little more ... a little more ...

On impulse she squeezed her breasts together and up, using her hands as a push-up bra. 'Fuck me hard, please. I have to come now or I'll die!'

She saw the surprise in his eyes, the pleasure in his smile, and then he was thrusting, withdrawing, thrusting again, his thumb still steady, moving in tiny circles, and now it was as if only his cock inside her and his thumb on her clit anchored her to the bed as the she-beast inside her unfurled its wings and soared.

Someone was making a lot of noise. Oh! It was her. Sarah yipped as each contraction caught and held her suspended for an obliterating moment, then yipped again as she was released to soar some more.

He was yelling now, and fucking her furiously. For a moment she focused on his face above her, dreamy dark eyes and a fabulous smile. Her orgasm was abating; paroxysms of pleasure had become pleasant tremors. Before she could gather her senses another one began, and she was helplessly yipping and soaring even higher.

More noise. Knocking? Cheering? Flashbulbs popping? Impossible.

Jack collapsed on top of her. His weight pinned her in place. On a bed. In a swanky hotel suite. She wrapped her arms around him and held him. They were both trembling.

She opened her eyes.

'Bravo!'

Bill and Silky and Andrea and Mimi, which was obviously what 'Me-Me' meant, she now realised, were standing naked in the doorway to the room.

Jack withdrew. She knew, for the very first time, how it felt to be achingly empty inside.

'Can we play, too?' Bill was grinning. The girls were also smiling, though some smiles seemed forced.

'Beat it,' said Jack.

'We thought maybe someone was being murdered,' said Silky.

'I said get out.'

They left, closing the door softly behind them.

Jack collapsed on the bed beside Sarah. 'Fuck, that was fantastic.'

'I thought flashbulbs were exploding, like those big boxy cameras the paparazzi used in the olden days.'

'Funny.'

'Yes, but true. Just like in the movies. I saw stars!'

'I saw a train disappearing into a tunnel.'

'You did not!' Sarah hadn't known him long, but she could already tell he was teasing.

'No. I saw a gorgeous young woman coming like a house on fire and it made me crazy. Made me come.'

Sarah sat up. 'I'm grateful,' she said. 'You made my first time special.'

'You're welcome,' he said, a wry smile on his lips.

'Now what?' Sarah grinned at him.

'Now we do it again,' he replied.

It was exactly the answer she'd hoped for but a playful impulse prompted her to roll onto her tummy, as if to deny him. To her shocked surprise, she felt the flat of his open palm come down hard across her bottom. It stung. Was he angry with her? But no, he couldn't be, because his hands gripped her hips and pulled her up on all fours. Sarah wriggled her bum encouragingly. He whacked her again.

She didn't know how to respond. Should she at least act offended until she decided if she was? She should probably say or do something before – too late. A third deliberate sharp slap landed and the happy moan that escaped her lips made any pretence at being annoyed impossible.

'What a bad little schoolgirl you are,' he told her. His voice was warm with admiration.

'I know,' she whispered. 'Please, Jack, make me badder.'

Sarah hollowed her back, blatantly presenting her sex like a vixen inviting the attentions of a dog fox. She watched over her shoulder as he slid a fresh condom onto his erection. The few spanks he'd heated her bum with had obviously turned him on, too. Interesting. She looked forward to thinking about everything that was transpiring, later. But right now . . .

Jack's big hands took her hips once more. She spread her knees further apart and braced herself. He entered her, the position affording him a deeper penetration. Sarah's thoughts scattered like tossed Scrabble tiles. She was free.

2

A sharp, most unwelcome, rat-a-tatting yanked Sarah from a deep, dreamless sleep. She moaned into her pillow. She had a splitting headache, the kind any nascent drinker would experience when she drank, not a split of champagne, but almost a magnum. Oh God. Was that awful noise merely the sound of her pulse pounding at her temples? No. There it was again. Probably Bill and company trying to move in on them again. But why wasn't Jack telling them to get lost? Oh God. Bill. Jack. Those girls. She opened her eyes.

Where Jack's head had lain the previous night there was an envelope with her name on it. She was alone. 'Jack?' Her voice was hoarse and no wonder. Her mouth was dry, as if she'd eaten sand the night before, and not the marvellous midnight meal the two of them had enjoyed.

A glass of water and two Tylenol sat on the bedside table. She gratefully sipped the water, popped the tablets into her mouth and sipped again. 'Oh God.' It was all coming back to her now.

The knocking had blessedly stopped. The doorknob to the room turned. She hoped it was Jack, coming back to her, but no, it was a rather large woman with an unmistakably disapproving look on her face.

'Housekeeping.' Her voice was flat. Her eyes took in the messy bedroom, the rumpled sheets, the empty bottle, the girl alone in the big bed.

'Have you seen my friends?'

'They go. You go too.'

'Fine. Two minutes.'

The big woman closed the door. Sarah heard a vacuum start up. Ouch.

She got up. Got dressed. Grabbed the envelope from the pillow. Left the bedroom.

The living room was a terrible mess, even worse than the bedroom. No wonder the housekeeper was disgusted. Still, weren't they supposed to be polite to guests? Everyone had been so nice the night before, serving and bowing with professional flair.

Sarah brushed a few half-eaten crab legs off her knapsack, pretending not to see that one ragged shell had fallen inside it. She hoisted the knapsack to her shoulder. The housekeeper was ignoring her. Good.

It was all so difficult: the ride down the elevator; the eyes of tourists checking in and out all seemed to be checking her out, as if they'd never seen a dishevelled girl in a rumpled kilt before.

Coffee. Desperate for coffee. But not here. Sarah was in danger of swelling to twice her normal size – not literally, but it might just as well be. When she was supremely uncomfortable in her surroundings she sometimes felt huge, clumsy, uncoordinated. It was a trick of her mind, she knew, but knowing neither kept it from happening nor made it bearable. Best to get out of this elegant hotel and find a greasy spoon somewhere, a place where she wouldn't stand out like a huge sore thumb on an exquisitely manicured hand.

Outside, brutal sunlight punished her skull. Oh God. Oh God. 'I'll never drink again,' she muttered. Half prayer, half oath. It was horrible to feel like this. Horrible to be so ruined after such a magical night. Her legs creaked.

Her bum hurt when she plopped into a banquette in the first café she encountered. She knew why her legs hurt, and her crotch, but her bum? Right. He'd spanked her a little, once, and then a little more. Gripped her cheeks tight when he took her from behind. God. She felt like she'd spent the day before on a day-long ride, bareback on a stallion too big for her.

She dreaded the long walk back to her house. She could take

a bus but she'd probably throw up if she did. Oh God. If only she could take a cab. Sarah cursed her luck. She should never have bought that ancient Volvo. What good was a car when it was always in the shop? The mechanics had refused her any more credit, so, although her car was repaired now, it was as good as gone, except for the payments she was still making on it. David should never have co-signed that car loan. David. Oh God.

It wasn't until she'd finished her second cup of coffee that she remembered the envelope Jack had left behind. She fished it from her knapsack, confident that it contained his contact information. She was quite sure she was in love with him, and last night she'd have bet any amount that he felt the same.

There was no note. Just bills, a lot of them. She started to count. Two thousand five hundred dollars.

The penny dropped.

Four girls, three of them sexy and sophisticated, and her, but there'd only been two men. Sex from the moment the six of them were alone. Three of the girls willing to share one of the men.

Damn!

She'd been taken for a whore – a high-class one but still a whore. Her very first fuck and she'd been paid for it. If only she'd known; if only she'd understood. But that was Sarah's curse. IQ tests and her grades said she was smart – smart enough to have skipped grade eight – but socially, she was always a step and a half behind everyone else. Often, when other people seemed to understand the undercurrents in conversations, she'd just smile and nod while her brain squirrelled around, trying to catch up. It had got her into trouble often – like the first time she'd joined in a heavy-petting make-out party and been bewildered by the spinning bottle. Even before, when she'd agreed to play Post Office and had been pleasantly shocked when a boy kissed her – her first real kiss. And now, her first fuck, also the result of her lack of understanding.

But it hadn't been 'just a fuck'. It'd meant much more to her, and to Jack, she was sure. He hadn't treated her like a prostitute. He'd been kind, and gentle, except for the whacks on her bum, which had been playful, at least. Boy, did she have some explaining to do the next time she saw him. Maybe, years into the future, they'd look back on the misunderstanding that had brought them together and laugh. Yes, she was sure they would.

Poor David! He'd blown his chance with her and pretty well pushed her into Jack's arms.

Newly and exhilaratingly rich, she called a cab and had it take her to the Volvo dealership, where she paid her bill and filled up the tank. On the drive home she successfully resisted the desire to stop and shop a half-dozen times before finally succumbing. For the first time, she visited a sexy lingerie shop. Sarah chose a couple of daring pale-blue thongs, delicate as smoke caught in cobwebs, and a matching half-cup bra. The next time Jack reached up under her skirt, he wasn't going to find plain old white cotton panties.

Unless that was what he preferred? Hmm! Being sexually active was more complicated than she'd thought.

Sarah drove home to the big old house on Maple that she shared with five other students.

The front hallway was cluttered with suitcases and carry-on bags. She stared at them for a moment, her mouth open. Sarah recognised that blue duffel as her dad's. Her folks were here from St Paul? But where? She called David's number on the hall payphone that the student residents shared.

He answered with, 'Where the hell were you last night?'

'I – um – Andrea's? My friend – you don't know her. We had some drinks. I – um – slept over?' Why was she explaining and apologising when it was all David's fault? Her voice changed. 'Where was I supposed to be? You thought I'd stay in and mope after you forgot my damn birthday?'

'Oh!' It was his turn to be apologetic, or halfway apologetic, anyway. 'Did you really think I'd forget your special day? It was supposed to be a surprise. Your parents flew in. We were going to make a big night of it. I made reservations. When you didn't show, they went to their hotel.'

'Their luggage is here.'

'Most of the stuff at your place is presents. For you.'

'You should have told me.'

'*You* should have trusted me.'

That was hard to argue with. Still, he knew she'd planned to go all the way with him for the first time on her birthday. Why complicate it by bringing her folks in? Maybe he wasn't as hot for her as she'd thought.

Keeping her voice cool, she told David, 'Well, you really screwed up this time. If you think you know me, how come you didn't know I'd take you literally when you pretended to forget my birthday?' She hung up quickly while she still had the moral high ground.

In her bedroom, Sarah succumbed to the blues that beckoned to her from her bed. She fell face down, muffling her sobs so none of her housemates would interrupt the flow of her thoughts, and her tears.

'Jack,' she whispered into her pillow, pounding it with her fists, 'come back, come back for me.' And so on, and on, until she fell asleep.

That evening, David took Sarah and her parents to a Thai restaurant for her favourite food. She wore a short black skirt with a matching turtleneck. Now that Jack had released her womanhood, it seemed right to dress in a more sophisticated style. Even so, she went bare-legged.

The meal likely strained David's budget, especially the champagne, even if it was domestic and vastly inferior to the Dom that Jack had bought for her. With her new wealth she could have offered to pay part of the bill, at least, but that would have raised questions she wasn't prepared to answer. Anyway, he deserved the hit on his pocket.

It was uncomfortable, taking that first sip of bubbly and declaring it delightful, when it was too sweet and just about the last thing in the world she wanted in her mouth after last night. Sarah hated lying and she was lousy at it, or, at least, she'd always considered herself lousy at it. But everyone seemed to buy her lies, so perhaps it was just something that required a little effort, or perhaps it was because, for the first time, the truth she was protecting was worthwhile.

'Did you open your gifts yet?' Sarah's mom was smiling but her bright blue eyes weren't. 'It wasn't easy getting them here but as we were only invited for the weekend, I knew there'd be no time to shop.'

'I haven't opened them. You're welcome to stay longer if you like.' Sarah should be placating her parents after last night's no-show, but she wasn't in the mood.

'We can't. We dare not leave Donna for more than a day.'

Mr Meadows jumped in. 'She's probably already turned the place into a flophouse.' He turned his palms up on the table in a gesture of helplessness.

'What's her latest illness?' Sarah glanced at David. 'Donna's a cyberchondriac.'

'What's that?' Mr Meadows looked from Sarah to David.

'A hypochondriac who searches the web for diseases,' said David. Sarah was relieved that he didn't mention that he knew this because that's what she sometimes called him.

'She thinks she has Alzheimer's,' said Mrs Meadows.

'Surely not! She must know she's too young –'

'Not Alzheimer's,' said Mr Meadows. 'Asperger's syndrome.'

'Right,' said Mrs Meadows. 'Well, they both start with an "A". What difference does it make? It's not like she really has it, any more than she had chronic fatigue or Fibromyalgia or any of the other syndromes *de jour* she finds online.'

'Is Donna working?'

'She's filling the house with junk for "found art",' said Mr Meadows. He laughed. His cheeks were flushed, likely from the wine.

'Some of that sort of stuff does get into the art galleries,' said David.

'You're very sweet,' said Mrs Meadows. She covered David's hand with her bony ones. 'A keeper.' She gave Sarah a meaningful look.

Sarah bit back sharp words. Mrs Meadows, after spending

most of her life an ardent feminist, had become, overnight it seemed, a proponent of tradition. She, who'd once said, 'Never marry, never have children,' to her little girls, now sought new roles to play – specifically, Mother of the Bride and Grand-mother.

'Oh, I'm not going anywhere,' said David.

David and Sarah's dads were alike, both dedicated to keeping things pleasant. Why had she never seen it before?

Her dad came through with a birthday cheque for $200. This, on top of the gifts her mother had likely chosen and the air fare and hotel bill, made their visit to Toledo an expensive attempt to make her happy. She pasted a happy smile on her face and ate a big piece of cake, choking it down with more of the dreadful wine.

The trip to the airport took for ever. Sarah was in the back seat of David's Astra, beside her mother, so her dad could sit in the front and point out places he recognised.

Mrs Meadows fanned her face as she flushed beet red, the metamorphosis as startling for the speed in which it took place as it was for the depth of its hue.

'David, please –'

David glanced back at Sarah. 'What?'

'She needs air.' Mr Meadows cranked up the air conditioning to maximum. 'Menopause,' he added.

Mrs Meadows said, 'I just have to speak up. I'm proud of you, sweetheart. I am. But when you graduate in the spring, well, a degree in philosophy isn't going to get you much of a job, is it? Look at the economy. Look at –'

'The big picture. I will, I promise.'

'Just make sure to cover your bases, that's all I'm saying. Don't squander the opportunities so many women paid so dearly for. For the first time ever, a girl like you really *can* have it all.' She glanced meaningfully at the back of David's head.

'I know. I'm grateful, I really am.' Sarah kept her voice carefully sarcasm free. 'I'll try.'

Sarah considered the mass of contradictions that was her mother. One minute burning her bra, the next stuffing her breasts into a push-up to please her man. That thought led to another – the way she'd compressed her breasts with her hands to push them up to Jack. Christ. She felt her own cheeks start to flush. What would her mom have to say about that?

'You could use a little make-up,' said Mrs Meadows. She was patting powder on her face and now she dabbed Sarah's nose with her orange-streaked puff. 'Maybe buy some with your birthday money.'

'I guess,' said Sarah.

Her mother tapped Sarah's bare knee. 'You need pantyhose, too, it seems. Although your father wants you to buy a cellphone with that money.'

'He didn't say so.'

'He wouldn't, would he? But that's what he wants. We'd like to know that you're safe.'

'You do anything you want with that money.' Mr Meadows twisted in his seat to look at Sarah and her mother. 'Treat yourself, baby. OK?'

'OK, Dad,' said Sarah.

'I ate there once,' said her dad, pointing out a steak joint.

The airport was too bright and too hectic. Sarah recalled the joy she'd felt when she'd watched a plane take off from the penthouse suite of the Royal. It had seemed so peaceful without sound. She preferred a long-distance view of busy places, maybe even of life itself. She'd have to think about that later, when she was finally alone. It might mean something.

Hugs, kisses, waves. After the interminable car ride, the send-off went fast. Sarah's eyes filled with tears as she watched her parents clear security. As usual, her dad had to go through twice, setting off the alarm the first time because, as usual, he'd forgotten to empty the coins from his pocket. Mrs Meadows waited for him on the other side. She shook her head at her forgetful husband, but there was a smile on her lips. She took his arm. Then they were gone.

'They're getting older,' Sarah murmured to David. She felt the need to explain the tears in her eyes.

'They're pretty cool, for parents.'

Sarah let him hold her hand. She felt a rush of affection. Maybe David really was a 'keeper'.

On the way back, David rested his hand on Sarah's bare knee. She let him leave it there until it began to wander up her thigh.

'Don't!' she said.

'I thought ...?'

'*Did* you?'

He looked so downhearted she almost relented, but she steeled herself against pity. Sex wasn't supposed to be about pity. It was supposed to be about being carried away by a masterful man, like Jack.

David parked a little way from her door, under a towering Crimson King maple that blocked most of the light from the street lamps. That was where he'd stopped in the early days of dating, before he'd earned the privilege of being invited in. Good. It showed that David understood that their relationship had backtracked several months.

He half turned and reached back into the rear of his Astra. 'I got you a present.'

'My birthday was yesterday, remember?'

'I wanted us to be alone when I gave it to you.' He handed her a big box wrapped in golden paper.

Alone? Why? Had he bought her something sexy to wear, that he didn't want her folks to see? If so, how should she react?

David asked, 'Aren't you going to open it?'

'Sure.' Sarah's fingers trembled as she ripped the paper away. When she lifted the lid, she discovered a pale-green sweater that her touch told her had to be pure cashmere.

She loved cashmere. And the cost! Poor David, what with the expensive meal and this lovely gift, he must have spent close to a thousand dollars on her birthday. For him, that was a fortune. How could she stay angry with him?

How could she not? She'd pretty much decided to dump him as soon as, or maybe even before, Jack tracked her down. Being mad at David would make that easy. Reconciling with him and then dumping him would be both hard to do and cruel. Maybe she could make it up to him by fucking him first? That seemed fair. It was what he wanted the most from her, wasn't it? She wouldn't have to tell Jack. But Jack thought she was a whore, so he wouldn't care. But Jack would soon find out that her act had been genuine, so he might care. But . . .

It was all so damned complicated.

For now, she half decided, she'd make out with David but not go all the way till she'd thought things through.

Not looking at her, David asked, 'Do you like it?'

'Love it.'

'Going to try it on?'

'Here, in the car?'

'We could go in, like always.'

'I don't think so.' Stripping her top off, alone with David in the privacy of her room, where there was a bed, could only lead to one thing. Sarah compromised. She took hold of the hem of her top and lifted it up above her head. David's gulp when she revealed her breasts, nestled prettily in their gauzy half-cups, was most satisfactory. Sarah paused for a moment to give him the full effect.

He lay a tentative palm on her midriff. She quickly discarded her top and pulled the dreamy cashmere over her head. Smoothing it down dislodged his hand. He sighed.

Sarah twisted towards him, wrapping an arm around him and making sure that her elbow 'accidentally' brushed across his straining erection. 'You deserve a thank-you kiss.'

Her lips stayed closed to his tongue until he turned in his seat and pushed her back against hers. Sarah was still determined to make him earn every inch of progress. She almost giggled. Her night with Jack had proved she wasn't cheap and now, with David, she wasn't going to be easy, either.

His arm reached passed her and down to the seat control. It dropped her back, with him half sprawled on top of her. That was more like it. Sarah parted her lips for him. Her tongue met his. He still tasted of coriander, but then so must she.

She loved to kiss. Once she started, she could never get enough. As David's kisses stoked her passion, she became voracious, licking him, giving him her tongue to suck, each of them breathing the other's heated breath. His hand slipped up under her sweater, caressed her ribcage and slithered higher. Her nipples tightened in anticipation. When he finally reached and then gently rolled her right nipple, she almost yelped, but swallowed it. Only Jack was welcome to make her squeal.

David was moaning into her mouth. Where he was pressed against her hip, she could feel the hardness of his erection. Should she break it off now, before his, and her, excitement took them all the way? Should she take him up to her room and into her bed after all? As usual, when undecided, she chose neither course. Besides, the kisses were intoxicating.

David's hand withdrew. Sarah knew what that meant. He'd decided that she was excited enough that she'd allow him to touch her between her legs. Yes, his hand slid up under her skirt. Even though she'd expected that caress, she still hadn't made her mind up if she was going to let him or not. Her thighs parted, making her decision for her.

'You're not wearing any . . .' David whispered when his fingers reached their goal.

'Yes I am.'

'Oh?' He fumbled at the delicate fabric of her new thong. 'New?' he asked.

'A birthday present.'

He froze. 'From . . .?'

'From me to myself.'

He relaxed. 'To wear for me?'

'Like I said, for myself.'

He kissed her again, with renewed passion. David always did that when he was about to touch her *there*. Maybe he thought his lips and tongue would distract her from what his fingers were doing. Dumb. Perhaps she wasn't good at multitasking but she wasn't such a ditz that she couldn't pay attention to a probing tongue and an exploring finger at the same time.

The lips of her sex had engorged and parted. She was already wet. His finger slid up into her. Sarah allowed herself a quick gasp.

'Nice?' he asked, smugly.

She didn't answer. Her thoughts were in turmoil again. The last time David had penetrated her with a finger, she'd been a virgin. What if she felt different now that she was a woman?

'You twitched – inside.'

'Girls do.' She wasn't going to explain that the sudden contraction had been for fear he'd be able to tell she'd been fucked, hard and deep and for a long time, just the night before. The memory of the things that her Jack had done to her excited Sarah. 'Do me like I like it,' she said.

He found the nub of her clit and rubbed it. Sarah slumped down further and strained her thighs apart. David didn't know it, but for a few moments, if he'd rolled fully on top of her and entered her, she wouldn't have been able to resist. Nor would she have wanted to.

Then he was rubbing in the wrong place at the wrong angle and too hard, so she was able to take back her self-control. It'd been a close thing. Sarah had a defence that had become a reflex. She squirmed a hand between their bodies, found the tab of his zipper and pulled it down.

David gasped, 'Oh Sarah! I love you *so* much.'

He always declared his love for her when her hand got close to his cock. She'd have preferred an honest, 'Jerk me off, please.' That's what he really meant.

She said, 'Lie back.'

He rolled away, lowered the back of his seat and went down with it. Sarah leant over him, put her hand inside the fly of his jeans, found his burning shaft and pulled it out.

'You're so beautiful,' he said. She translated that as, 'Please don't stop.'

Businesslike, she spat into her palm and wrapped her fingers around him. It did feel good in her hand, she had to admit, but it was no comparison to Jack's. What she really wanted was to be alone in her bed in her room, going over her date with Jack in minute detail and maybe masturbating, if she liked. She wanted to whisper his name, as she had that afternoon, until she went to sleep. Well, she'd get there soon enough. With her fingers loose, she stroked David's foreskin up and down, going faster than he probably wanted. His hand settled on the top of her head and pressed down lightly. She resisted. No way, David. My mouth belongs to another. She gripped him tighter and pumped faster. He began to groan. His hips jerked up at her. Any minute now . . .

He erupted. Warm cream flowed down over her fingers and the back of her hand. She wiped them off on his denim-clad thigh, retrieved her old top, opened her door and was out of his car before he recovered from his climax.

'Goodnight, David, and thanks again for the sweater.'

3

The next morning, between lectures, she managed to squeeze in a trip to her bank to deposit her funds, legitimate and otherwise, and pay off her current debts. Sarah had lived with debt for so long she'd become used to it. She floated on the freedom she felt, no longer hung-over and no longer in arrears on payments.

Sarah was in her last year of an honours degree in philosophy. Now that they were well into September, her classes were taking shape and her professors were adequate to wonderful, with the exception of her maniacal existentialism professor. She was taking an improvisation class as a final credit towards her minor, drama, and it looked like it would be fun, at least, if not actually useful as a means of bridging the gap she perceived between herself and everybody else.

Indian summer still held Toledo in its stultifying grip, but most of her classes were in air-conditioned rooms and now that she had wheels again, there'd be no more pavement stomping for Sarah Meadows. Soon, autumn would nudge the heatwave aside and paint the campus with the rich red and gold hues that always raised her spirits.

It was only while lingering over an apple pie and coffee in a McDonald's that she acknowledged her reluctance to go home. Sarah wanted a call to have come in for her while she was gone – a call from Jack. Somewhere during their decadent night together, she'd fallen in love with him. If he hadn't called by the time she got home she knew she'd run a serious risk of sliding into despair. It was stupid, plain and simple, and she was not a stupid girl. But she knew herself well enough to know that once she'd painted a picture in her mind it was pointless to try to erase it. Ignore it, avoid it, rationalise it? Sure. But she'd yet to develop the skill set not to let it happen and, once it did, she could not so much as dilute it with reason, let alone eliminate it. She left the coffee half-drunk and headed to her car.

There was a yellow Post-it note on her door when she got upstairs. 'Call them', and a local number. Sarah's heart leapt with joy. Yes! She was so used to having her hopes dashed she'd forgotten that sometimes dreams come true. Sarah didn't recognise the number so it had to be Jack's. He'd found her, just as she'd known he would.

She ran back downstairs and dropped fifty cents into the payphone before she stopped to think about how late it was. She'd managed to waste so much time not coming home that it was after ten, and her mother had drummed into her the folly of phoning folks past that hour. But this was Jack, her lover. He wouldn't mind her waking him, even if he was asleep. Maybe he was dreaming of her and, like her, he'd be surprised and overjoyed to have his dream come true.

An answering machine picked up with, 'Classique – leave a message.' Confused, Sarah hung up. Classique? That didn't sound like the name of a dot-com company; it sounded more like the name of an escort agency.

She'd half expected something like this, though she'd success-fully ignored the possibility until now. She had a pretty good idea what they wanted. A cut of the profit she'd unwittingly earned by going to bed with Jack. Was she in some kind of trouble? Or would she be, once she confessed she'd spent every penny of it? Damn. On the other hand, maybe their clients paid up front. That'd mean the money in the envelope had all been meant for her, in which case she was in the clear. Perhaps, no, obviously, Jack had contacted them to find her. That made sense.

She called again the next morning, at around ten, and got the same message. Her third try was answered by a crisp female voice.

'Sarah Meadows. I got a message . . .'

'Yes, Ms Meadows. My boss, Ms Veronica Kane, would very much like to meet with you. When would be convenient?'

'There isn't a problem, is there?'

'Problem? Not that I'm aware of. When's good for you? Any day, any time between noon and ten in the evening.'

They settled on Thursday, at seven. The address was on Prince Rupert Drive, Suite 1911, the Imperial Building. Sarah knew where that was; close to Westfield Franklin Park Mall, her favourite place to window-shop. That was a comfort. She'd have been nervous of an address in some dingy slum area.

She wore skinny black pants and her new cashmere sweater to give herself confidence. A uniformed security guard had her sign in and directed her to the bank of elevators. Again, Sarah was comforted. White slavers didn't have you sign in before they shipped you off to Far Eastern brothels, she didn't think.

The elevator was lined with dove-grey moiré silk and pink mirrors. The Muzak was classical. The luxury was intimidating, but Sarah braced herself.

Classique's receptionist, she of the crisply efficient voice, had hair like scrolls of pewter, pale-grey eyes and obsidian-sharp cheekbones. She greeted Sarah by name and told her to go right on through to the waiting room and take a seat.

There were three doors off the waiting room, each made of frosted glass that was etched with cavorting naked sylphs. Two of those doors were dark so Sarah assumed the third was to Ms Kane's office. She could hear voices but not make out the words. One was deep, male and stern. One was contralto, with a 'more hurt than angry' tone in it that reminded Sarah of her mother. The third voice was high pitched and protesting.

There was a pause, then a protesting sound from the high-pitched voice. After another pause there was the sound of a slap. Intimidated, but too curious to resist, Sarah crept up to the door where its hinges left a narrow gap between the glass and its frame.

There was an armless chair directly in her line of sight. A distinguished-looking silver-haired man had a girl pinned across his thighs, facing away from Sarah. Her skirt was rucked up to her waist, baring her bottom. One cheek was crimson. The man's open hand came down on the other, hard. The girl kicked and whimpered but to no avail. He slapped her again, and again, in a steady rhythm.

Now that she was closer, Sarah could hear him say, 'Ten minutes late is too late. Ten minutes late is too late,' repeating it like a mantra, once for each time his hand came down.

Poor girl. She must feel awful, both from the pain and from the humiliation. Sarah imagined herself in the same position, being punished and being helpless to resist. She'd be so ashamed to be treated like that, ashamed and . . .

Mmm. There was that familiar feeling, not a tingle, not exactly, more like the ghost of a tingle, between her thighs. It was something she sometimes felt just before making out with David, a subtle harbinger of the more intense sensations she anticipated enjoying – a sure sign that she was really looking forward to being held and touched.

The man released the girl. Sarah back-pedalled. Maybe she should make a run for it? She was getting confused, and that wasn't good. She needed her wits about her. Sarah sat down on the bench seat. The door opened. The girl, her skirt in place now, her face red and streaked with tears, burst through.

She threw Sarah a fiery glare and spat, 'You!' before exiting.

What on earth did that mean? There was something familiar about the girl but Sarah couldn't recall ever meeting her. Oh – yes she did! That straw-coloured hair. That snub nose. It was the girl Sarah had misdirected to the Royal Avenue Hotel.

The man came out. He said, very calmly, 'Ms Kane will see you now, young lady,' and followed the girl into the reception area.

The inner office was huge, Art Deco, black and pink, with floor-to-ceiling windows on two sides.

Veronica Kane was a tiny but voluptuous blonde with big blue eyes, a turned-up nose and an over-wide, full-lipped mouth. Despite her tailored black suit, she looked like a sexy youngish wife, the kind who'd bake pies every Sunday and make her husband deliriously happy in bed, often. Sarah felt herself relaxing.

Veronica waved Sarah to a chair. There was a sparkle in her eyes as she observed, 'We've had quite the mix-up, Sarah, haven't we?'

'We sure have. I'm sorry, Ms Kane, but . . .'

'Call me Veronica. All my young ladies do.'

'But I'm not . . .'

'Of course you aren't. You're a lovely girl who just happened to accidentally get caught up in a little adventure. No harm done. Your "client", by the way, was effusive in his praise for you. You might be an amateur but you are obviously a gifted one.'

Sarah blushed. 'Jack said nice things about me?'

'Jack? Oh yes. He was very pleased.'

'How did he . . . you . . . how did you know who I am?'

Veronica smiled warmly. 'I could tell you that I have psychic powers but it's much simpler. You showed your ID to the bartender. He didn't recognise you as one of my employees, so your name stuck in his memory. The way you were dressed told us where you were studying, and *voila*!' She opened a ledger and picked up a pen. 'Now, let's get the boring business out of the way and then we can have a nice little chat.'

'Business?'

'My fee. Classique charges its clients two thousand dollars a date. That's a thousand for the agency and a thousand for the escort, plus the escort keeps any tips, gifts, or whatever. Fair, don't you think?'

'Oh yes, very fair, only –'

'Good. Then I'll take my thousand now, if you don't mind.'

Sarah blurted, 'I don't have it. I spent it.'

A tiny crease appeared between Veronica's eyes. 'Spent it? All of it, including *my* money?'

'I didn't know it was yours, and I had some bills to pay, and . . .'

Veronica closed the ledger. 'I quite understand – a young college girl – it must have seemed like quite the windfall. I'm not the least bit cross with you, my dear. We'll work out some easy terms, at say, ten per cent? You can pay me back a hundred a week for eleven weeks. How does that suit you?'

'I . . . I . . .'

'Yes?'

'Can I get in touch with Jack? I'm sure he'd straighten this out.'

'"Jack" is the name he gave you? I'm sure you understand that our clients often use names that aren't their own.' She paused, toying with her pen while Sarah squirmed. 'I'm sorry, Sarah, but we have a strict confidentiality rule. Both our clients' and our staff's personal information are sacrosanct. We don't give them your names, nor you theirs.' She put her pen down with a 'click'. 'Of course, if "Jack" came back to us, and if he asked for you, what transpired between you two while you were on your date would be your own business.'

Sarah blurted, 'He'll be back for me. I know it. When he does, you can keep the whole two thousand, and then we'll be square, right?'

'And if he doesn't? Some clients are regulars, some occasional and some one time only. It was his first engagement with Classique. He very well might call me next week or I might never hear from him again. I don't feel I can allow you extended credit on the basis of something that might never happen.'

Sarah's fingers knotted in her lap. 'But I don't have any money!'

'Oh dear.' Veronica got up from behind her desk and went to the window. With her back to Sarah, she continued, 'Let me explain a little bit about how we work, my dear. My agency provides escorts, nothing more. Our charges cover a client enjoying eye candy and charming company for an evening. We don't sell sex. That, as I'm sure you know, would be illegal.'

She seemed to be waiting for a response, but Sarah had none. Her mind was scrambling and coming up empty. Thoughts tried to form but no matter how intently she tried to find the words, nothing came. *Illegal.* Why hadn't she considered, until this very moment, the fact that she'd broken the law?

Veronica shrugged and resumed talking. 'If, however, a client and one of my girls are compatible and they mutually agree to some degree of intimacy, that's their business. When that happens, as I understand it, it often leads to gifts or tips, substantial tips.'

'But the girl doesn't have to ...'

'No, never. It's always her choice, and the client's, of course. Just out of consideration to my girls, I sometimes get an inkling of what a client expects. Then I pass the information to his date. That way there's less embarrassment all round if he happened to want something the girl wasn't ready to offer.'

She turned to smile at Sarah. 'Want to give it a try? You look younger than your years, so you'd be very popular. You could make a thousand plus tips every week, or more often, when we're busy. Would fifty-odd thousand a year help put you through college?'

'I don't know – I mean, it would, of course, but I don't know about the work.'

'You seemed to show a natural inclination for it, judging from the reports I received after your visit to the Royal Avenue Hotel.'

'That was ... I wasn't ... I didn't know ...'

'Why don't you try it, just the once? You could pay off your debt to me, and see how you feel after that.'

'I wouldn't have to ...?'

'Not unless you wanted to.' Veronica marched to her desk and pushed the button on an intercom. Into it, she asked, 'Mr V., Debra. When's the appointment?'

Debra answered, 'Next Friday, Veronica.'

Veronica turned to Sarah. 'You're in luck. I have a client who not only wouldn't so much as touch you, sexually, but who specifically requires that you don't do any touching. You'd be doing me a favour. He's a regular, only twice a year, but every year. He likes us to provide a different girl every time, which isn't always easy. It's a simple gig, I promise. All you have to do is be there for a few hours.'

'Do I have to be naked or something?'

'No, silly, not naked. That school uniform of yours would do nicely. What do you say? You could be debt free and you might even make a hundred or so for doing virtually nothing.'

'It sounds too good to be true.'

'Working for me can be just that. Are you free next Friday?'

'Is that the day after tomorrow or –'

'No.' A smile played on Veronica's lips. 'The day after tomorrow is this Friday. A week from this Friday is next Friday.'

'I get confused. I'm sorry.'

'Don't be. It's rather appealing, actually.'

'Just the once?'

'That'd be up to you.'

'And if Jack comes back?'

'If he comes back looking for you, I'll contact you immediately. You wouldn't be the first of my girls to land a man that way.'

Sarah stood up, shoulders back, and looked Veronica straight in the eyes. 'I'll do it.'

'Then I'll explain the details of my client's requirements, so there's no misunderstanding. At eight o'clock, a week from Friday, that's nine days from today, you'll go to . . .'

4

On the weekend, David, as pitiful as a whipped puppy, begged Sarah for a date. She suggested he stay home and nurse his cold, but agreed to see a movie with him early in the week. He thanked her for her concern and didn't suggest, as he would've not long before, that she come to his place and nurse him back to health. She spent the time studying. She'd decided to do a paper on 'Love', for her epistemology course, starting with Plato's definitions of *eros*, *philia* and *agape* and moving to more contemporary considerations of the possibility, or impossibility, of a knowledge of love.

The closest Sarah had come to the kind of thing described by the sages was her night with Jack, though maybe she was confusing lust with love. Sarah didn't think so, but her academic mind insisted she explore the possibility, and so she would, for a credit.

David took her to the movies on an off-night when the theatre was almost empty. They sat in the back row. She knew what that meant, and so, obligingly, she buttered her hand from the tub of popcorn and jerked him off.

When they parked under the Crimson King maple, he had to content himself with a few tepid kisses.

Well, what did he expect, for free?

Sarah went in and up to her room, grateful for her lonely bed. Tonight, as she did every night, she relived her time with Jack in detail until lust overtook her and her fingers played at being his fingers and brought her release. Whenever she remembered something she'd forgotten before, she felt a frisson greater than anything she'd ever felt with David.

Anyone would think, to see her writhing on her bed mumbling, 'Jack, come back,' that she was half-crazy. But no one ever did see her, so she was safe.

Someday she'd share a bed with the man of her dreams. Until then, she'd sleep alone, not bitter, but young, female and free.

Sarah 'mmm-d' her lips. She'd purchased make-up with some of her money, just as her mother had suggested, though not with the intention her mother had had in mind, but Ms Veronica had told her to keep her make-up 'invisible', just clear lipgloss, a delicate brush of blush and the faintest trace of eyeliner. She had been told to look younger rather than older and to wear her page's uniform.

Well, here she was, outside the hotel-room door, ready for her debut as a genuine, deliberate, not accidental escort. To be honest, as a call girl – even if she had been promised there would be no physical contact. That didn't mean that her 'date' wasn't to be a sexual one. From what Ms Veronica had told her, it was certainly going to be that, in a weird way.

She asked herself how she felt about doing what she and Classique were to be paid two thousand dollars for, and decided that she was both excited and nervous, like a virgin bride. In a way, she was a virgin, where this sort of sex was concerned. She'd never even watched porn, apart from what her sister sneered at as 'soft core'.

She took a deep breath, squared her shoulders and rapped on the door. Seconds later, it was opened by a big sandy-haired man, in his mid-forties, she guessed, who looked like he'd been something of a jock in college, a line-backer, maybe, and who was just beginning to soften. He was in a bathrobe and barefoot.

Sarah said, 'I'm from . . .'

He put a finger to his lips and backed away, beckoning her to follow him. It was a nice suite, not up to the one Jack had had at the Royal Avenue, but spacious, with a king-sized bed dominating the area plus ample room for an armchair and some side tables and a credenza with a TV. The man pointed to the armchair. Sarah sat.

Next to the chair was a small table with a bucket of ice, glasses and half a dozen assorted cans of pop. There was also a platter of tiny sandwiches, a bowl with mixed nuts and another with some nibbly-salty things. What really caught her attention, though, was the very lifelike pink plastic replica of a large gnarly cock that lay atop a box of tissues. Her sister owned one of those, though Sarah wasn't supposed to know that. As she remembered it, when you twisted its base, it vibrated. She'd never had the chance nor the inclination to actually try it.

Her every need had been anticipated and catered to, though the vibrator was a bit presumptuous. Still, the customer is always right, right?

The man seemed to forget she was there. He thumbed a remote. The TV came on. Sarah was at the wrong angle to see the screen properly but the sound of rhythmic grunting, squealing and squelching told her that it had to be porn. The man dropped his robe and threw himself onto the bed, absolutely naked. He had a thick, solid body and an erect cock to match. Just as if he'd been alone, he watched the screen and stroked himself, almost idly.

Sarah watched him. That was what she was there for, Veronica had explained, just to watch. In any case, in her whole life, Sarah had only seen three real cocks: David's, the one that belonged to the boy she'd dated before him and Jack's. She was curious about them and the differences between them. That was only natural, wasn't it? This one was as long as Jack's but quite a bit thicker. Looking at it, she couldn't help but wonder what it'd feel like – in her hand, in her mouth, or pushing up inside her.

The bathroom door opened. A woman, stark naked but heavily made-up, entered. She looked to be a couple of years younger than the man, tall, slender, very fit, almost no body fat, like she worked out at a gym and counted carbs. She was a freckled redhead, with her hair cut in a feathery boyish style.

Her breasts were a bit smaller than Sarah's and certainly not as pert, but still attractive, with prominent maroon nipples. Her waist was slender, with hints of taut abdominal muscles moving just below her skin. There was a ring through her navel, with a diamanté pendant. She had narrow hips with deep hollows, lean muscular flanks and long, almost thin, legs. Her shaved mound was quite plump, divided by a double crease that framed the ridge of a prominent clitoral shaft.

It felt strange, appraising a nude woman as a requirement for an assignment. In her high school gym's showers, girls made sure not to look as if they were sizing each other up, though they did, of course, surreptitiously.

The woman sat on the edge of the bed, beyond the man, who was still stroking himself. 'Playing with yourself, James?' she asked. 'The pretty little schoolgirl is watching you, you know.'

'She wants to learn how grown-ups do it, Daphne.'

'And so she shall. We'll show her. We'll give her a show she won't ever forget, right?'

Well, they'd acknowledged her presence at last. So, she wasn't supposed to be invisible. It seemed that her role was to be that of a silent but appreciative audience. Sarah played her part by leaning forwards, elbows on knees, chin in her hands, and staring openly.

Daphne said, 'Let me do that for you, James.' She arched over him, making the skin of her waist wrinkle. Her long-fingered right hand cupped his balls. He relinquished his grip on his shaft. Her hand replaced it, but delicately, just fingertips and thumb. As she stroked, she said, 'This is how you like me to start, right, James? Teasing?'

He grunted and lay back.

'Nice and easy,' Daphne crooned.

His hand lifted up under her to her pendent left breast, gave it a little jiggle and then toyed with her nipple. 'Love your tits, Daphne.'

'Thank you, darling. Feel free.' She chuckled. 'Fondle at will.'

'Like this?' He rolled her nipple between his index finger and his thumb.

'Harder.'

He pinched and rolled. Daphne gasped. Her lips parted. It seemed that she liked the pain. Sarah dropped a hand to her own breast and pinched her own nipple experimentally through her thin shirt. It made her wince but she persevered. Hot little sparks of sensation radiated from her peak. Interesting. David had always been so gentle when he'd touched her there, and she'd thought that was considerate of him, but now she was learning about something different, somehow naughtier. Gentle caresses were nice but it seemed that there were other sorts of pleasure to be coaxed from her body. It was her second lesson in that, she realised. She'd enjoyed those few spanks that Jack had given her, even if they had come as a bit of a shock.

Daphne pulled her legs up to kneel beside James but didn't miss a stroke. As his torment of her nipple increased in intensity, so did the speed and strength of the fingers she was masturbating him with. Looking close up at his glossy plum but obviously directing her words at Sarah, she said, 'Don't worry about him coming too soon. That's the advantage of a mature man. He can hold back for a long time, right, James?'

He grunted again. Arousal seemed to have stolen his power of speech.

Daphne continued, 'But I'm different. I can come again and again, each time getting better and better. Make me come, please, James.'

She lifted one knee up and set it down on the other side of his head, facing forwards. She grinned at Sarah as she lowered her sex onto his mouth.

'He's got a wonderful tongue and he loves to use it.'

David had never done that for Sarah, though he really enjoyed it when she used her mouth on him. Jack had offered to but somehow they'd never got round to it. By the intense, almost angry, expression on Daphne's face, it had to feel very good. Sarah decided that when she and Jack finally got together again, she'd make sure to get him to do it to her. He'd be good at it, she was certain.

Daphne was undulating on James's face. Sarah wished she could see what the man was doing with his tongue in more detail. The serpentine woman lowered her face towards James's cock. She threw Sarah a glance, as if to say, 'Watch this,' and worked its head between her stretched lips. There was a pause, and then she plunged down.

Oh hell! She'd taken him so deeply that her lips were buried in his pubic hair. With a thing that size – it had to be pressed against the back of her throat.

James put his hand on the back of Daphne's head, holding it in place, and jerked up at her, driving his shaft even deeper.

How did the woman take it? Why didn't she gag, Sarah wondered.

He thrust up again and again before relenting and letting her mouth rise completely off his shaft. Daphne grinned, licked her lips, and ducked down again.

She enjoyed it?

He was still buried in her mouth, to the hilt, when her hips gyrated and then began to thrust as if she were riding a stallion at a gallop. Well, in a way, she was.

Sarah's fingers seemed to have found their way inside her shirt and were flickering on her nipple. Her thighs squeezed together.

Daphne made an obscene snorting sound. She pulled back off James's shaft. The muscles in her belly convulsed. Her diamanté pendant bounced against her tummy. She said, 'Oh yes, my darling, oh, oh, oh, fucking yes!' She toppled sideways, her left leg straight and pointing upwards at a forty-five degree angle. Daphne held that pose, giving Sarah a clear view of her glistening flaccid sex.

The bitch was showing off! *Look at me! I just came, hard and wet and glorious!*

Daphne wasn't the only one who was wet. Sarah's new thong panties were saturated. Nobody had touched her but the exhibition she'd just witnessed had made her incredibly horny. And girls weren't supposed to be 'visual'? Maybe some weren't but she certainly was, it seemed.

It couldn't be over. Daphne had climaxed but James was still stiff and, it looked to Sarah, even bigger than before.

He threw Sarah a glance and then rolled sideways away from her, but just long enough to take Daphne by her hips and heave her body over him and plonk her down between himself and Sarah. Their legs splayed apart, her right one overlapping his left. She took hold of his shaft again. He cupped her mound and curled two fingers down into her sex.

This was their interlude, Sarah surmised. Daphne was recovering her lust, if she'd ever lost it, and she was maintaining his. His dabbling fingers made wet sounds. They lay, just toying, for a few minutes before his free hand came up, reached over and 'pinged' Daphne's nipple with a flick of his finger.

Her 'Ouch' was a pleased one. 'Want a reverse cowgirl next?' she asked him.

'Mmm.'

She sat up and straddled her man again, facing his feet. Her hand took hold of him and steered him to nestle between the petals of her sex. Rotating her hips, she sank down, slowly impaling herself. James put his hands behind his neck, ready to just lie there and enjoy.

Daphne leant forwards to grip his thick thighs just above his knees. She rocked slowly to and fro, building up speed until her breasts were bouncing wildly, then switched to rotating her hips. James put a flat palm on the small of her back and pushed her down gently until her face was between his ankles.

'He loves this angle,' Daphne mumbled into the bedclothes. 'It does nice things for me, as well.'

James's hips rose off the bed, bearing Daphne with them. Very slowly, his face contorted with restrained glee, he lowered and raised her, over and over.

Sarah imagined where the pressure would be, inside Daphne, and what it might feel like. She made another mental note for when she saw Jack again.

Still lifting and lowering, James sucked on his own index finger and reached out to the crease of Daphne's bottom. Sarah squirmed. She knew that some people had anal sex but it wasn't something she'd thought about. In fact, it was something she'd avoided contemplating.

James's wrist turned. Jesus! He was working his finger into Daphne's bottom!

The woman gasped, 'Two fingers, please, darling.'

Sarah could hardly believe it. How incredibly full Daphne had to feel. Not even thinking about it, Sarah slid the hand that wasn't toying with her breast up under her short kilt. It was only when Daphne caught her eye and grinned that Sarah realised what she'd been caught doing. She blushed and almost withdrew her hand but stopped herself. The horny couple had hired her to watch them because they wanted to be appreciated. It was actually part of Sarah's job to show them that what they were doing excited her. If she was going to earn her pay, she mustn't be modest.

She could play the slut. How hard could it be? What would a slut do under these circumstances? That was easy. Instead of pulling her hand back and pretending it hadn't been up her kilt, she reached up higher, got a grip on her thong and pulled it down her thighs, over her knees and off.

'She's such a bad little schoolgirl,' Daphne said. 'I think she's going to play with herself.'

Sarah could take a hint. Bold, now that she'd decided to give them their money's worth, she slumped back in the chair, legs spread wide, and pulled her kilt right up to her tummy. There! They weren't the only exhibitionists here!

Now that she'd exposed herself, what next? For now, a little fondling. After that, well, she'd see where the spirit moved her. Feeling incredibly liberated, Sarah bracketed her clit between two fingers and slowly worked its sheath up and down.

Daphne didn't say anything but she sat up, reached down and began to caress herself in exactly the same way. That was better than words. Sarah felt warm emotions flood her. She'd never seriously considered sex with another girl and what she and Daphne were doing was a sort of Sapphic exchange, but it was a safe one, because they weren't actually touching each other.

Daphne panted, 'She's bad, James, perhaps the naughtiest little schoolgirl we've ever had. Oh, so bad, so very, very bad, so ...' Her belly writhed. She sucked air, made a sound that was almost a giggle but from very deep inside, and flopped sideways.

Sarah had done that to her, or at least, she'd contributed. How could she not feel proud?

And James's erection still stood, glistening and angry. Without thinking, Sarah reached out to the waiting vibrator and caressed it, comparing it to the real shaft not five feet away. They were about the same size. The imitation one was cool but yielding. Still stroking her clit, she raised the pink plastic to her lips and gave its dome a flat-tongued lick.

James groaned. Because of what she'd done? Experimenting, she worked the blunt end between her lips and gave it a hollow-cheeked suck.

James groaned again.

Daphne sat up and looked across his body towards Sarah. 'She wants you, James. I can see it in her eyes, the bad, bad girl! I'd better cover your eyes so that she can't tempt you.' Daphne climbed to her feet on the bed.

James sat up against the pile of pillows at the bed's head. Daphne braced herself with one hand on the wall and the other knotted in his hair. The foot furthest from Sarah lifted up, its toes pointed elegantly, and Daphne stepped over James's right shoulder. Her legs bent, bringing her sex down to the level of his face. The hand in his hair twisted his head away from Sarah and to Daphne's sex.

'I'm so strung out on sex,' Daphne said, 'that I'll come very quickly this time. Tongue me, darling! Hard and fast!'

His tongue extended. The angle gave Sarah a clear view. It slithered between Daphne's lips, flattened, and flipped up, right across his lover's engorged clit. It lapped, long and strong, but as fast as a kitten at a bowl of cream. Daphne had been right to brag about his skills.

James couldn't see Sarah, not with his face half turned away. Daphne's head had fallen back and her eyes were screwed tight shut. Sarah didn't know if she'd have dared do it with their eyes on her, but she dropped the hand that held the vibrator to her lap, turned its base to make it hum and worked its head between the lips of her own sex.

She gave a little start. The shaft was pressed against her clit. The effect of the vibrations was almost, but not quite, overwhelming. Why hadn't someone told her?

Daphne took hold of James's head with both hands. Her other leg bent up and passed over his shoulder. His big hands cupped her bottom to hold her in place. The tall slender woman bent her back, leaning herself away from her man while pressing her mound harder against his mouth. And still she bent, folding her back like it was hinged at her waist. Her head dipped lower and lower, to level with her bum, then further, all the way down and tucking in until the top of her head rested on his belly and his shaft's head was touching her just under her chin. Her hands flattened on the bed beside his thick thighs. The upside-down position spread her ribs like a fan and hollowed her tummy. Gravity removed the slight sag of her breasts so that her nipples pointed almost towards her face.

Jesus! Sarah was half Daphne's age but she doubted she was that flexible. In fact, she knew she wasn't. And to think that she'd assumed, like many her age, that if older people still made love, it was missionary style, once a month.

Daphne's mouth opened wide. James's cock just naturally slid between her lips.

Sarah pressed the vibrator hard against her pubic bone with her clit trapped between them.

James's hands lifted Daphne's bottom a few inches, moving her entire body upwards, drawing her lips back up his shaft. He lowered her, impaling her mouth. Again, faster. And again. Daphne wasn't moving a muscle. She hung limp, just letting him use her mouth to masturbate with.

Her breasts jiggled. Her belly button pendant glittered as it shook. James accelerated and now his hips were coming up as he lowered Daphne, driving his shaft deeper and deeper into her mouth.

A sudden urge made Sarah push the vibrating dildo up inside herself while the fingers of her free hand strummed her straining clit. The timing was perfect for, at that moment, James threw his head back, jerked his hips up and roared.

As Sarah was riding her own internal convulsions, Daphne's throat was working. She was swallowing.

The image triggered Sarah's aftershock.

Daphne raised her calves up from behind James, pointed her legs straight up, then tumbled away from him onto her tummy. James slumped down and rolled onto his side.

Daphne slithered off the bed and patted her man's shoulder. 'Take a little nap, darling. We've got all evening.' She sauntered over to where Sarah sat.

Sarah brushed her kilt down, just in case the 'no contact' rule was about to be broken, but Daphne ignored her and helped herself to a sandwich and a can of cola.

'How on earth can you bend yourself like that?'

'Yoga, sweet cheeks.' Daphne gestured to the snacks. 'Take a break. His second climax always takes much longer. You're booked till midnight, I believe, but if we go past that, there'll be a nice little bonus in it for you.'

5

Ms Veronica told Sarah, 'Now you don't owe me a penny and I imagine you got a nice tip as well, right?'

Sarah nodded.

'How was it?'

'I think they were pleased.'

'I meant, how was it for you?'

Sarah blushed and shuffled. 'It was OK.'

'Just OK? You didn't enjoy yourself, not even a little bit?'

'Um . . .'

'They're exhibitionists, remember. They like to talk about what they do. According to them, you got off, three times.'

Sarah couldn't help grinning. 'Four. They missed one. Too busy.'

'I'm pleased. Was it educational?'

'Those two – they're very – um – inventive.'

'That's a perk in this business. You learn all sorts of things. Your boyfriend will be happy about that.'

'About my boyfriend – did Jack call you?'

'Not yet. Who knows, he might call tomorrow, or the next day, but meanwhile, seeing that you had such a good time, shall I sign you up?'

Sarah sank into the office chair. 'I don't know. I was very lucky with that couple. I wasn't expected to do anything . . .'

'Thank me. I never send a girl out on a date unless I'm sure she can handle it.'

'You get many like those two? I'd date them, anytime.'

'I told you, they're twice a year, her birthday and his. As you can probably guess, your date was in celebration of *his* birthday. Our clients are all different. We get a lot of corporate business – escorting out-of-town visitors. Half the time, all they want is eye candy on their arms.'

'The other half?'

'My girls only ever do what they're comfortable with. As it happens, I have two clients to match up this coming weekend, both of them well within your comfort range.'

Two dates meant two thousand dollars, plus tips. Sarah couldn't help being curious. 'They don't want to touch their escorts?' she asked.

'One's new. He'll be in a wheelchair, I'm told. He wants a pretty nurse to push him and act as if she dotes on him at a banquet. He doesn't want people to feel sorry for him.'

'Poor old man.'

'No, I've seen his picture. He's not at all old. He's quite young and good-looking.'

'But in a wheelchair?'

'Yes, in a wheelchair.'

'I could do that, I think, if I had a nurse's uniform.'

Veronica looked Sarah up and down. 'We could fit you out of wardrobe, I'm sure.'

'Wardrobe?'

'We keep some evening gowns and cocktail dresses but mainly fantasy costumes and so on, right here. Quite a few of our clients make special requests about what their dates are to wear, and we don't expect you to have a closet full of fancy gowns, not yet, at least.'

'You said you had two clients that you haven't matched up yet for this weekend. What does the other one expect from his date?'

'He's something like your date last night. He doesn't want to fuck you, if you'll excuse the expression. Like them, he just wants you to be there.'

'Watching?'

'No. He wants to touch his date. In fact, he wants to touch her a lot, but he's very gentle and he's not interested in penetration, not with his dick, at least.'

'I'm confused.'

'He worships women's bodies. He likes to look at them, stroke them, kiss and caress them, even make them climax, but his date wouldn't have to do anything to him and, as I said, no penetration. I'm not sure if he jerks off or not, but you could handle that, after last night.'

'*Handle* what?'

'Not his cock, silly. He does that for himself. You'd never have any contact with his genitals, none at all.'

'James – last night – he stroked himself.'

'And how was that for you?'

Sarah thought about how she'd felt. 'Interesting.'

'Good. I'm glad you have an open mind. You could go a long way in this business, Sarah.'

'I'm not sure that I want to.'

'But two thousand dollars, for two nights' easy work, *that* interests you.'

'It does,' Sarah admitted.

'Then that's settled. Let's go check wardrobe, shall we?'

'Wardrobe' proved to be a large room that was lined with racks of dresses and costumes, all in plastic bags. It was fascinating. Apart from prom night at high school, Sarah hadn't had any occasions to wear formal dresses, and certainly not any in the slinky and sophisticated styles she saw here. There were velvet gowns and some in fabrics that Veronica told her were called 'liquid metal', because that was exactly what they looked like. Several were trimmed with lace and a few were all lace, mainly in black. A woman would have to be extremely daring to wear one of those in public. The thought of doing that brought a warm glow to Sarah's cheeks, and to her sex.

One section was for what Veronica called 'fantasy wear'. There were schoolgirl outfits that would get a girl expelled – micro-skirts and see-through skimpy shirts, ditto cheerleader costumes. 'Nurses' had an entire rack to themselves. Most of those were totally unsuitable for Sarah's date. She couldn't very well show up for the client's banquet in clinging white rubber, even if it did come with a tiny cap with a red cross on it.

'Nurses don't wear uniforms any more,' Sarah said. 'Not even the decent ones. They all wear scrubs or tracksuits.'

'In men's dreams,' Veronica explained, 'all nurses are pretty and horny, and wear white button-through uniforms over skimpy lingerie and thigh-high hose. We can lend you the uniform but you'll need to come up with your own underwear, white preferably, and you'll need white shoes. For a fantasy, white high heels are fine but you're supposed to be the real thing, so trainers or flats of some kind, OK?'

'OK.' Sarah caught her breath. Until that moment, she hadn't actually committed herself to going through with it. That 'OK' changed everything. She'd gone from an 'accidental' escort to 'just this once' to 'this is going to be my part-time job, for some time to come'.

Veronica found Sarah a uniform that was attractive but decent enough to wear in public and added a broad elasticised black belt.

Sarah asked, 'If he wants to show me off to his colleagues, why doesn't he want me to go as his girlfriend instead of as his nurse?'

'People are funny, Sarah. You'll find out just how true that is working for Classique. We get requests for things that even I don't understand.'

'Oh? I don't think I could do anything really kinky.'

'We don't talk about "kink". We prefer the expression "sexual preferences".' She gave Sarah a knowing smile. 'You have those, I'm sure, just like the rest of us. Remember, I'm very careful to match the client to the escort. You'll never be asked to do anything you'd find difficult.'

'But how do you find girls for the clients who have "sexual preferences" that are really, well, different?'

'You'd be amazed at the things some of my girls are into. The only complaints that I get from them is that a client is too vanilla.'

'I'm "vanilla", aren't I?'

'Are you? We'll see, won't we?'

Veronica had arranged an appointment for Sarah with Carlo, who had a beauty salon on the ground floor of the same building. She was to report to Carlo on Saturday, for 'the works'.

As Sarah left the University Pages' office that Saturday, David was waiting for her.

'I'll buy you lunch,' he said.

'Can't, sorry.' She walked fast, forcing him to hurry to match her pace.

'Why not?'

'I'm busy. How's your cold?' Normally, David could be counted on to be distracted from any topic by an enquiry after his health. Not this time, though.

'Gone. Sarah.' David grabbed her forearm, forcing her to a full stop. 'Are you seeing someone else behind my back?'

Ouch! Sarah blushed. 'No.' It was sort of true, she wasn't seeing 'someone' but many 'someones'.

'What's going on?'

Sarah conjured up a lie based on an ad she'd read a few days before. 'Catering,' she blurted.

'Catering?'

'I've found a part-time job with a catering service, working weddings on weekends. You can still take me out on weekdays though.'

Surely he would see through her flimsy story? Sarah steadied herself for the barrage of outrage that was surely coming.

'I see.' David released her arm. 'OK.'

Amazing. It seemed that half the success of lying lay with the one being lied to. David didn't want to face the truth, so he swallowed anything she gave him as an alternative, however sketchy. What a fascinating insight into the human psyche. She decided then and there to do her final epistemology paper on the topic.

Sarah pecked David on the cheek and made her escape.

She delivered herself into the expert hands of Carlo. For the first time in her young life, Sarah submitted to the happy ordeal of a manicure, a pedicure, a seaweed wrap, a facial and the full range of hair treatments including blonde highlights, something she'd always longed for but never tried. Her hairstyle stayed basically the same, on her insistence. A new one would have made David suspicious.

He really was beginning to get in her way.

She left Carlo's with her hair burnished and her face subtly transformed from 'very pretty' to 'absolutely stunning'. Perhaps it was the pink mirrors in the elevator fooling her, but she didn't think so.

Veronica wasn't in her office but Debra had Sarah's nurse's outfit waiting. The receptionist didn't offer anywhere private for Sarah to change, and watched her as she stripped off her page's uniform and everyday undies and put on her new sexy lingerie and white Dim stay-up stockings. Stay-up stockings! They were nothing like the pantyhose she'd worn to the prom, the last time she'd worn hose. Stay-ups were comfortable once she got them on and the lacy tops were pretty; they'd be even prettier in a colour less institutional than nurse white.

At first, Sarah was uncomfortable dressing in front of Debra, but by the time she was pinning her little starched cap in place she'd adjusted. A professional escort can't very well allow herself to feel embarrassed about showing her body, after all.

In a breach of standard practice, Sarah was given a private address. As his nurse, she'd be expected to arrive with him at their destination.

'Take this,' Debra said. She held out a sleek black plastic rectangle.

'What is it?'

'A BlackBerry.' Debra shook her head. 'It's a cellphone. And a lot more.'

Sarah blushed. Debra had already explained how to put on stay-ups, and now she had to explain what a cellphone was. Sarah wouldn't blame her if Debra thought she was stupid, but the other woman's voice was patient as she explained. 'Now that you're on the books, you have to carry a cellphone. You won't need it, but speed-dial number one will always bring you help, twenty-four/seven.'

'Help?' Sarah's tummy felt queasy.

'In case you get stranded somewhere, or something. Ms Veronica looks after her girls.'

Reassured, Sarah tucked the compact phone into her white beaded clutch. There was a cab waiting for her outside. The traffic was heavy so it took a while for her to get to the high-rise apartment building. Her date was waiting in the lobby.

He looked to be in his late thirties. His thinning hair was slicked back from a broad forehead. Either he wasn't at all bad looking or it was the effect of his immaculately cut tuxedo, but when he smiled up at her, his face lit up in a way that Sarah found endearing.

He said, 'George. George Patros. You are?'

'Sarah. Nice to meet you, George.'

'Nurse Sarah. I like that. Would you wheel me down to the underground parking, please?'

There was a van and driver waiting. The driver locked George's chair onto a tailgate, made it go up and then pushed it into the back of the van. There was a seat for Sarah facing her client.

'You have lovely legs,' he told her.

'Thank you, George.'

'Would you mind . . .' He paused as if embarrassed.

'Mind what, George?'

'I shouldn't.'

'Go ahead. Ask me.'

'I don't get to be with beautiful women very often and I do admire . . .'

'Admire what?' she encouraged.

'Nice legs. Would you mind?' He mimed pulling an invisible skirt up.

'Well, George, I really enjoy being admired, so . . .' She tugged her skirt up high enough that its hem rested on her thighs just above the lacy tops of her hose. 'How's that?'

'Oh my God! They're absolutely perfect!'

Sarah blushed and pulled her skirt a couple of inches higher. What a sweetheart he was! Poor man – to get so excited over her legs. He had to live a very lonely life.

As they travelled, George briefed her. He worked from his apartment as a programmer for GeoMancy, which was a subsidiary of O.M.E. She guessed that the 'O' was for Ohio but she'd never heard of the company. O.M.E. hosted two employee functions a year, one on its founder's birthday and one at Christmas. George had only been with the company for a matter of months so the people he knew there he only knew by phone and email.

'I'm a bit self-conscious of people staring at me,' he explained. 'Having you with me, I won't have to worry. All their eyes will be on you.'

The doll! Sarah decided then and there that she'd make the date extra special for him. If he wanted to look at her legs, she'd gladly show them off. Come to that, whatever he wanted to look at, he'd get to see.

She wondered whether he could fuck. Having lost the use of his legs didn't necessarily mean that he couldn't get an erection, did it? And if it did, maybe he could still feel. He might like to be touched, or it might embarrass him. Somehow or another, she'd find out.

There was a handicapped ramp into the banquet hall. They picked up nametags and went on inside. The men were almost all in tuxedos and the women wore cocktail or evening dresses. So what? Sarah was dressed up, though in a way she doubted anyone would suspect.

A crowd had gathered around the free bar. Sarah wheeled George up to it. It parted like the Red Sea for him. The barkeep took their orders out of turn. So there was an upside to not being able to walk.

A man with 'Carl' on his jacket and a woman with 'Liz' over her left breast introduced themselves. Both worked in a department that George programmed for.

Carl said, 'I didn't know ...' He twirled a finger at George's wheelchair.

George shrugged. 'Why would you? It's one of the advantages of e-commuting, everyone's equal.'

The talk turned to technical stuff that was far beyond Sarah's limited computer literacy. George's hand was resting on his chair's armrest. Sarah pressed her thigh against the backs of his fingers. He threw her a grateful glance and pressed back. From then on, from time to time, his fingers wriggled. Sarah glanced down into his lap. There was no sign that he was getting an erection, but that didn't mean that he couldn't.

An MC announced that dinner was served. Sarah wheeled George in. Carl removed the chair that was in front of George's name card. Sarah's card read 'Guest'. There was minestrone or antipasto followed by either buffalo steak or squab. Sarah didn't think she could eat pigeon meat so they both had the steak, which came with a plum sauce and was decorated with what Sarah took to be blades of grass.

George ordered a bottle of Chianti for them to share. It was dry enough to make her tongue stick to the roof of her mouth but she found that she quite liked it.

The white linen cloth draped onto their thighs. In the spirit of giving George good value for his two thousand bucks, and as an experiment, Sarah rested her hand on his thigh under the cloth's concealment. His leg twitched. It felt quite muscular. Perhaps he hadn't been crippled for long enough for it to atrophy.

So, his legs could feel, which had to mean ...

His fingers touched her nyloned thigh just above her knee and stroked up to the top of her stocking. Sarah hitched forwards in her chair so that his fingertips brushed her bare skin. They half turned to look at each other, a question in his eyes and an answering promise in hers. She thought she actually felt something for the poor man, not love exactly but at least something close to affection. Was that weird? Was it something hormonal or psychological? She'd made up her mind that she was going to make George happy that night. Had that decision triggered an emotional response in her? If it had, being an escort could be more satisfying than just the money and the sex.

How had she felt towards the exhibitionists, James and Daphne? Warm. Definitely warm. She considered them her friends now, even though she wasn't likely to see them ever again.

Jack, of course, was something else again. She'd fallen in genuine love with him, her first.

Because he'd been her first?

She'd have to think about that, but later. For now, George's fingertips were making little circles on her bare skin and she was thoroughly enjoying it. That ghost of a tingle was starting. *Carpe diem*, she told herself. 'Seize the day.' A line from a song her dad sometimes sang came into her mind: 'If you can't be with the one that you love, love the one that you're with.' For the first time in her life, the lyrics made perfect sense.

There were speeches about things and people that didn't interest Sarah so she concentrated on what George's fingers were doing and daydreamed about what they'd do to her when they got back to his apartment. A man who couldn't walk could still kiss, and she doted on kissing. He could still use his fingers, as well, and George seemed to have a very delicate touch.

But she should be thinking about what she could do to please George, not about what he could do for her. He was the customer, after all.

Daphne had done some incredible things to James with her mouth. Sarah didn't know if she was up to doing the same things, but she could certainly try. What sort of a cock did George have, she wondered.

Everyone but George stood up. Sarah hurried to copy them and drank a toast to someone or something. Waiters cleared away and then came round with coffee and liqueurs. Sarah would have liked to try her first liqueur but she whispered to George, 'What time does this finish?'

'Bored?'

'No,' she lied, 'but wouldn't you like us to be alone?'

George arched his back. Louder than necessary, he announced, 'I'm getting pangs, Sarah. My back's seizing up. I'm sorry to drag you away from all the fun but could you take me home and give me my medicine?'

As she wheeled him out, she whispered, 'Are you really in pain, George?'

'Of a sort, but my stiffness isn't in my back. I was hoping you'd have the right treatment to cure it.'

Sarah chuckled. 'I'll think of something, I promise.'

'Sweet nurse.'

On the ride back, Sarah posed her legs and pulled her skirt up high enough to show George glimpses of her gossamer white panties. He groaned. If it hadn't been for the driver up front, she'd have unbuttoned her uniform to see if he liked her matching bra and its contents.

Was she becoming an exhibitionist or didn't it count if there were just the two of you?

George said, 'This ride is taking for ever.'

'It'll be worth the wait, George, I promise.' She really meant that.

George's apartment was nothing like Sarah expected. With him being a computer geek, she'd thought it'd either be a total mess, with tottering stacks of books and papers scattered everywhere, or obsessive-compulsive neat. It was neat and tidy, but lived in, quite ordinary, really.

The couch looked as if it was used, so she asked him, 'Would you like me to help you to the couch, or to your bed?' She made her voice throaty on 'bed', so he'd understand the implications.

'I'm comfortable in my wheelchair, thanks. Nurse Sarah?'

'Yes, George?'

'Could I see those lovely legs of yours again, please?'

'Of course.' She stepped back a little, to give him a full view. Working slowly from the lowest up, she undid the buttons on her uniform one at a time, till she came to its broad elasticised belt.

When she put her fingers to the buckle, George said, 'Leave the belt, please?'

'Whatever pleases you, George. Shall I . . .?' She reached for the top button.

'Yes, please.'

Sarah posed, one knee before the other, as she'd seen models do, and unbuttoned down to her belt. That, she guessed, was part of his kink – or 'sexual preference' as Veronica had insisted it be called.

'I could take my uniform off but leave the belt on, if you'd like.'

'No, I like the uniform on you, Nurse Sarah.'

Ah, so it was her being a nurse that he was fixated on.

'Is there anything else that your naughty little nurse can do for you, George? I'm here to look after you, and –' she paused to tilt the little watch pinned to her breast pocket up so she could glance at it '– I see the night shift has started.' Sarah parted the skirt to her uniform to give him a better look at her legs.

It was strange, she felt, for a professional escort to be seducing her client. After all, she was bought and paid for. He was entitled, whether Veronica was willing to admit or not, to any relatively normal sexual services he fancied.

How did she feel about that – being 'bought and paid for'? Should she be ashamed? She wasn't. In fact, she was sort of proud of herself. Almost any girl could 'give it away'. Not many could sell their good looks and erotic skills at $2,000 plus tips per time.

George's voice was creaky when he asked, 'Could you come closer?'

She sauntered towards him, deliberately teasing, until her thighs were inches from the armrest of his chair.

His eyes opened wide. He licked his lips. 'May I touch you?'

'I'd like that, George.'

'You would?' He seemed both pleased and surprised.

'Nurses have needs too, George.'

'Oh!' His hand reached out hesitantly. His fingers rested lightly on Sarah's stocking, just above and on the inside of her knee. George looked up into her eyes, as if questioning his right to be fondling her.

'You have a delicate touch, George. I like that.'

Encouraged, he made tiny circles on the white nylon, slowly travelling upwards. Sarah sighed and half hooded her eyes. Poor man, she thought. He needed all the encouragement he could get. Her excitement wasn't all fake. It was a sexy situation. Here she was, with a man who was virtually a stranger, blatantly showing herself off and offering herself. If that made her a slut, then being a slut was fun!

When she compared, she realised that George's diffident caresses excited her far more than David's had ever done. The difference, she thought, was that with David she'd always felt that she had to hold back, not get carried away by her own lust. In her new role, getting totally hot was an asset, not a liability.

George's little circles seemed to have stalled at her lacy stocking top. Perhaps that was what he liked, but she decided to take a chance. Sarah reached down, took hold of his wrist and moved his hand higher.

When George's fingers touched the bare skin of Sarah's thigh he sucked in a deep breath. To encourage him, she moved her feet further apart and pushed her mound an inch closer to his face. Even so, his circles moved no higher than to brush the backs of his fingers against the thin fabric that was stretched over her sex. Didn't he want to finger her? With David, it was always a kiss and an exploring finger at the same time. Could that be it?

Sarah made her voice husky and asked, 'May I kiss you, George?'

'You want to?'

'You're a very attractive man, George. I like kissing, don't you?'

'Y-yes.'

She closed the gap, forcing the back of his hand to press up against her sex, and leant over him, holding the far arm of his chair and its back. He turned his face up. Her lips descended. She brushed them lightly across his.

George's lips were softer and smoother than she expected,

more like a girl's than a man's. That wasn't unpleasant at all. When he didn't respond to her 'little girl' kiss, she let her lips part slightly in invitation. He still didn't react. She took his lower lip between her two and tugged at it gently. His free hand came up to hold the back of her neck, as if he was afraid she'd pull back, but his mouth was still passive. OK, in that case . . .

Sarah extended the tip of her tongue. His lips parted just enough to allow it entrance but his tongue didn't reciprocate.

Hmm. She'd heard boys complain that some girls didn't 'kiss back' but she'd never heard any girls gripe about the reverse. It had to be because of his insecurity, from being confined to his chair. Sarah stabbed her tongue into his mouth, thrusting it in as deeply as she could.

George moaned and gripped her tighter, both her thigh and the back of her neck. It was obvious that she was pleasing him but he remained the passive recipient, taking but not giving.

She could handle that.

Sarah let her tongue go wild, exploring, lapping and sucking, feasting on his mouth. He made more noises. The hand between her legs cupped and kneaded her. The hand on her neck moved higher, knocking her little cap off and knotting in her hair. There was no way he was going to let her escape but she had to do all the work, and it was becoming uncomfortable, being bent over him awkwardly and immobile. Partly for a change in position and partly to check if she was really getting to him, she dropped her right hand into his lap.

Yes, she was getting to him all right. Under the serge of his tuxedo pants, he was rigid. Still dominating his mouth, Sarah fumbled for and found his zipper's tab. George held his breath. Sarah tugged downwards, very slowly, deliberately teasing him. To extend his torment, she rested her open palm over where his erection lay and massaged it gently through the fabric.

His fly was open and he no doubt expected her hand to slide inside. Let him wait!

Each little squeeze of her hand brought a pleading moan

from him. She gripped and rubbed, but not hard. Up and down. Up and down. Perhaps it was cruel, him being in a wheelchair, but Sarah was determined to make him suffer.

Eventually, he gasped into her mouth, 'Please, nurse?'

'This?' she asked. Her fingers parted his fly, found the slit in his boxers, and crept slowly inside.

His shaft was burning hot. She just held it for a long moment before working it out into the open air.

'I want to see it,' she told him.

His hand released her hair. Sarah dropped to her knees in front of his chair, denying him easy access to her sex. He hadn't been doing much about that, anyway. Sarah reminded herself that she was there for his pleasure, not hers. She couldn't expect every client to be as giving as Jack.

Still holding his shaft and gazing at it as fondly as she could, she murmured, 'It's so handsome.'

Smugly, he said, 'You'd know. You must see a lot of cocks in your line of work.' He paused before adding, 'Nursing.'

'Yours is extra special.' In fact, judging by the few she'd seen, there was nothing special about it at all. It was neither particularly long nor thick, but it still attracted her. She'd thought that maybe some cocks would be ugly but she hadn't seen a repulsive one yet.

Sarah remembered Daphne stroking James. She'd held him delicately between thumb and finger and said, 'This is how you like me to start, right, James? Teasing?'

Sarah took hold of George in a similar fashion, stroked him from base to head once, and said, 'Is this how you like it at first, George, teasing?'

He grunted.

Very well. She continued with her gentle caresses until George's hips twitched at her. She asked, 'Harder?'

She felt his vigorous nod. Her fingers wrapped him. Using a little more force, she worked her hand up and down again, slowly accelerating her strokes. A tiny bead of clear fluid extruded from the eye of his cock's head. Sarah smoothed over it, smearing her palm with his essence. She changed her strokes to slower but stronger, each one culminating with a gloss over his glans. She'd learnt a lot from Daphne. Now she was honing her skills against the day she'd be able to use them on her Jack. When that day came, she was going to be the best, she'd decided.

But she'd been denying David her mouth and her oral skills were important. OK. She changed her mind. She had been going to give George the best handjob she knew how to give, but having him helpless, totally at her mercy, made him an ideal subject to practise what her mouth and tongue could do. Sarah cast her mind back to Daphne and James. That lithe redhead had done incredible things with her mouth. Maybe Sarah couldn't perform as well as Daphne had, not yet, but she could start learning, right now.

Holding just the head of George's cock between finger and thumb, Sarah flattened her tongue and slurped it up his full length, from his scrotum to that little knot just below its head. In that second love-making session, Daphne had paid particular attention to that tiny area, to James's obvious delight.

Sarah changed her grip to a firm grasp around George's shaft, pointed her tongue and swirled its tip on that delicate spot. He went rigid. Sarah smoothed her tongue over his dome once more before returning to tantalise his knot. He tasted salty-lemony sweet. Jack had as well. Perhaps the flavour was universal.

Her tongue went from knot to dome and back again, over and over, for what she judged was a full five minutes. By then, George was making unintelligible yearning noises and his cock was leaking copiously. Mentally, she commanded him not to climax yet, not before she'd got some practice with her mouth. Her lips parted. She took his head gently between them and tried to work the point of her tongue into his cock's eye.

George made a choking noise.

Not yet, George.

She took a little more of his shaft into her mouth. Her tongue pressed up on its underside. She nodded, rubbing his dome against her hard palate. George groaned. Soon, George, but not just yet. Sarah set her hands on the seat of his chair, one beside each thigh, and pushed herself higher, into an arc over his lap. Now was the test. She relaxed her throat and commanded her gag reflex to cease functioning. Little by little, she lowered herself. His knob pressed her tongue down. Lower. Her mouth was full of him, and he wasn't as big as Jack. She took a deep breath in through her nose and thrust down. His cock's head butted the back of her mouth. Sarah felt a brief moment of triumph before her throat spasmed and she had to snatch back.

She was going to need more practice, but it was a good start. Sarah had learnt all she felt she could for now, so she slurped off George's cock and began masturbating him again. Still using what she'd learnt from Daphne, she extended the flat of her tongue so that each stroke rubbed his dome on it. She strained her eyes upwards to meet George's, just as Daphne had done with James.

Between vigorous strokes, she begged, 'Give it to me, George. Give me all your lovely hot cream.'

And he did. His body shook so hard his wheelchair rattled.

Sarah licked her lips and swallowed, making sure that George saw what she was doing. She stood and began to button her dress up before she remembered that he had her till midnight, and it was barely eleven. 'More?' she asked him. 'What would you like me to do next?'

'I'm drained,' he admitted. 'You were wonderful.'

'Thank you.'

'Oh, your pay.' And George stood up, walked to the sideboard and brought back a thick envelope.

Sarah was still in a state of utter confusion when the apartment door closed behind her.

6

Veronica had warned Sarah that 'Peter' might seem a little weird at first but she'd promised her that he was completely harmless. In fact, some of the girls competed for a date with him. Veronica had said she was only giving the date to Sarah because she thought it would be educational for her.

As instructed, Sarah arrived at Peter's motel wearing loafers, no hose, no underwear, no make-up, not even lipgloss, with just a simple floral-print button-through dress under her fall topcoat.

'Just do everything he asks,' Veronica had said. 'You don't even have to speak, though some appreciative moans would please him. When you climax, make it as loud and dramatic as possible. Can do?'

'I didn't get there on my date with George. I did with James and Daphne, but not because of anything they did to me. I had to take care of it myself. What if I don't climax with this client? Do I fake it?'

'You won't have to fake it with Peter. I guarantee it. Enjoy, my dear. I envy you this one.'

'But you said he wouldn't want to fuck me?' Sarah was becoming more at ease with the word. It was what she was paid to do, after all.

'He won't. You'll see. There are more things people can do to make each other happy than you can dream of, Sarah.'

Sarah doubted that. She'd had some pretty wild fantasies since she'd hit puberty. Still, she wasn't going to argue.

It was a nice motel, which was encouraging but not surprising. People who could afford what Classique charged could afford nice places for their assignations. That familiar ghost of a tingle started between her thighs. Anticipation always did that.

Peter opened the door on her first knock. Like James, he beckoned her in without a word. Her date looked kind of young at first glance, with a shock of dark curls over a round boyish face, but the creases around his eyes hinted that he was mature. Like James, he was in a robe and barefoot, but Peter's robe was much fancier, crimson silk, with black grosgrain lapels. Sarah wondered what the texture would feel like, but she'd been warned about showing any initiative.

There was a masseur's portable table set up in the middle of the room. It would certainly take her weight easily enough but she doubted it would bear two people at once, particularly if they were moving vigorously. That confirmed what Veronica had said about him not wanting to fuck her.

He took her coat and laid it aside, then stood behind her with his hands hovering above her shoulders. Right – he wanted her naked, no striptease, just bare, and quickly. Sarah unbuttoned her dress. He took it from her and set it with her coat. By reflex, Sarah posed, but he walked right past her to the bed, to a glossy mottled-chocolate pile of what looked like fur.

Peter flourished it like a toreador executing a veronica and cast it over the massage table. He added a matching pillow. A broad wave invited Sarah to climb on top. Closer up, she was sure that the cover was either mink or an excellent imitation. Sarah stretched out flat on her tummy. How decadent! Naked, on mink. She shivered. The slight movement caressed her tummy and thighs with the tips of a thousand tiny mink hairs.

In Psych 101, they'd touched on the works of Leopold von Sacher-Masoch, who'd given his name to masochism and who'd written a notorious novel *Venus in Furs*. Was Peter a masochist? Couldn't be. Veronica would have primed her for that, not that Sarah could have managed that sort of encounter, not as the dominant sadist. As the submissive masochist? Her first thought was, Of course not, but she'd enjoyed Jack's few spanks and his less-than-gentle treatment of her nipples, so . . .

Sarah turned her head, her eyes slitted. Peter was pulling a glove, mink again, on to his right hand. Lying on mink, being stroked by mink – she'd never even fantasised such a scene but now that it was obviously about to happen to her – that ghost of a tingle between her thighs intensified into a real tingle.

But what if she seeped onto his mink?

Peter's left hand lifted her hair from her nape. The glove stroked across the skin at the back of her neck, as delicately as a sprinkling of talcum powder. Sarah wanted to squirm but made herself lie perfectly still. The tickling caress ran down her spine to the pad of muscle at its base. His bare hand followed, skimming very lightly, as if, perhaps, he was assessing the quality of the goosebumps his glove was raising.

There was a pause. The glove lifted. Sarah didn't tense, but she wanted to. Anticipating where she'd be touched next was sweet torture. She became very aware of the nap of the fur she lay on, particularly where it almost tickled her mound.

The glove descended onto the exact spot it had lifted from and then swiftly ran up the full length of her spine, back to her nape. Sarah couldn't help it. She shivered and let out a tiny moan.

Peter gave a grunt of satisfaction.

Right. Reaction was good. It was initiative that was forbidden.

He stroked down her left side. There was a spot at her waist that made her want to squirm and giggle. The glove lingered there, making little circles, driving her to the edge of begging for mercy. Perhaps Peter was a sadist, of sorts. Was it still sadism if tormenting pleasure was what was inflicted?

His glove brushed across the undersides of her bottom cheeks before moving up again, travelling the length of her right side, once more executing an arabesque where she was the most ticklish. From there, it was light swirling movements, her shoulder blades, nape, the right cheek of her bottom, nape again, left cheek. He returned to her bottom again and again, sometimes drawing the fur up its crease but always so gently that she felt no pressure, no indication that he was interested in touching her between her cheeks.

Perversely, Sarah couldn't help but wonder what that tormenting glove might feel like if it did stroke her there.

She was twitching a lot, sometimes from an actual caress and sometimes from the anticipation of one. Those tiny movements conspired, without her volition, to move her thighs subtly further apart, just a couple of inches. Sarah couldn't control her involuntary movements, could she?

Then his glove was on her left ankle. If he started on the soles of her feet, she wouldn't be able to control herself. That would be unfair of him.

But he travelled slowly up her leg, stroking her calf and then behind her knee. That area made her gulp and knot her fists. Sarah stayed tense as the fur wandered up the back of her thigh. It was nearing an area that both desired and dreaded its touch. What would mink feel like, smoothing over, not her mound, she'd felt that, but those sensitive lips that had already parted slightly, Sarah wondered.

But he switched to her right ankle and subjected her to the same torture again, almost excruciating behind her knee, thrilling as it moved higher, pausing an inch from her sex.

Huh? Had he touched that sensitive area between her sex and her anus? If he had, it had been too lightly for her to be sure.

Then there was nothing. The back of a bare hand nudged her hip gently. Sarah opened her eyes a little wider, letting him see that they were open. He made a 'roll over' signal.

Oh God! It'd been hard enough to endure the things he'd done to her back. How would she bear the same treatment on the front of her body? The mere thought of it made her clit tingle and her tummy clench. Still, she had no choice. Sarah rolled onto her back, letting her arms flop sideways and her legs part even wider. She closed her eyes for real and took a deep breath.

A smile twitched her lips. What sacrifices a girl had to make to please a man!

He started at the hollow of her throat. The touches there made her want to crook her neck but she forced herself to relax. The glove's fingertips trailed downwards, passing between her breasts, past her diaphragm, to her navel. That made her suck air. It wandered a little lower but paused just short of her mound again.

Up once more, but making circles, the biggest one of which encompassed both of her breasts, just brushing the sides and undersides of their globes. But then it circled her left breast, with a touch so light he might have been trailing cobwebs across her skin, and spiralled in, towards her erect nipple. She peeked again. The flat furry palm of the glove was hovering over her nub, again making circles, but in the air, and it was descending with agonising slowness.

It felt to Sarah that her nipple was stretching up to meet the fur. Minute hairs brushed her flesh. She gasped and resisted the urge to push her chest up. The phantom brushing became a definite caress, but not hard enough, nowhere near hard enough. She was panting, she realised. Her ribcage was heaving.

The bastard was driving her out of her fucking mind!

He switched to her right breast. This time, she could anticipate every movement, every touch, and that made it so much worse.

Sarah endured the excruciating pleasure somehow. The glove crept down her body, moving more slowly than ever before. The skin in its path cringed in anticipation. Her insides clenched. Sarah whimpered, which elicited a chuckle from Peter. His free hand touched the insides of her thighs, suggesting that she spread them more. Mink reached the delicate fuzz on her mound. She couldn't help it. Sarah peered down the length of her body. The glove was hovering again, right over her sex. It was cupped, ready to fit her curves. It descended. Lower. Closer. Lower. Closer. Could she feel it?

Then she knew that she could, and she knew that her sex lips had parted on their own, exposing their sensitive inner surfaces. She knew because those delicate internal membranes were being tickled.

Somehow, Sarah resisted the urge to hump up against her

tormentor. Despite her attempts to control herself, her head whipped from side to side. Wet hair flailed her cheeks. She had to have been sweating. Sarah whimpered, pleading wordlessly for mercy, but to no avail.

Peter grunted. Sarah slitted her eyes. He was peeling the mink glove off.

How could he? Did he mean to leave her like that? That'd be too, too cruel.

He nudged her hip. Obediently, she rolled over again but with her head turned so that she could spy on him. He had a bottle of oil in his hands. Peter leant over her, pressing close enough that if he hadn't been wearing that robe she could have got her mouth to his cock. She could taste its aroma, though, in the air. It hadn't occurred to her before, but the torment he'd put her through had to have teased him almost as much as it had her.

Oil dribbled across her shoulders and in a line from her nape down to the base of her spine again. Strong fingers took hold of her trapezius muscles. Powerful thumbs pressed into her flesh, separating those muscles. They kneaded. Sarah sighed. She was still taut with lust, but those hands, working so artfully, were relaxing her. They moved lower, one to each shoulder blade, and somehow worked those flat bones in little circles. She sighed again. The knuckles of both of his hands pressed on each side of her spine.

It felt so good that he had to have had training in massage. Perhaps he was a therapist of some sort, or a chiropractor. Sarah suppressed a giggle. Women would give good money for what she was experiencing, and here she was, being paid to endure it.

The knuckles worked down, down to the pad of her tailbone. He poured more oil. Some of it trickled into the crease of her bum. Was he going to touch her there now? She'd been thinking about that sort of thing, ever since James and Daphne, but she hadn't made up her mind if she was ready to be touched in that taboo place.

A hand encompassed each cheek of her bottom. They

kneaded. Pressing down firmly, they rotated, moving her buttocks independently. As they moved, they were squeezed together and then pulled wide apart. Sarah felt herself blush. When her bottom was spread, her anus was exposed. He'd be looking at it! No one had ever inspected her there.

His hands moved on, to her relief. Peter worked the long muscles in the backs of her thighs, passed on to her calves and then, this time, he paid attention to the soles of her feet. Strong probing thumbs separated tiny bones, working between them. It was absolute bliss. It occurred to Sarah that the first massage Peter had given her was aimed at awakening her skin. Now he was stimulating her at a much deeper level, inside and between her muscles. It felt as if his fingers were investigating her very bones.

Peter took hold of the baby toe of her left foot and tugged it. She felt a 'crack' but it was too soft to hear. He passed on to the next toe and so on, each tiny digit getting its own dose of therapy. Although Sarah's sex was still in a state of arousal, the rest of her body, and her mind, were lulled into a dreamy torpor.

But his touch on her hip awakened her. Roll over? Those clever hands were going to manipulate the front of her body? Would he . . .? She decided that yes, he would, but she'd have to wait for that. Impatiently. Fuck! Sarah really needed to be touched there, in that intimate place that so far he'd only threatened to fondle. Or promised?

Peter anointed her body again, a drizzled cross that drew a line from nipple to nipple, from the hollow of her throat down to her mound – and beyond. Oil dribbled onto her swollen outer lips and trickled between them.

She was going to be massaged there! But when? Soon? Please, soon.

His fingertips came to rest on her collarbones. The heels of his hands pressed lightly down on the upper slopes of her breasts. He rotated. The movements wobbled her breasts. His touch became firmer. Peter's fingers moved a little lower and manipulated her pectoral muscles, making her very aware that they were her breasts' support. By ignoring those parts of her breasts that men doted on the most, her nipples, he was demonstrating his complete mastery over them, and her.

He was in control. She was being controlled. That thought was simultaneously relaxing and exciting.

His massage wandered down her sides. Once more she squirmed when he reached her waist but he didn't linger there. He compressed the fleshiest parts of her hips, palpitating, and moved lower, when she really wanted him to pay attention to her sex. The large muscles of her thighs were pliant under his firm ministrations. It was a contradiction in a way: he was making her very aware that those muscles were strong but at the same time soothing them so completely that they felt like jelly.

Peter moved her kneecaps. That felt weird, but not at all unpleasant. The fingertips of both of his hands pressed against the insides of her knees, not massaging now, just urging them further apart.

At last!

Sarah whimpered, to encourage him, and spread her thighs wide. From her knees down her legs dangled over the sides of the table. Inside, she twitched with nervous thrills. She'd endured the longest and most elaborate foreplay she could imagine and was so fucking ready to be fingered that she could have screamed.

He was standing at the far end of the table, pouring oil over his own hands. With a movement so sudden that it made her flinch, he reached up the table at her, took her behind her knees and dragged her down towards him. More oil was poured, directly onto her sex now, onto and into it. She could feel the oil trickling into her intimate crevices and secret depths.

Peter came round to her side again. His hands lifted high to shake his sleeves back to his elbows. He inspected his own hands, fronts and backs.

In her head, Sarah screeched, Get on with it!

There was a sly little grin on his face as he reached over her.

Peter did that little 'hovering over' that was so maddening. Sarah couldn't help it. Her hips rolled slightly. Her back arched. The long muscles in her thighs knotted and relaxed. Her belly clenched.

One hand descended and came to a gentle rest, its heel on the base of her pubic mound, its fingers cupping her sex. His thumb and little finger moved, pressing down on her outer lips, tugging them further apart. Three fingers curled under, and into, her.

Hell! They didn't have to push or probe. Her pussy had to have been gaping wide, waiting. Fingers dabbled in the softness of her sex's vestibule. The heel of his hand pressed down and rotated.

It was on her clit, her bare, engorged, exposed clit. Thank Christ!

Inside her, the fingers curled up behind her pubic bone. There, they explored. They came to rest on the area she'd read about in a magazine, her G-spot. There'd been some debate over whether it really existed and if it did, did all women have them.

Whatever 'all' women had, she certainly had one, though no one had ever touched hers before now. Fingertips palpitated. Their pressure became firmer, more insistent. It was as if he were trying to make something happen.

Sarah gasped. Something *was* happening. The insides of her sex, its walls, were oozing.

Peter chuckled softly.

It was a cliché but he really was playing her body like a musical instrument. He was a maestro. All she could do, all she wanted to do, was surrender, just feel, just let him have his way with her. With a long sigh, she went limp.

The hand that had taken possession of her sex pressed and rotated, rolling her clit under its heel while three fingers coaxed her fluids to flow. His thumb seemed to be stroking her labia and one finger, his smallest, see-sawed between the cheeks of her bottom. Its tip stroked her bum hole. Before now, she'd have clenched and jerked at that contact, but given the state she was in, she had no emotional responses. She simply absorbed sensations. There were no rights or wrongs apart from 'feel good' or 'feel bad'. Nothing he'd done had felt bad. If his little finger had pushed up into her rectum, she'd have accepted it. He didn't. All the oily pad of his finger did was circle her sphincter. It felt nice but those sensations were minor compared to the divine thrills that the fingers inside her and his stroking thumb and the palm pressing on her clit were giving her.

But he'd oiled both of his hands, and he was only using one.

Sarah let her head flop to the side and her eyelids part a fraction. So, that was why. Peter's free hand was inside his robe. By the movements of his elbow, he was masturbating.

She'd enjoy watching but it was hard to concentrate because the heel of his other hand pressed down harder, pushing her clit against her pubic bone. She'd never in her life been handled like this. Not even Jack had shown such incredible ability, even when using two hands. Peter was done playing now, she was sure of it. His hand beneath his robe was pumping, but it was the hand inside her, the fingers and thumb that pressed and rubbed and stroked and plunged, moving ever faster, that she couldn't have escaped if she'd wanted to. She was held down by the force of his hand on her clit as surely as if she were bound to the table.

'Oh God, Peter, you're good, you're so good ...' She was starting to rave now, the words tumbling from her mouth as the sensations piled on top of each other. Each thrust of his fingers made her ache for the next. Each stroke of his thumb made her labia swell. Her clit was thick beneath his palm, her head was thick with words and her groin was thick with boiling blood that had to, had to be released.

He grunted, once, and bore down harder. Sarah yipped. Her entire body folded up around his arm like an elapsed-time film of a closing flower. The release was complete. Sarah could do nothing but hump and judder and yip until the paroxysms ceased and she lay limp on the wet mink.

Wet?

Peter cleaned his hands on a small towel and handed her a big one. She wiped the oil off her body and sat up. Yes, the mink beneath her was soaked. She dabbed between her legs. Also wet. 'I'm sorry,' she mumbled.

'Silly,' he said. 'You ejaculated.'

'Oh.'

He fetched her dress for her. She climbed off the massage table onto trembling legs.

'That was nice,' he said. He barely looked at her. He was captivated by the wet fur. His hands twitched above it. 'There's something for you on the table by the door.'

Sarah picked up the generous tip on her way out. As she closed the door, she caught a glimpse of him climbing up onto the massage table. He stretched out face-down on the wet fur with a sigh and closed his eyes.

Another satisfied client for Sarah Meadows. She headed for the elevators with a jaunty spring in her step.

7

Professor Braun wrote furiously on the second of three black-boards at the front of the classroom. Many of the students attempted to keep up, but not Sarah. She'd figured out his *modus operandi*. He was teaching them existentialism by example. Long before even the keenest of her classmates had managed to copy his scribbling, he'd run out of blackboard space, erase everything and start over.

They'd been through this before. Every moment in his classroom was meaningless torture, but since the only requirement for a pass was perfect attendance, not showing up was not an option.

On the one hand, she hated him and his arrogant teaching approach. On the other, she had to hand it to him. How better to teach the 'futility of life' than this?

Penny slid into the vacant desk beside her. She'd been in many of Sarah's classes over the past three years but they'd rarely talked, until lately. For some reason, perhaps because of Sarah's new style, she'd become one of the gang in a way she never had before.

It hadn't bothered her, she didn't think. Or had it? She'd always been a loner. But it was fun, much more fun than she'd have imagined, having a give and take sort of friendship with the other students.

'Hi,' said Penny. She jerked her head towards Professor Braun. 'Back at it, I see.'

'Mmm.'

'Suckers,' muttered Penny, glancing at the bent heads of the keeners. 'None of it makes any sense. Have you noticed?'

'Yep,' Sarah replied.

'Some of us are hitting the pub night tonight. Wanna come? Thirty-five cent chicken wings.'

Sarah's reflexive response would have been to beg off, but she hesitated. Her best friend through her school days had been Alice, another bright, odd-girl-out type who was now studying archaeology at Luxor University. Their communication was limited to emails and occasional phone calls.

Sarah had always been content with one friend, and once she'd come to university David had filled that spot quite nicely. Now, however, she avoided him as much as she could.

Since she kept her escort work for weekends and only acted as a tour guide Saturday mornings she was free to play the part of the student tonight. She almost laughed out loud. It wasn't, after all, a 'part', not the way 'voyeur' or 'nurse' was. It was what she was.

'Jeez,' said Penny. 'It's an invitation to the bar, not a question about the meaning of life.'

'Yes to the bar,' whispered Sarah. 'And, since you obviously haven't been paying attention to Professor Brain: life, my child, is meaningless.' She jotted in her notebook. There might be something worth investigation in her musings about the roles she played. All the world's a stage, Shakespeare wrote, and all the men and women merely players ... What, one might ask, does it mean?

That evening, Christopher shouted, 'You got to drink lager, mon.' He was West Indian, slender and fine-boned, the colour of quality toffee.

'OK! If it means that much to you, I'll drink lager.' Sarah held her hands up in mock surrender. When she put them down, she let her arm rest on the table, a hair's breadth from his. The contrast in the colour of their hands was fascinating.

'A lager for the lady and one for me,' called Christopher. He seemed to have only one volume level, although in the noisy students' union pub it made sense.

Sarah wondered if he shouted when he came, or did he get

quiet during sex, the way some men did? She felt the familiar stirring of desire in the pit of her belly. What would it be like to have sex without an agenda? Had she ever? Even the first time, with Jack, she'd wanted to celebrate her birthday by losing her virginity. Since then, she'd either participated in sex for money, or given David the bare minimum to keep him quasi-satisfied.

Christopher grinned at her when their bottles were delivered. He lifted his and tipped it to her in a brief toast, before putting it to his mouth.

He had a beautiful mouth: generous pink lips and a perfect set of gleaming white teeth. He wore a sweater, though the bar was hot. Being from the West Indies, he'd feel the cold. He didn't look to have much meat on his bones. She wondered if he had hair on his chest, or would it be as smooth and toffee tinted as his hands?

Sarah had to quell the impulse to simply run her hands up the inside of his sweater and find out. She reached for her beer instead, and, imitating Christopher, took a long draught. In truth, it tasted as repulsive as any other beer she'd tried since she'd started drinking. It fizzed up her nose. She swallowed quickly. In answer to Christopher's questioning look she said gamely, 'The king of beers.'

'You got that right!'

Penny grinned at Sarah from the other side of the table, where she'd been deep in conversation with Dan since he'd arrived. Penny, Dan, Christopher – Sarah had known them all for years. Why hadn't she noticed them before?

'Where are you from?' She directed the question to Christopher.

'I'm Bajan.'

'I don't know –'

'From Barbados.'

'Oh. Bajan. Neat.' Should she have known that? She felt dumb, suddenly. Why was she even here, trying to socialise with her classmates for the first time when graduation was imminent?

'It's OK. Don't look so devastated. I'm not vex with you, mon.'

Sarah laughed. She'd only ever heard Christopher speak the most beautiful English, the Queen's English, until tonight, when most of what he'd said was in a patois she could hardly understand. The combination of the two, spoken in as many sentences, was disarming.

'Relax,' murmured Christopher. He rubbed her bare arm, which made the fine hairs on it stand up and sent a shiver travelling through her. 'I'm not going to eat you, girl.'

'I should hope not. Not when you can have all the wings you want for thirty-five cents each.'

'Well said! More wings!' Christopher waved at their harried waitress, but she had only smiles for him. He was popular, Sarah realised. Probably a regular. But she knew he maintained high grades, at least in the Phil Honours courses they had in common. More than once she'd battled him for first place, and she'd not always won.

She supposed he was well rounded while she – well, she was not. But maybe it wasn't too late? She was here, wasn't she, eating wings and drinking beer with her classmates? Surely if she wanted to, there was enough time left for her to feel like 'one of the gang'. But what would that entail? Time, of course, and lots of conversation. Probably the telling of secrets. She'd never had anything to hide, before, and yet she'd always been so quiet. Now that she definitely had secrets to keep, did it make sense to throw herself into uncharted waters?

'You are being philosophical,' Christopher said. He tapped the side of his head, just below his close-cropped hair. 'Your eyes are as glazed as two Krispy Kremes.'

'Charming image, Christopher.'

'Accurate as well.'

'I was just wondering, if we each suddenly stood up and shouted out our secrets, what would be revealed.'

'I have only one,' he said. He pressed his hand to his chest. 'One I have kept close to my heart for years. I have a crush on you.'

Sarah flushed. 'I didn't mean we should, only that if we did –'

'But I was shy, in the beginning. And before I could approach, that fast-talking historian had scooped you up.'

'David?'

Christopher nodded. 'I have waited for you to lose interest in his fusty musings on the past. And finally, you have!'

'Well we're still ... seeing each other.'

'You must, like me, prefer musing on the future, else you wouldn't be a philosophy major.'

'Is that what we do?'

'I think it is. We take the events of the day and apply critical thinking so we may separate foolishness from wisdom and, perhaps, prevent the past from repeating itself. It isn't merely remembering it, as the historians would have you believe. Don't you agree?'

'Maybe. If we are heard.' Sarah felt awkward, as if she'd suddenly doubled in mass. It happened when she was uncomfortable in her surroundings, and suddenly, in this bar, with this gorgeous young man who had just confessed his feelings for her, she felt very uncomfortable. 'I should go.'

Christopher thudded his forehead on the table. 'I've ruined everything.'

'No.' Sarah stood. From what seemed a great height, she touched his head. His hair was incredibly soft, not at all what she'd expected. 'I'm strange, Christopher. Sorry.'

'But –'

She threw a few bills onto the table and grabbed her knapsack, ignoring the protests of her tablemates. It was suddenly imperative to her that she get out, quickly, before she became so huge she wouldn't fit through the doors.

She scurried out into the cold night air, intent on getting home as quickly as possible, given her sudden girth. 'I'm strange,' she'd said, to the gorgeous young Bajan man who'd shown an interest in her. How ridiculous! She almost batted her head with her fists in frustration, but she held back, for fear the other pedestrians would see, and think, Oh, how strange.

'Well, it's true,' she muttered. Ah. Talking out loud. She

pressed her lips together in a thin, exasperated line. She was a call girl. Veronica was her pimp, albeit a bubbly, blonde one. In a few short months her new profession had become as much a part of her as being a philosophy student was, though she'd been the latter for years. Christopher had spoken of critical thinking. Had she ever applied it to her 'decision' to trade sex for money?

What if she were found out? How long would it take for the whole campus to be abuzz with the news? What about the legality of what she did with her clients, never mind the morality? She could go to jail!

Sarah's feet, in their $400 boots, pounded the pavement as she quickened her gait until she was almost running. She'd expected Jack to come back for her but he hadn't and quite likely never would. He'd enjoyed her virgin schoolgirl 'act' and paid handsomely for it and that, in his mind, was that. Over. Meanwhile she'd continued to play the part of the mooning nubile maiden. That is, when she wasn't hiring herself out to other men. Where was the logic in any of it?

'It's not too late,' she whispered, consoling herself. Again, she pressed her lips resolutely together. But it wasn't, was it? Nobody knew. Nothing had actually happened. Just a night out with her friends, a few drinks. She could call Veronica (nothing more or less than a pimp!) as soon as she got home and put a quick end to all this. Sure, she'd miss the money, and maybe the excitement. And it was fun to be adored, but Christopher adored her. She could dump David and take up with Christopher if she wanted, but even that seemed dangerous. No, best to get out of the escort business and patch things up with David. Turn up the heat and get a ring. Graduate. Get married. Teach, maybe, have kids.

She rounded the corner. As if her thoughts had summoned him, David was on the porch of the house where she rented a room. Coming? Or going? Sarah ducked behind a bush. David was leaving.

She should call out to him. Run into his arms. Go, she urged herself, go. But she stayed put. Run into his arms and then what? Take him upstairs and make love to him and never mind that the thought neither excited her, as the thought of Jack did, nor even stirred her interest, as Christopher had.

He'd called David 'fusty'. That wasn't David's fault, any more than it was her fault that she felt physically huge whenever she was extremely uncomfortable. Nevertheless, she *did* feel that way from time to time and David *was* fusty.

David. Marriage. Teaching. Babies. None of it appealed. Not in the least. So she stayed where she was while David descended the front stairs and slouched into the night.

What was the difference between trading one's body for a diamond ring and a big party and a lot of stuff, and trading it for cold hard cash? Except that one required a lifetime commitment and the other only a night? God, it was hard to know which thoughts were stupid and which were wise.

When David finally disappeared, Sarah stepped from her hiding space. She no longer felt huge; she was just Sarah, shapely and, if anything, on the skinny side. Weird, maybe, but she'd never really been a pawn in this game called life. She'd been making decisions all along, so it wasn't all that difficult, now that the coast was clear, to simply acknowledge that and accept it. She was a student, she was an escort, she was a page, and more, a daughter and a sister and a friend. Parts of a whole. She didn't need Jack and she didn't love David and she didn't want Christopher. Not really. Perhaps she did tend to compartmentalise but all the compartments made up a whole, and it was Sarah, and she was just fine with that.

'Onwards,' she ordered herself.

8

There was an article in the *Toledo Blade* about GeoMancy having to lay off twenty per cent of its employees. Perhaps that was why that George had wanted to appear at his company's function in a wheelchair. It's harder to fire the handicapped.

Sarah was getting more comfortable with her new popularity at the university. She didn't, after all, have to join in every pub night or study session in order to be a part of the gang; she just had to pay a little more attention to her fellow Phil. Honours classmates. Christopher, likely humiliated by his confession of a crush, kept his distance. Sarah was fine with that. She didn't need the complication.

Sometimes she idly wondered what exactly had happened to cause this surge in popularity. Hair and make-up could only be credited with so much. Part of it must be from her new confidence. Each date she went on reconfirmed her power to please men and nurtured her blossoming sensuality. That made her approachable by both sexes. Interesting.

She'd upgraded her wardrobe as well, but subtly. Her fellow students would have been shocked if they'd known what she'd paid for her flared shortie boots, stretch-fit jeans and scarlet kid-leather bomber jacket. Sarah had also splurged on a $2,000 laptop that she'd distressed so she could pass it off as second-hand. For the first time, she had money. That made her more confident, too.

Though she was still a loner by nature she'd become more at ease with other people, as well as in her own skin. Since her night out at the student pub she'd not felt that strange 'hugeness' that came over her when she was outside her comfort zone. She hadn't been back to the pub but she'd found other ways to spend time with new friends. Even loners need study partners and someone to eat lunch with or argue philosophy with or sit with in lectures. It became easier for her to greet a guy or wave a girl over to the lunch table or scrunch along a study bench to make room for one more.

David had preferred her as an outsider. Well, she'd preferred him then, too. Perhaps he suspected that the one date a week she allowed him, always climaxed by a perfunctory handjob, was charity on her part. She knew she had to do something about him but she held back for fear of hurting him. One day, Sarah had decided, she'd let him fuck her and then she'd let him go. If she played her cards right he'd be riding high on his sexual abilities and eager to test them on other girls. He'd barely notice she was gone. That was the plan anyway. David was a nice guy, but she'd outgrown him, pure and simple.

Sarah's newly elevated self-esteem took a knock when she found herself in Veronica's waiting room with two other escorts. They looked to be in their mid- to late-twenties. One had geometric-cut glossy black hair, the other an upsweep in molten honey. They wore more make-up than Sarah, but carried it well, as if they were in a beauty-related business. In a way, they were.

One's suit was charcoal with a faint chalk stripe; the other's two-piece was emerald, worn over a yellow silk blouse. Both suits had to be by famous designers, Chanel or Givenchy or the like. Sarah didn't know style well enough to recognise them. Perhaps she should start reading *Vogue*?

The women ignored her. She eavesdropped on their chatter. The blonde had flown in on a private jet the previous night, from a party in Montreal where there'd been a number of Hollywood celebrities whose names she managed to drop into every sentence. The raven-haired one had spent the weekend at a 'simply fabulous' house party that'd been thrown by a mysterious someone 'in oil'.

Neither mentioned getting fucked, as far as Sarah could tell. They sprinkled their conversations with foreign words and phrases, so she couldn't understand it all. What she could follow was about five-star restaurants, movie premieres, the latest exhibitions at art galleries and so on.

By the time the two of them went in to see Veronica, Sarah felt like a junior apprentice in a profession she'd begun to think herself a mistress of. She'd had a few memorable experiences with kinky guys and a few forgettable fucks with regular guys, but nothing swanky or sophisticated. She'd never actually been an escort, except with George, and then she'd been dressed as a nurse. Nothing fancy about that.

When she got her turn with Veronica, Sarah blurted, 'How come I never get the glamorous dates?'

Veronica smiled. 'Patience, my dear. Do you remember how you got into this business, and why?'

'Um . . .'

'Because you look so young and innocent. There's a demand for that. Don't rush yourself. As time goes by you will become more sophisticated. At your age and experience, do you really think you could hold your end up in a conversation about politics, art or literature, with politicians, artists and writers? Besides, you've sampled some of my best clients. Peter was a real peach, don't you think?'

'Yes.' Sarah blushed. 'I ejaculated,' she blurted.

'Did you like it?'

'I didn't even know at the time. But I was incredibly sensitive for a few hours afterwards. It was . . . interesting. But I want dates where the guy actually talks to me. I don't know much about politics or literature but I am familiar with philosophy and drama. The rest I can learn.'

'And so you shall. Look, if you really want a public gig where all you need do is look pretty, no physical contact required, I've got just the thing coming up.'

'What sort of gig?'

'The Exotic Auto Show starts in a few weeks. I could get you a job as a model. All you'd have to do is pose prettily next to cars and have your picture taken. The pay isn't what you're used to and the hours are longer, but it's easy work and you'd get to meet all sorts of interesting people.'

'Pay?'

'Eight hundred a day, and no tips. It's from ten in the morning till ten at night, but with lots of breaks. There'd be two of you spelling each other, so you'd actually only work about six hours.' She paused. 'And one other advantage; this'd be work you could tell your friends about. It'd help explain why you have so much more money to spend these days.'

Sarah considered. Her grades were fine. She could afford to skip lectures for two days, one before and one after the weekend. And it had been difficult, pretending to still be dirt poor when her bank account was fat and she was carrying more cash in her purse each day than she'd spent in an entire semester last year. Every so often, she and her housemates had pooled their resources to get a pizza and a bottle of wine and she'd just tossed in small change to pretend that she was still poor. It made her feel guilty. If she had a legitimate source of income, she could treat the others once in a while.

'I'll do it,' Sarah said.

'Excellent!' Veronica went to the door. 'You'll be working with Nancy.' She called the girl's name.

Nancy came in. Sarah's heart dropped. She'd recognise that straw-coloured hair, snub nose and wide thin-lipped mouth anywhere. She was the girl Sarah had misdirected.

Before Nancy could speak, Sarah blurted, 'I'm so sorry about the mix-up that day. What an idiot I was! I had no idea about the new hotel.'

'Yeah, silly you, so silly you stole my date, "by accident".'

'It really was an honest mistake,' Sarah protested.

Veronica put in, 'That's all in the past, girls. Kiss and make up. Sarah's going to be working the Auto Show with you, Nancy, so you two had better get along.'

Sarah made a tentative move in the girl's direction. Nancy's face relaxed into a smile that Sarah hoped was sincere and reached out for Sarah. Each kissed the air beside the other's cheek.

Veronica said, 'That's better. Now, Sarah, you'll be working in costume, so I need your shoe size and your measurements.'

'A six shoe, and "small".'

'"Small" isn't very exact. Run along to the wardrobe room. Craig will take your measurements.'

'Craig' turned out to be the older gentleman who'd spanked Nancy. The memory of that scene brought another ghost of a tingle to Sarah's clit. It was strange, now that Sarah was so much more practised in sexual matters than she'd been back then, that the mental image of a bare bottom and a hard hand coming together still affected her so strongly. She'd have to think about that.

'You're the other Auto Show girl?' he asked.

'Yes . . .' She paused. 'Sir.' Now why had she called him 'sir'?

'Strip off then and I'll measure you. It's for a bikini, by the way.'

How odd that she should feel nervous about undressing in front of this man, when so many others had seen her naked. 'I already have a bikini, sir.'

'A magenta one?'

She raised her eyebrows.

'The car you'll be working with is a new Italian model, called, the "Magenta". Your bikini and your go-go boots will be in that colour. You'll match the car.'

'Oh.' She waited.

'Now? Please?'

'Oh, right.' Sarah unzipped her bomber and laid it aside. She pulled her cashmere sweater over her head and turned her back to him to take her bra off. Silly! He was going to measure her, for goodness sake! As matter-of-factly as she could, she stripped down to her plain 'off-duty' panties.

Craig gave her an amused look but said nothing. He picked up a tape measure and passed it around her chest. The backs of his hands brushed her breasts but he didn't seem the least affected by the contact. Was he gay?

'You get to keep the outfits, two of them,' he told her as he noted the measurement of her waist.

'That's nice.'

'The boots are very good, Italian kid leather, very supple.'

So he *was* gay. A straight man wouldn't have known that.

He continued, 'Can you manage four-inch heels OK, for a longish period?'

'That's a bit higher than I'm used to, but I'll cope.'

'Be sure that you do. Classique has a reputation to uphold. We don't want you looking awkward.'

'No, sir.' Gay or not, there had been steel in his voice as he'd said that. Once more, Sarah had a flashback to him spanking Nancy.

The tape was around her hips. Just testing, she gave a little wriggle.

'Be still.'

Any straight man would have given her bum a little slap, at least.

He noted her last measurement in his book, and said, 'And no, I'm not gay. No offence, Sarah, but you're too young for me to be interested in you that way, and you're an employee, so off-limits.'

Pouting, she said, 'I saw you and Nancy, and she's not much older than me.'

'Me spanking her? Silly girl, that wasn't sexual. She hates to be spanked. That was just a matter of discipline. You, if I'm not mistaken, would enjoy it, but I'm not going to give you that pleasure.'

'Enjoy being beaten, me? No way.'

Craig shrugged. 'Before the show, get a bikini wax.' He closed his notebook with a snap.

'Wax?'

'Best make it a Brazilian. Your bikinis will be skimpy. Off with you then.'

Driving home, Sarah thought about what Craig had said. What was it about her that had given him the impression that she'd enjoy being spanked? She replayed the scene she'd spied on in her mind. What if it had been her across his knee? What if Veronica sent her on a date where the man wanted to do that to her? What if . . .

Unlike the $5 tickets to the regular Toledo Auto Show, entrance to the Exotic Auto Show was either by invitation or at $150 a ticket, to keep the public out. That price, Sarah was sure, was steep enough to keep anyone she knew from attending. She'd decided not to announce the gig to her pals. If some of them showed up to tease her she'd die.

Craig had driven Nancy and her to the show and had promised to pick them both up after it closed at ten. As he'd dropped them off, he'd handed them a suitcase each, with their costumes. 'FedEx didn't deliver them until last night,' he explained. 'Don't worry. They'll fit just fine.'

The autos on show were mainly 'concept' cars out of Detroit but with a dozen or so production models from abroad, all 'high end', priced in the hundreds of thousands of dollars. The Magenta was a new model from the Albina Automobile Company in Milan. Sarah and Nancy reported to Signor Aldo Fulvio, a florid little man in a suit that looked as if it'd been sewn directly onto his body piece by immaculate piece. His title was long and impressive but Sarah could never remember it, let alone pronounce it.

Nancy could though. To Sarah's annoyance, it turned out that Nancy spoke Italian fluently. From the moment the girl greeted Signor Fulvio in his own language, he only spoke to her, leaving Nancy to pass his instructions on to Sarah.

'He says he's sorry that we don't have our own private room but there's a cot for us in the storage room behind his office and it can be locked from inside. Anything we need, he says, just ask. All he requires is that there should be at least one of us on the stand at all times, with the car, posing prettily and drawing lots of attention from the visitors and the journalists. We start at ten and it's nine-thirty already, so would we please go and get changed *pronto*.'

The storage room wasn't as small as Sarah had feared. Apart from cartons of brochures, all it held was the cot, a dressing table with a mirror, a small fridge and a table with an elaborate coffee machine that was already burbling, some good china and assorted snacks.

'Espresso and cappuccino,' Nancy said. 'My favourites.'

Nancy matter-of-factly stripped down to her panties and sat at the dressing table. Sarah undressed more slowly. As she stripped, she surreptitiously checked out the girl she thought of as her rival. Nancy was less rounded than Sarah, with wide-apart cupcake breasts that actually tilted upwards, like her tiny nose. The cherries on those cupcakes were very pale, too pale, in Sarah's opinion.

The kits they'd been given included magenta wraps, plus some make-up: magenta eye gloss and lipstick. Nancy smeared some onto her nipples, which certainly needed colour, but what for? No one was going to see them. Perhaps tinting her nipples gave the girl confidence.

Their bikinis were even more daring than Sarah had imagined. The bottom halves were tiny and diamond-shaped, with tapes that passed between their thighs and up through the creases of their bums and three more tapes from each side that stretched up to the tapes that circled their hips.

Thank goodness she'd taken Craig's advice and been waxed bald. It'd been a painful process, but justified. She'd have hated to have little curls poking out.

The bras were similar to the bottoms: pairs of diamonds that barely covered their nipples, held in place by tapes that ran around their backs and up to form halters.

And they were to appear in public dressed like that! Thank goodness her folks lived far away.

Sarah returned to the dressing table to apply more make-up – enough, she hoped, to make her unrecognisable. Much as she hated to disturb the hairdo that Carlo had lavished time on, she took a brush and gave herself bangs and flip-ups. The look was a bit old-fashioned, but so were the go-go boots. Maybe they'd play some disco?

Nancy, ready first, left the room with a steaming mug of espresso and a biscotti on a little plate. When Sarah followed, Aldo Fulvio had the coffee and the crispy biscuit on his desk. Nancy was already draped across the Magenta's hood. The little suck-up!

The platform was made to revolve and was elevated by about a foot. The car was long, sleek and sexy. Parked, it looked like it was speeding.

Aldo motioned to Sarah to join Nancy. He tapped his watch. It was a full minute after ten. A stream of visitors was pouring in through the doors but hadn't reached the Albina stand yet. As Sarah stepped up, a little uncertain in four-inch heels, the stand began to turn. She stumbled. Nancy giggled. Signor Fulvio scowled.

As quickly as she could, being careful not to scratch it with her boots, Sarah hitched up onto the car's trunk to sit leaning back on straight arms, shoulders slightly turned in. She'd practised her poses in front of a mirror. Apart from kneeling on all fours, that was the one that showed her breasts off best.

Let Nancy's puny cupcakes compete with these plump puppies!

The crowd reached their stand, photographers first. Cameras flashed. Perhaps it was Sarah's imagination, but after the first few revolutions, it seemed like there were more pictures being taken of the trunk, with Sarah, than of the hood, with Nancy.

Sarah rolled onto her tummy and lifted herself up on her arms again to deepen her cleavage. The flashes began to strobe, with definitely more pics being taken of her than of Nancy. Sarah knelt up and into her best pose, on her hands and knees, back deeply hollowed. From the directions the flashes came, it seemed as many photographers were focusing on her bottom as on her chest. Well, in that minute bikini, her bum was as good as bare.

Someone touched her shoulder. Sarah blinked the glare away. It was Signor Fulvio. He was signalling for her to go to the hood to replace Nancy. That made sense. He'd want more shots of the car's hood than its trunk to appear in the magazines, and she was the model who was attracting the lenses.

As the girls passed each other, Nancy swung a hip-check at Sarah. Sarah was ready for it and simply swayed out of range.

On the hood, and encouraged by shouts from the bystanders, Sarah moved from sexy pose to sexier pose, almost hoping for a 'wardrobe malfunction'. The applause, mainly from men but with the occasional whoop or 'You go, girl,' from a woman, was intoxicating. So this was what motivated Daphne and James to pay for an audience.

Sarah smiled and licked her lips seductively. She wriggled her bottom and swayed her breasts. The more her audience reacted, the sexier she felt. Hell, a girl could get off on this!

She lay on her back, legs spread wide to either side, and let herself slither into a perilous backbend over the car's snarling grille, hooking her fingers through it to hold herself in position. A photographer knelt up on the edge of the moving platform to snap half a dozen close-up shots before a behemoth in a Magenta Security T-shirt tapped his shoulder and invited him to dismount, 'For his own safety's sake.'

There was a Brazilian car on show on the other side of the aisle. It had three girls, in even briefer bikinis than Sarah's, but she was the one who was getting the most attention.

Nancy took the first lunch break. When it was Sarah's turn, she found there was prosciutto and Provolone in soft buns and individual salads waiting. As she ate, she browsed the Magenta's brochure. When she was done eating, though she was entitled to more time, she went back to work. Being ogled was fun.

There was another man at the sales desk with Signor Fulvio – a younger and better-looking one. The newcomer had a stubble-shadowed lantern jaw, broad shoulders and a narrow waist. He introduced himself in pretty good English as Luigi Volpone, sales manager, and insisted on giving Sarah a hand up onto the revolving platform.

Nancy had taken up residence on the hood, so Sarah perched on the trunk and blew kisses at every man who passed by.

After a while, Nancy came back to where Sarah was. 'Signor Fulvio wants us to demonstrate how roomy the trunk is,' she said. 'You're to lie down in it.'

'OK.'

Nancy lifted the lid. Sarah climbed in and posed as best she could.

'How's this?' she asked, just before Nancy lowered the lid. That didn't seem right. How was anyone to see her? How were the photographers to snap her? Sarah rapped up on the underside of the lid before she remembered that the car boasted of being soundproof.

She shivered as the first intimations of claustrophobia crept up on her. Silly! She'd read the brochure. The inside release handle had been pictured just about ... She fumbled. There! Sarah tugged the lever. The mechanism gave a comforting click. She pushed up. The lid moved, but just a fraction of an inch. Something was holding it down.

Sarah wriggled and squirmed, certainly not panicking, until she managed to get her knees beneath her and her back pressed up against the padding that lined the hard metal. She took a deep breath, and heaved.

The lid flew up. There was a squeal of fear. Sarah stood up and looked down. Nancy was sprawled on the ground beside the stand and suddenly the girl was the centre of attraction. Photographers were running to her, cameras flashing.

And no wonder. Her precipitous descent had parted the delicate tapes that held her bra in place. She was topless.

Nancy started to scowl but it seemed that her being the cameramen's focus dissolved her anger. She stood with a flourish and posed for the photographers, not even trying to cover her silly little tits up. Signor Fulvio rushed up with one of their wraps and draped it round her before he led Nancy away through the office and to the storage room, screaming at her in rapid-fire Italian.

Luigi Volpone stepped up onto the platform and gave Sarah a hand climbing out of the trunk. 'She's not so nice to you,' he told Sarah. 'Perhaps Signor Fulvio will send her away, I think.'

'I hope not. I'm sure she only meant it as a little joke.'

'Not so little. Are you all right? You need to take a break?'

'I'll be fine. We mustn't leave the Magenta without its cheesecake.'

'Cheesecake? Please?'

'Girl. Pin-up girl,' Sarah explained.

'I see.' He grinned. '*Ragazza copertina, si*? And you are the most tasty "cheesecake" in the *panetterria*, no?'

Sarah didn't know what a '*panetterria*' was, but he was obviously paying her a compliment, so she smiled and said, 'Thank you, Signor Volpone.'

'Luigi, please.'

'Luigi.'

'I must get back to work.'

'Of course.'

Luigi paused before stepping off the platform. 'A girl like Nancy, she deserve a – how you say?' He made a bum-swatting motion.

'A spanking.'

'Yes, a good *forte* spanking.'

Why was it always Nancy that men thought about spanking? Sarah had a rounder bum, which ought to have been more tempting, right? She returned to her poses feeling flushed. It had to be because she'd been trapped in the trunk for a while.

Although there was no one to relieve her, after half an hour, Sarah felt the need for a trip to the ladies' room. She asked Luigi's permission, promised to hurry, and went to fetch her wrap from the storage room. When she tried the door, it was locked.

Signor Fulvio's voice, kind of strangled, called out, '*Tra un minuto!*' A few seconds later, he sighed and grunted. There were fumbling sounds and the door opened. Signor Fulvio emerged, more florid than before. He pushed past Sarah, avoiding her eyes.

Sarah went in and found Nancy repairing her lipstick. The scent of sex was in the air.

'I take it that you aren't being fired,' Sarah said.

'Me and Aldo – we have an understanding.' Nancy grinned. 'We've come to an *oral* agreement.'

Sarah took her robe without commenting but she couldn't help thinking about the incredible power that the promise, or better, the delivery, of a blow job had over men.

The next day of the exhibition was quieter. There were fewer photographers but more serious business people, keeping Aldo and Luigi busy at their desks. Nancy shirked her duties, leaving the bulk of the work to Sarah. When Aldo took his lunch break in the storage room, Nancy accompanied him.

Luigi looked at Sarah and shrugged. He seemed so nice but it was his boss who was getting all the action. That didn't seem fair. She went out of her way to flirt with the handsome Italian, who, whenever he wasn't with a client, went out of his way to help her on and off the revolving stand.

It didn't hurt to blow him a kiss from time to time, did it?

Sunday, the third day, was disastrous for Sarah. She'd been sure that no one she knew was going to pay $150 to get in but she'd underestimated the power of infatuation. She was demonstrating her 'dangling backwards over the grille' pose when a familiar but upside-down face swung into view.

David said, 'Sarah!'

Shocked, she lost her grip and slithered down onto her back on the platform.

'How could you!' he demanded.

Sarah scrambled to her feet. 'How could I? I'm just modelling.'

'In that?'

'There are girls here wearing less.' She motioned to the Brazilian stand.

'They aren't my girl.'

'You can't –' she began, but he grabbed her wrist and tugged.

Luigi appeared at David's side. 'Young man, I think you should go away and leave the young lady very much all alone.'

David pulled a fist back but dropped it to his side as the Magenta Security behemoth materialised behind Luigi. Scowling, David backed away.

Sarah felt sick.

Luigi asked her, 'Your boyfriend?'

'He thinks he is.'

'You don't?'

'No.'

'Take a break. I'll get Nancy to take over for you.'

'I think she's busy.'

'She and Aldo have been in the back room for half of an hour now. They'll be finished. Aldo, he doesn't last so long.'

Sarah and Luigi exchanged knowing looks. Angry at David's presumption of ownership, Sarah said, 'When do you get your next break, Luigi?'

He smiled. 'For me, for a lady like you, Sarah, the half-hour in a storage room does not seem enough time or the right place for *un appuntamento tra amanti*.'

'That's a shame.'

Luigi's brow wrinkled in thought. 'You like our Magenta?'

'It's magnificent.'

'Sexy, no?'

'Sexy, *si*.'

'We have two here, did you know?'

'No, I didn't.'

'One to show, another in case of accidents.'

'I see.'

'The other one is in the storage, here at the exhibition. Would you like to see it?'

'Very much. When?'

'After we close, eleven tonight? Not too late for you?'

'I'll look forward to it.'

At her next chance, Sarah used her Classique cellphone and told Craig that she wouldn't be outside to be picked up at ten-thirty, as usual. 'It's a matter of client relations, ' she explained.

Craig laughed. 'Any idea when you'll be done taking care of "client relations"?'

'About one in the morning?'

'I'll be waiting outside. That's too late for a girl to be out alone without a car. Don't worry if you're a little tardy. I'll bring a book.'

9

The show closed at ten but there were always lingerers. Nancy and Aldo disappeared into the storage room so Sarah stayed on duty for the benefit of the last few stragglers, even though she wasn't on the clock. Her clothes were in that back room so she didn't have much choice. As Luigi had said, Aldo couldn't last long. He and Nancy were on their way out by ten-thirty. Sarah collected her things and headed for the ladies' room to freshen up and change into a short jean skirt and a cropped top. She didn't bother with underwear. What'd be the point?

It was kind of eerie, heading back to the Magenta stand with no one around but cleaners. It occurred to her that she was about to go all the way just for the fun of it, no cash involved, for the very first time. She'd be under no obligation to make it good for the man while ignoring her own needs. And this was a man who'd be flying far away in a matter of days. She'd likely never see him again. That was liberating. She could be completely selfish, make demands even.

She could try her techniques out and it wouldn't matter a damn if she screwed up.

It also occurred to her that no one had seen her newly bald little pussy, not yet. Luigi would be the first. How would he react?

Luigi had changed as well, into tight blue jeans and a tighter magenta T-shirt. Both suited him. He had the body to carry them off; a body that she was eager to get to know.

They strolled across the vast echoing open space, not touching, just casually chatting, for the benefit of the cleaners. Luigi led her to enormous lift-up doors with a normal door beside them. Inside, it was very utilitarian and only lit by exit signs. The spare Magenta was at the far end of a row of shiny new cars.

Sarah said, 'I'd like its headlights on, please.'

He shrugged, opened the driver's door and reached in. Covers lifted off the headlights like slowly opening eyes. They glowed into life, on dim. Sarah dropped her skirt to the floor. She took a wide-legged stance in front of the car's grinning grille, between the headlights, and lay back across the sloping hood.

'What do you think?' She pointed down at her hairless mound.

Luigi knelt in front of her as if in awe. 'Che bella fighetta! Bellisimo!'

Sarah didn't need to know Italian to understand that he approved. There was a word in Italian that she'd picked up from movies. She told him, 'Mangiare.'

'Si, si!' His hands spread on the hood to each side of her hips. Luigi leant forwards, tongue extended and flat, to lap Sarah's smooth skin from halfway up the inside of her left thigh to the crease of her groin – and back halfway down her right thigh.

So, he was going to make her wait for it, was he? That suited Sarah just fine. She stretched her arms up above her head. The movement raised the hem of her abbreviated top up to her nipples. Luigi's eyes followed and widened. His head lifted and moved from side to side, dragging the point of his tongue along the creases at the tops of Sarah's thighs.

She lay back and closed her eyes, surrendering to the tantalising sensations. How would it be if, instead of being free to move at will, she were chained – no, not chained, that'd be uncomfortable – maybe secured by soft leather straps, spread-eagled on the hood of this gorgeous car? She'd have to endure his tongue torture for as long as he cared to inflict it. Perhaps, when his tongue tired, one of Luigi's friends would take over, maybe a dark-haired Sicilian boy or a big red-faced farmer with large horny hands and a thick tongue?

Luigi's tongue was teasing the lips of her sex apart now. Sarah groaned softly to encourage him.

Perhaps there'd be more than two of them? She visualised a long line of exotic men, each eager to take his turn to taste her. And when they all had, they'd all want to fuck her, wouldn't they? One after another after another and she'd climax and climax, writhing but helpless to resist until every last one of them was sated and she was limp and numb.

Luigi's tongue had almost reached her clit and was spiralling in on it. His fingers were working up inside her, hooking up to that lovely spot behind her pubic bone. Hmm! The last time a man had done that, she'd made a lot of wet. Maybe she should warn the darling man? She should, but it seemed that her voice had become disconnected, somehow. Anyway, he was a sophisticated European, so he'd know all about 'female ejaculation'.

His tongue reached her clit. From the way it felt, his lips were pursed around her clit and he was sucking in and out, fucking his own mouth with it.

The tongue started. The tongue and those probing fingers. Sarah arched. Her thighs strained further apart. Her feet lifted until only her toes touched the floor. Half her weight pressed down on Luigi's fingers and tongue. The pressure on her clit and pubic bone became almost painful.

'Yip!' That was her, wasn't it? 'Yip, yip!' It was a silly little noise, but it was hers, and no man had objected to her making it, yet. 'Yip!' Oh yes!

Her climax flowed.

Luigi spluttered, laughed, and covered Sarah's sex with his mouth. When he was done sucking and Sarah's flesh was aching, he murmured, *'Delizioso! Squisito!'*

That was a relief!

He stood up. His zipper hissed. Sarah sat up to see what he had for her. The man was magnificent! She was tempted to simply lie back and enjoy but her plan had been to take this chance to experiment. What's the point of making plans if you don't carry them out? Before he could continue, she slithered off the hood and told him, 'Inside the car, please? You take the driver's side?'

He raised an eyebrow and slowly grinned, saying, without

words, I don't understand what you're up to but I'll play along with you, with pleasure.

Sarah had never been inside the display car, except its trunk, but she'd read the brochure several times. The 'new car' scent was intoxicating. Apart from the dash and the floor, everything seemed to be covered in buttery pale-yellow leather. She flipped on both the map lights, illuminating their laps. The Magenta was a two-seater but with ample room behind the seats. The criss-cross racing-style seat belts were anchored to the floor there. Luigi didn't resist as she buckled him in with his arms tucked inside the straps. She leant over him to get to his seat's controls and lowered him backwards until he was horizontal. The belts retracted automatically, so the illusion that he was strapped down and at her mercy was maintained. Sarah lowered her own seat to meet her 'prisoner of love' on his level.

His staff, still proudly projecting from his fly, directly in the spotlight, was very tempting but she'd get to it soon enough.

'You are now my love captive,' she told him.

'Si, si!'

Her left hand cradled the back of his neck. Her right tugged his T-shirt up as high as the straps allowed. Sarah lowered her lips to his. Luigi's mouth surrendered, which said a lot for him. She'd always thought of Italian men as very macho but this one was playing along with her game. Sarah nibbled on his lower lip with teasing little sucks. Her hand slid up under his shirt, across the smoothness of his torso, up to the curly pelt on his chest. As her tongue sampled his mouth, she tweaked one of his nipples. His sighs hinted that he liked that. David had never let her toy with his nipples. The other men she'd had sex with had paid well to be in charge, so somehow she'd never tested their reactions to that particular caress.

Still kissing Luigi, she shoved his shirt even higher, working it up under the straps, all the way to bunch up under his chin. Her lips left his mouth and wandered lower. She let her teeth drag across his chest until they reached the crinkled raisin of his left nipple. Sarah nibbled with slowly increasing pressure.

Luigi made little sounds, not displeased ones, but perhaps a little nervous, so she switched to rhythmic sucking, much as he'd made her clit endure. As she teased, her fingers found his belt buckle, undid it, popped the button of his jeans and pushed the denim down. He'd shown up for their assignation not wearing any underwear, just as she had, and likely for the same reason. With his jeans down to his knees, his movement was restricted further. Sarah trailed her fingernails up the inside of one muscular thigh. Luigi tensed and relaxed. His hampered knees pushed as far apart as his jeans allowed. She cupped his big warm balls and tickled him beneath them.

Suckling on his nipple reminded her that she enjoyed the same sort of attention. She scrunched up and over him and used his face to ruck her cropped top up. Sarah pressed down, squishing her breast on his lips. They parted. His tongue flickered on her nub. His lips closed on it, then his teeth, deliciously threatening and inflicting just the right amount of pleasure/pain.

She told him, 'Good boy,' and rewarded him by closing her fingers around the base of his shaft.

Her fist smoothed up to his knob, then down again. Luigi groaned. Veronica had told her that most men loved it if a girl talked dirty to them but she hadn't dared to test that advice before, for fear of offending her clients. Now she had no reason to worry about that.

Sarah asked, 'Would you like me to suck on you, Luigi? Would you like me to take your nice big cock into my soft wet mouth? Would that make you happy?'

He released her nipple for long enough to get out, '*Si, mia stracciamanci meraviglioso!*'

'Don't you dare come, not yet. I want you to stay nice and hard. Later, maybe I'll let you come in my mouth, understand me?'

'Come? Ah – *ejaculare, si?*'

That was close enough to the English. '*Si*,' she said, '*ejaculare* in my . . .'

'*Bocca* – is "mouth" – *bocca.*'

'*Bocca*,' she agreed. 'Mouth.'

'*Labbra* – is lips,' he continued.

Sarah almost giggled. Here she was, with a gorgeous male body to play with, taking time for lessons in Italian.

'*Suo labbra, per favore*,' he asked. '*Su pene mio*.'

'*Si*.' Sarah snuggled down into a ball on her seat with her head resting on Luigi's lower chest. That put the spotlit glossy crown of his shaft no more than half an inch from her lips. She pursed them and blew, very softly. Luigi shivered. Sarah stretched out her tongue and lapped a droplet of sweet dew from its eye. Luigi groaned.

This was fun! This had to be the same, but different, as the pleasure 'Peter the Masseur', as she thought of him, had got from tormenting her. This time, though, there was going to be fucking involved. But first, she'd work on her 'deep throat' skills and discover if the exercises she'd performed with bananas had improved her self-control.

She kissed his dome's eye and pushed down, letting its bulk spread her lips. Luigi twitched but restrained himself. Her lips closed just behind the flared head. He had to be excited, because the sweet wetness in her mouth certainly wasn't entirely her saliva. Her tongue swirled. Luigi's fists clenched but he lay still, very tense, but still. The warm living thickness of him pushed her tongue down. A little upward pressure clamped it against her hard palate.

Nod. Nod. Nod.

The sound he made was almost a whine.

Deeper, tongue relaxed, throat relaxed. It was on the back of her tongue now, making her salivate, but she wasn't gagging, not yet. Deeper. She squirmed round more, getting her knees up next to Luigi's head, lining her mouth and throat up. Could she? Sarah plunged. His dome plugged the back of her mouth. She gurgled around it. The muscles back there spasmed on him. Sarah sucked a deep snorting breath through her nose and twisted her head from side to side, working him in even deeper. Something in her throat twitched threateningly. Enough, for now at least. She pulled back with deliberate slowness, not letting him feel her desperation, until his dome was at the front of her mouth again and she could breathe past it.

'*Meraviglioso!*'

'*Grazie.*' The word was mangled but Sarah was sure he'd understand. She gave him a few more licks and sucks before releasing him. 'Now I'm going to fuck you.' She searched his jeans pocket for a condom and tore it open.

'*Fottere.*'

'*Si, fottere.*' This, she'd decided, was going to be for her, not for him. If he came, fine. If he didn't, she'd take care of him after. Sarah crawled down over Luigi's legs and pulled herself up by the leather-sheathed steering wheel. His shaft resisted her fingers' tugging but she was merciless. She forced it upright enough to nestle its sheathed head between her pussy lips. '*Fottere,*' she sighed as she sank down, impaling herself. '*Fottere, fottere.*' She reached down to fondle the base of his shaft where it emerged from her. '*Pene*, huh?'

'*Si, pene!*'

Her fingers lifted an inch or two to touch herself. '*Fighetta?*'

'*Si, fighetta squisito.*'

'*Squisito* – means squeeze?' she teased. Her vaginal muscles clamped tight.

'No, *stretta . . .*'

'No, squeeze – yes, squeeze. Make your mind up.' Before he could explain what she already understood, Sarah rammed down.

The map light shone on her pussy, with his balls dangling beneath it. She reached down again to cup them and leant forwards. The head of his cock pushed against the rear wall of her pussy. Her clit pressed down on the thick vein in the curved base of his shaft. Sarah rotated her hips. She tried a little hump forwards, then back. Eventually, she found the position that pleased her clit the most and rocked in it, grinding. Luigi said something but she wasn't listening. Sarah was feeling. The sensations became her entire being. Her hips twitched with increasing violence until she was punishing herself, and him. She climbed higher and higher, concentrating on the only thing that mattered right then and there, reaching the magical point where ...

'Yip!'

Sarah toppled sideways. As much as she'd needed to ride him to climax she needed him out, now that she'd come in one gut-wrenching spasm. Luigi was practically sobbing, thrusting his glistening shaft into the air. Poor man! She couldn't – didn't want to – leave him like that. Once she'd caught her breath, she lay her head back onto his lower chest. She told him, '*Fottere mia bocca, per favore.*' Whether or not she had the words and grammar right, he got the idea. 'Fuck my mouth, please,' is an invitation that a man will understand whatever the language it's given in.

Sarah slid the condom off before taking his shaft's head between her lips. She held his column tight in both of her hands. Luigi jerked at her, not penetrating her mouth deeply, but, from the sound of his babbling Italian, deeply enough. After a couple of dozen strokes, he stiffened. Her mouth was flooded with warm ambrosia. Sarah held him in her mouth through his aftershocks until he was still. One last strong suck made him groan. Mission accomplished.

Sarah reached down to where his jeans were bunched around his calves. She hit the steering wheel with her hip and the horn sounded four musical notes that Sarah recognised as being from some opera or another, likely an Italian one.

'I think,' she said, 'that the fat lady has sung.'

'*Che?*'

10

Monday night, Sarah left the Exotic Auto Show with a magenta – what other colour could it be? – plastic goodie bag. It contained a Magenta T-shirt that was far too big for her but would do for sleeping in; sunglasses; a mug; a pen and pencil set; two bottles of Limoncello soda; a miniature of Amaro Fernet-Branca liqueur; and, best of all, an iPod with a glossy magenta cover bearing the Albina Autos logo.

First chance she got she downloaded a freebie course in basic conversational Italian and two operas, *Rigoletto* and *La Traviata*. She didn't expect she'd ever see Luigi again but it never hurt to expand one's knowledge of culture, did it? Although she still planned to quit her career as an escort just as soon as she got her degree, what she learnt today would remain an asset for the rest of her life. Sarah imagined herself bumping into an important Italian in the course of her real career, whatever that'd be, and being able to chat with him in his own language, and make intelligent remarks about Italian opera.

How cool would that be?

For a few weeks she threw herself into her studies, taking on a few easy Classique gigs on the weekends. The improvisation class had proven far more difficult than she'd imagined, but she was learning to trust her instincts and her fellow students. It was a full year course so she was confident she could pull off a good grade by the end.

Her other courses were coming along beautifully, except for existentialism with Professor Braun. He'd abruptly changed his requirements and started testing the class every Friday. Since almost everyone had abandoned the pointless exercise of trying to keep up with his scribbling on the blackboard, there'd been some concern. But his tests had nothing to do with existentialism, or philosophy, or anything much at all. He'd ask questions like, 'If Schrödinger's cat walked into the room, would you pet it, ignore it, or tell it to scat?' One answer was deemed correct, the others wrong. As if that wasn't bad enough the students had compared papers and discovered that whereas one received a check mark for 'pet it' another received an 'x' for the very same answer.

The Phil. Honours students were particularly concerned. They were stuck with Professor Braun for existentialism this term and ethics next term. It would soon be time to apply to graduate school, and they needed top marks. Professor Braun was not just messing with their minds, he was messing with their futures.

He was impervious to their requests for an explanation. He refused to meet them in his office. What had once been amusing was becoming sad; at least, that's the way Sarah saw it. Others were less charitable.

'What should I do?' Sarah had outlined the situation to David while he walked her from the lecture hall to the library. She'd managed to avoid him since the car show, but he'd been waiting for her when she left the class, so she'd reluctantly bid goodbye to Penny and the other girls, calling loudly, 'Meet you in the library!' They'd nodded, though the girls had made no such plan. A gang, Sarah had come to realise, was useful as well as fun. Now she was simply trying to avoid (1) the hurt look on David's face and (2) a discussion of their future.

'It's pretty serious,' said David. 'You don't want to get a reputation as a troublemaker. I think you just have to make the best of it.'

'I guess ... but –' Sarah tried to come up with more to say on the topic but David cut her off.

'What are your plans, Sarah? If you don't mind my asking.' His voice betrayed bitterness, but he took her hand.

'I don't know. I was thinking graduate school, somewhere

. . .' In truth she'd been so busy she'd only just managed to focus on her final grades in terms of her education. She'd not given the future much thought.

'Will I be bumping into you naked on the hood of a car again soon?'

'I wasn't naked, David. The answer to your question is "No."' She'd already decided it was too risky to do that kind of work again. She'd best stay 'undercover'. Sarah almost laughed but one look at David's face squashed the impulse.

'Good. It's not seemly, sweetheart.'

She groaned inwardly. *Seemly*. How freakin' fusty could he get?

'How about Christmas?'

'I'm probably going home, like always.' She quickened her pace.

David kept up, kept her hand in his. 'Why don't you come with me? Spend some time with my family in Vermont? You'd like it, Sarah. They want to get to know you better.'

'I don't know.' Sarah wracked her brains for something else to say but came up empty. The library was close. She could see the happy-go-lucky students entering and exiting the double doors. She tried to tug her hand free but David held fast. She felt captured. She tugged harder.

'Do you still love me?' David was gripping her hand now. It hurt.

'I –' She stopped herself from saying she didn't know. 'I can't talk about it right now.'

'After I was ejected from the car show, which I paid a pretty penny to get into, I thought you'd come after me.'

'I was working!'

'I waited a long time. Until it closed, in fact. You never came out.'

'Obviously I did, David. I'm here, aren't I?' She tugged, hard, and freed her hand from his grip. She hastily stuffed both hands in the pockets of her jacket.

'What's going on? I think I have the right to know.' David blocked her escape. His face was set; he looked five years old. 'Talk to me.'

'Not now. Come over tonight. We'll have tea and talk in my room.'

'Fine.' He stepped out of her way.

Sarah darted off without a backwards look. She was both furious and guilty. Relieved to be free of him and full of dread about the evening ahead. Damn him. Why couldn't he just go away?

That afternoon, Sarah handed in her paper on 'Love' for her epistemology class. It wasn't everything she'd hoped it might be; though it was academic and properly annotated it lacked a definite position on her part. Not surprising. She'd come to realise that she didn't actually know much about love at all. Not something she'd want to admit in an essay. Not something she wanted to admit to herself. But true.

She arrived home early, bathed, slid into her wispy pale-blue bra and thong and dressed in the cashmere sweater David had given her and a stretchy denim skirt. She wanted to be *seemly*. Happily, she'd already ditched the pitiful 'Jack' paraphernalia she'd collected to fuel her obsession with her first client, including the crab claw that'd made its way into her knapsack and from there to her desk. It embarrassed her to even consider the way she'd called out to him every night. Incantations to Jack. Prayers? Christ!

For a girl who'd reached the age of majority a virgin, she'd accumulated a fair amount of sexual experience in a short time. Granted, there hadn't been a lot of 'Tab A into Slot B' sex, but each assignation the agency had sent her on had been sexual. She'd enjoyed every one and been well paid, too.

It was ironic to the extreme that she was about to have sex she didn't really want to have, and wasn't to be paid for it. She wondered how many women had had that experience. Most likely, quite a few. She'd sold her sexual favours the entire time she'd been sexually active, except with Luigi, but she'd never felt as ruthless as she did on this night, when she set about to seduce David.

He deserved as much from her and Sarah was intrinsically fair. Once she'd bolstered his fragile male ego she'd set him free. It made sense that he'd be mollified by having at last gotten what he'd wanted for so long: her 'virginity'. It would definitely ease the blow of a break-up. At least, she hoped so.

She set the kettle to boil and did her make-up. A little shadow here, a little gloss there – she'd perfected the natural look. At the last moment, she changed her mind about bare legs and slipped on a pair of black stay-ups with lacy tops. Surely, once David was aroused and she'd stripped to her underthings, he'd enjoy the surprise of stockings? Sarah had just finished adding the boiling water to the teapot when her intercom buzzed. She rang him in and tried to quell the butterflies in her belly. This was David. How could she possibly be more nervous about having sex with him than she was when dealing with the sexual penchants of a stranger?

'I'm coming,' she shouted, a few hours later.

Sarah and David had progressed from petting on the couch to stripping to the bed, where the ceremonial deflowering of the maiden had occurred. They'd been fucking for a while now and, though her orgasm was far from the best she'd had, at least it was real. She didn't want David to miss it so she made a bit of a show. 'Christ! Oh, David!'

Sarah was beneath David, missionary style, but in the past half-hour they'd moved from missionary to woman superior to a bit of doggy style and back to missionary, so it wasn't as if David wasn't an energetic or enthusiastic partner. She'd always known his cock was a good one, a nice length and width and pleasantly smooth, and that he was very capable of a rock-hard erection, but she'd never seen David display such stamina. In truth, he had the makings of a good lover; he just needed more experience.

Laughable, really. Perhaps he was holding back for fear of frightening his nubile partner. Sarah giggled. Turned it into a guttural sound. Squeezed his cock with her internal muscles a few times to add oomph to the fluttering spasms of her lukewarm orgasm.

'Yeah! Go for it, Sarah!' David gazed down at her with such

love in his eyes that she had to close hers. She felt his hand squirm between them and then his fingers on her clit, straight on the head, his stroke too hard, too much, almost painful and not in a good way.

'God! Jesus!' She was scared to swear in case it turned him off, so she was stuck with crying out to the Lord above. She silently added a swift ending to the prayer, 'Make him come soon, Lord.'

She dropped her hands to his bum and clutched his cheeks. A little pain, perhaps? He soldiered on. When she squirmed her fingers into the cleft between his cheeks he grunted and reached back to push her away, which thwarted her plan but did get him off her clit.

David sputtered, 'Look at me.' At last, a command.

Her eyes opened. She granted him the mistiest look she could muster, but stopped short of saying what she was pretty sure he wanted to hear. 'I love you.' But if he didn't come in the next few minutes, goddamit, she would. Thank God for her drama classes. The improvisation game 'Let's pretend' had come in very handy in the last couple of hours. Her body bucked up against him but he held on.

'I love you, Sarah,' he whispered. And came.

Well, that was different.

After an acceptable time, Sarah slid out from under him. She slipped on her robe and padded barefoot down the passage to the communal bathroom. Across the hall, her floor-mate was partying. It usually got on her nerves but this time she was happy for the noise. She'd have been embarrassed to have the other tenants hear her fucking David in her room.

Christ, she could use a shower. Sarah had never felt so dirty, or perhaps the word was unclean. She sat on the toilet for a few minutes after she'd peed, listening to the hypnotic hip hop booming from the party room. There was no way, no way she could go back to her room without washing David off her body. Finally she succumbed, took a quick, soapy shower and pulled her robe back on. Maybe he'd think she was still wet from her first fuck.

David was face down where she'd left him. For a moment she feared he'd fallen asleep, but when she approached the bed he rolled over to gaze at her. 'You look beautiful,' he said.

'Thank you.' This was the part where she was supposed to break up with him, but she hastily revised the plan. Better to let him bask in his prowess for a while so he wouldn't think the break-up was because of his bedside manner. 'You were great, David. Worth waiting for.' She batted her lashes.

'Was there much blood, dove? I see you've taken a shower.'

Dove? 'Oh. No. Not a lot.' Did he think there wouldn't be evidence on the bed sheets, or on the condom he'd worn, if she'd bled? 'All those summers at riding camp, I guess.'

David nodded. He stretched. 'Come back to bed, babe,' he said. 'I've got a few more tricks up my sleeve.' He wiggled his eyebrows and twirled an imaginary moustache like a vaudeville villain.

Fuck. There was no way she could survive another session with him. Certainly not tonight and probably not ever. 'David –' she began, but she was cut off by the blaring of a stereo turned up even louder from the party room. Even with David in the bed it trembled from the shaking of the old wood floor of her bedroom.

'I hate hip hop,' said David. 'Let's go to my place.' He jumped up and pulled on his jeans.

'I have an epistemology paper due tomorrow,' lied Sarah. 'I really should get it done, David.'

'Why didn't you tell me? I would've waited, Sarah. I've waited this long.' David took her in his arms.

She pressed her head to his shoulder, hoping to avoid a kiss, but he turned his face to hers and kissed her for what seemed like for ever. All she could think was, Horrible, horrible, though whether she meant the kiss itself or her deceitful response to it, she couldn't tell.

The hip hop hammered. David winced. 'That garbage is giving me a headache. I hope it's not the beginning of a migraine.'

'You should go,' murmured Sarah.

'If you want me to stay and help with your paper, I will.' He squared his shoulders; such a good, brave soldier.

'No, no, it's OK.' Sarah practically pushed him towards the door.

'Are you all right, my love?'

'Yes. You're a very skilled lover, David. The best a girl could ever hope for. Any girl.' She opened the door, doubling the noise from the party room.

'I love you,' shouted David.

Sarah nodded. 'Me too,' she mouthed, hoping the fact that she hadn't really said it would buy her some points at the Pearly Gates. Fuck. She'd called on God for help and now she couldn't seem to shake Him.

David was still lingering in the doorway. She kissed him hard on the mouth and playfully pushed him into the hall, but she forced herself not to close the door until he'd started towards the stairs, a jaunty spring in his step.

Finally. She. Shut. The. Door.

If Sarah hoped it would be as easy to shut her conscience up, she was mistaken. A lot of badness had just happened, all of it instigated by her. She was a liar, a manipulator, a coward, a phoney. Worst of all, she was still fucking horny!

At first she thought the sound of a siren was part of the hip hop music but when it stopped abruptly, in front of her house, she knew it was real. Christmas break was approaching and, though she lived in a community of students, their usual tolerance for noise was lost during the crunch at the end of term. Apparently, David wasn't the only one who didn't like loud hip hop.

Sarah peeked out into the hallway just as her neighbour's door flew open. A stream of drunken students staggered forth. She was about to shut her door again when she saw Christopher among them. The only way out was down into the waiting arms of the police, and though no one was likely to be charged, it wasn't going to be fun.

Sarah beckoned to Christopher. A moment later he was safe

inside her room. 'Are you drunk?' she asked. He shook his head. So she took him to bed.

It was a fast fuck, no artifice and not a lot of foreplay. Just the way Sarah wanted it.

Once he was naked she pushed him back on the bed, slid a condom onto his already erect manhood, and climbed aboard. He held her hips and humped up in long hard thrusts. She leant forwards a little to get some friction between her clit and his cock, then back to establish contact between his cock and her G-spot. It felt good to show off her prowess in bed, instead of masking it behind the façade of innocence, as she had with David.

When she stopped riding him and simply sat atop him, Christopher stirred her tunnel with his cock, adding a little gentle clitoral play with his right hand, keeping the left lightly on her hip. Their movement was minimal but focused. Sarah felt her orgasm welling up inside her, so welcome and wild it made her eyes well too. 'Thank you,' she whispered to Christopher as she started to come.

He didn't speak, just watched her writhe and yip, using his cock and hand to bring her off again immediately, so that when she collapsed on his chest she was sated. Then he reversed their positions and fucked her hard and fast, eyes closed, with a beatific grin on his face. Sarah thrust up to meet his cock, slammed her wet pussy against him, urged him on with wild words and travelling fingers until his eyes opened, as if in surprise, and he gasped a few filthy words of his own. Five more furious strokes. Christopher groaning, shuddering, coming, sinking down to cover her lips with his, their mouths wet and open, panting hard between kisses. Christopher tumbled free of her body to lie beside her.

Now this was a horse of a different colour. Sarah stretched languorously, running her hand from the top of his spine down to the base, just above the jutting curve of his bum. There hadn't been a lot of finesse to their fucking, yet it had been anything but artless. The contrast of Christopher's toffee complexion and her rosy one was as pleasing as she'd imagined it might be. His chest was hairless, also as she'd guessed it might be, but she'd not thought to imagine the beauty of his cock. So that had been an entirely pleasant surprise.

'Christ,' she muttered. The last orgasm she'd had, the magic number three, had been bone rattling. 'I love honest sex.'

Christopher laughed. He sat up, the better to stroke her spine, sending shivers in all directions. 'Is there any other kind?'

'There're all kinds of sex,' she replied.

'There's goodbye sex,' he said. His incredible black eyelashes closed. He sighed.

'We have another semester,' she protested.

'Not me. I've been stupid and now I must pay. I won't be back after Christmas.' Christopher flopped onto his back and patted his chest. Sarah obliged, resting her head on him and gazing up. It was funny, how comfortable they were with each other after just one intimate encounter. Perhaps it was because they were so good at sex, confident that the other was satisfied?

'Explain,' she ordered when he stayed silent.

'My student loan is gone and there's no more money for Christopher.'

'Gone?' She gave him a stern look. 'What did you spend it on? Beer?'

He shrugged.

'Parties?'

He shrugged again.

'Shame on you.'

'I confess, I am ashamed, and will be more so when I have to face my family in Barbados.' He shuddered. 'Their disappointment will be crushing.'

'How much do you need to make it to the end of the year?'

'What difference does it make?'

'Answer.'

'I suppose a few thousand. I could move in with Dan; he's already offered. But there are the fees and the books and ...' He shrugged. 'Too much, even if I got another part-time job.'

'I'll give it to you.' Sarah hopped up and fetched her wallet.

'Don't be stupid. I know you don't have that kind of money to spare.'

'You do?' She pulled out her chequebook and a pen. 'You have access to my banking information?'

'Of course not. But ... I've known you for years ... you've never had much money. Although ... your new leather jacket looks pricey and you have been spotted in cashmere. I assumed they were gifts from Mr Fusty.'

'Wrong. Here you go.' She tore the cheque from her book and handed it to him.

'I can't.'

'You must.'

'Sarah –'

'Christopher. You're smart, maybe even smarter than me.'

'Impossible!'

They both laughed.

'You must graduate, Christopher. I can afford it. Let me do this for you.'

'I can't. It's too much, and I have no idea when I could pay you back.' Christopher flipped the cheque onto the bedclothes. 'But thank you, sweet.' He caressed her cheek.

Sarah grinned. 'I have another idea then. A way for you to work off your debt.'

'Are you about to make me an immoral proposition?'

'I am. One you can't possibly refuse.'

'Goody.'

'But first, fuck me again.'

'I have a feeling,' he said, tiptoeing his fingers down her neck to pinch her nipples, each in turn and none too gently, 'I'm going to have to get used to following orders.'

11

Sarah was sitting in the food court at the mall with a serving of General Po chicken, conducting 'The Anvil Chorus' with her plastic fork. Veronica sat down in the space opposite, somehow managing to look elegant and sophisticated but warm and motherly at the same time, like a wealthy socialite might look while bandaging the grazed knee of a future president.

Sarah's boss mouthed something. Sarah took an ear bud out.

'I was asking if you were alone here?'

'All alone, thanks, Veronica.'

'If anyone you know shows up, I'm just a stranger with whom you struck up a casual conversation.'

'Oh, right. Thanks.'

'Discretion, my dear.' Veronica took a sip from a polystyrene cup, made a face and set it aside. 'Dreadful.' She leant closer. 'I'm so glad I ran into you, Sarah. I wanted to talk to you about a potential date.'

'Oh?'

'You know you're always free to refuse a date, right?'

'You explained that at the beginning, Veronica. I never have, have I?'

'I've always been able to advise you what the client might expect. This time, I'm not sure.'

'Oh?'

'On the plus side, it's a corporate gig and it pays extra. It's from next Saturday at two in the afternoon – "precisely two" for some reason – until ten Sunday evening, so it counts as two and a half dates. Two-thousand five hundred for you, plus whatever the tip will be. It'd be at your favourite hotel, the Royal Avenue.'

What if she bumped into Jack there? Stupid. He didn't live there, for goodness sake! Sarah said, 'That sounds good.'

'And your looks would suit this client perfectly. I was asked to provide a "naughty schoolgirl".'

'My page's uniform?'

'Not this time. This time it'll be more of a fantasy schoolgirl outfit, like those in wardrobe.'

'I can do that.'

'I don't know what the rest of the requirements might be, but often, when they ask for a naughty schoolgirl, it means they want . . .' Veronica raised an elegant eyebrow.

'Want what?'

'Spanking.'

'For me to spank him . . . Oh? He might want to spank me?'

'Possibly. Not for sure. How'd you be with that, Sarah? Have you ever played that game?'

'No, never. I never even got spanked as a kid.'

'Do you ever have any spanking fantasies?'

'No – yes – I mean, not actual fantasies, but I've wondered about what it might be like, once in a while.'

'A lot of women do fantasise about it. Come to that, a lot of women enjoy the real thing.'

'We're talking about by hand, right? Slaps on the bum? Not canes or whips or anything?'

Veronica shrugged. 'Maybe he won't want to whack your bum at all, but he might, and, if so, I don't know what he'd want to do it with.' Veronica's eyes narrowed. 'We make it very clear to our clients that they mustn't damage their dates and that if they want something the girl isn't ready for, she can refuse. If this one seems like he's going too far, you may simply walk away and you'll still get paid in full. I don't want that to happen, though. This is a new corporate account – one I'd like to keep.'

'Why me?' Sarah asked. 'Don't you have any girls who you know are into being spanked?'

'Three, but none of them looks young enough. Apart from

you, there's only Nancy who can play a halfway convincing schoolgirl, and she hates to be spanked.'

'Two and a half thousand bucks?'

'Plus tip.'

'I'll do it.'

'Wonderful!'

'But please remember after that I'll be gone for Christmas. Though I'd be happy to take a New Year's gig if something suitable comes up.'

'Understood. If this works for you, it could mean a lot of extra business for both of us.' Veronica stood up. 'Let's celebrate. You are going to need a ta-da! coat. My treat.'

'A "ta-da!" coat?' Sarah asked.

'Winter is here and you certainly can't walk around in public wearing a fantasy schoolgirl costume. You'll need something that's both warm and dramatic to go over it, so that when you meet your client, you can . . .' Veronica mimed parting a coat with a theatrical flourish. 'Ta-da!'

After dragging Sarah through a dozen or so boutiques, Veronica settled on an ankle-length scarlet-silk-lined black leather duster, at just over $1,800. Sarah modelled it, throwing it wide with a loud 'Ta-da!' She and Veronica doubled over with laughter. If their behaviour confused the saleswoman she didn't show it. It was a nice sale for her and she was likely on commission.

When the day came Sarah dressed in the fantasy schoolgirl costume that Veronica had picked out for her: a blue and gold striped tie, knotted loosely around her throat, a gauzy white shirt-blouse that fastened by tying its tails just beneath her breasts, a parody of a tartan kilt that started four inches below her navel and finished at the very tops of her thighs, over-the-knee thin white socks and Mary Jane shoes. Under it, Sarah wore a white net thong because, to men, a thong on a woman is like black – it goes with anything. She carried a boxy pink purse.

Her hair was in ribbon-tied bunches that she wore very

high, like a Harajuku Girl. Sarah's only fragrance was pink bubblegum-scented lipstick.

She went up to the penthouse level of the Royal again but it was the other suite, not the one where Jack's party had been, thank goodness. Having sex with another man in the same room and bed as she'd shared with Jack would have felt too weird.

Before she knocked, she undid all the buttons of her duster. A tall man opened the door. He had silver streaks in his black hair and a face that looked slightly rumpled and studious, in a nice way. His irises were as dark as his pupils. Sarah had never seen eyes quite like them. She found his gaze pleasantly intimidating. Her client's grey tie was woollen, worn with a grey check shirt, under a hairy tweed jacket that had leather elbow patches. His pants were grey flannel. He was shod in gleaming black Florsheim loafers with tassels.

Sarah stepped inside. 'Ta-da!'

He laughed.

She said, 'I'm sorry . . .'

In an English accent he said, 'No, I'm the one who should apologise. You look absolutely stunning, adorable, irresistible and so on. I laughed because whoever had you dress in that cute outfit – well, it's an inside joke that I won't explain.' His eyes narrowed. 'That same someone is being very crafty, as well.'

'Crafty?' Sarah asked.

'I have to go out, right now, for a meeting where some people are going to try to get me to agree to something. Their idea is, if I know that you, looking like this, are here waiting for me, I'll agree quickly so that I can rush right back.'

Sarah smiled. 'And will you – rush back?'

'What they don't know is that I've already decided to agree to what they want. For me, the meeting will be just about whatever extra concessions I can squeeze out of them. I'm relieved that they've set me up to be in a hurry. That means I won't have to waste time pretending to be reluctant but they'll think they've won what they want because of you.'

'It sounds complicated.'

'Business politics, my dear. Plot and counterplot. It's all very tiresome really, except for you being used as bait to catch a man who wants to be caught. I really regret leaving you all alone for a while, but I promise I'll be very attentive when I get back.' He took her coat and hung it in the closet. 'Help yourself to whatever you want from the minibar. There's a TV with two hundred channels, plus pay-per-view. Don't worry about the bill. Everything is on "them", you included.'

He left. He hadn't so much as touched her. She didn't even have a name to call him by.

The suite was similar to the one she'd been in with Jack, but in this one the closet to the left of the king-sized ornate brass bed had mirror doors. Sarah tried a couple of schoolgirl poses, sucking her thumb with a knee turned in; pigeon-toed and pouting. Very cute. If she was a man, she'd do her.

She renewed her pale-pink bubblegum lipstick and smoothed her over-the-knee hose and took a look around. The minibar was interesting. She wasn't hungry but she loved smoked almonds and it'd been ages since she'd nibbled on a Twinkie. There had to be three-dozen miniatures of booze. She'd made it a rule not to get tipsy on a paid date, but she'd never tried Cointreau. Sarah settled down on the end of the king-sized bed and thumbed the TV's remote. *The Mikado* was listed as a 'free-on-demand' movie. She knew it was an opera of some sort so she tried it. She'd thought that all opera was Italian or German but, strangely, it was in English. Even so, though the tunes were nice, she couldn't understand all the words. The singers had accents and they sang too fast a lot of the time.

After a while she got herself a Coke to wash the Cointreau down, and a Benedictine, just to further her education. She was eating, so the booze, drunk slowly, wouldn't affect her. *The Mikado* ended. The pay-per-view menu offered 'adult' movies. Sarah picked one at random.

A skinny blonde with unreal breasts, which were each bigger than her head, was sucking on the gigantic cock of a muscular man who was covered to the top of his bald head with tattoos. After a while, another man joined them, then a third. Maybe some people would have found it sexy, watching a woman sucking one man, being fucked by another and taking a third up her bum, but Sarah found it boring. There was no plot. There was no reason to care about any of the characters. It wasn't even as if anyone got seduced or had any feelings about what they were doing. OK, she herself had sex for pay, but she'd always found it fun. She got the impression that any of the characters she was watching could have simply walked away at any time, without regrets and without being missed. Except the woman, of course. Sarah giggled at her mental picture of the three men, still thrusting away, with the woman missing.

Was this all that porn was about? She switched to another adult movie.

This time, in a restaurant, a hot-looking but sophisticated woman, who was either a spy or a thief – Sarah wasn't sure about the plot – was trying to seduce a rather handsome business man. That was better! He was trying to resist her wiles but she was too much for him. There was a scene in a cab with some really sexy kissing. Sarah liked that part. Instead of them getting naked the moment they got to a hotel room, there was extended fondling that led to well-simulated passion. That was more like it. They ended up in bed, making love in a variety of positions, though none that Sarah hadn't tried. After the man came all over the woman's breasts, he turned out to be another thief or spy, a rival one. He tied her up on the bed, still naked but for her stockings, spreadeagled, and started to fondle her as he questioned her.

Now that was sexy! Sarah could imagine herself as the woman, totally helpless, at the mercy of a man who was torturing her, sexually. If she were that woman, she'd hold out for a long, long time.

Sarah's hand found its own way up under her tiny kilt. She was already damp.

The man on the screen was using a vibrator on the woman. He was driving her to the edge, making her beg, then switching off. He wasn't going to let her climax again until she told him where the thing they were both after – whatever it was – was.

Sarah's fingernails scratched the net of her thong, right over her clit. When the man took the vibrator away, Sarah made herself stop scratching. When he put it back, she started again. It was like the movie was interactive. It would have been even better if she'd had a vibrator of her own – and better again if she was tied up like the woman and a lover was mimicking what happened on the screen.

A stern voice demanded, 'What do you think you're doing?' The man in the tweed jacket had come quietly back to the room.

She stammered, 'Y-you said I could watch movies.'

'Did I tell you that you could masturbate?'

'N-no.'

'What a naughty little schoolgirl you are!'

Ah! He wasn't really angry. He was playing a game with her. This could be fun. Sarah stood up and looked at the floor, her hands behind her back. 'Sorry, sir.' She dared peep up at him from under her lashes. 'Did your meeting go well, sir?'

'Don't try to change the subject.' His voice softened, as did his expression. 'As it happens, it went extremely well, thank you.' He became stern again. 'Now, explain yourself, miss.'

'I was – I was watching a movie, like you said I could, and I sort of got carried away. I didn't know I wasn't supposed to.'

'You're here to serve me, not to get off without me.'

'Sorry.'

He looked at the TV screen, where the woman, still tied to the bed, was now giving the man an enthusiastic blow job.

'Kinky,' Sarah's client drawled. 'Is that what you like?' He tossed his jacket onto a chair and loosened his tie.

'I've never tried that sort of thing.'

He grinned sardonically. 'Of course not, you being just a schoolgirl, even if you are a naughty one.'

Obviously, he thought she was lying about never having tried being tied up and that her protests were part of the role she was playing. She asked, 'What should I call you, sir?'

'Call me John and lose the "sir". Now, about your punishment. What do you think would be appropriate?'

Before her mind could process his question, Sarah blurted, 'A spanking?'

'I agree. How many slaps do you think you deserve?'

She'd thought about it, and she'd been warned he might want to do it to her, but now that it seemed inevitable and so close, her knees trembled and her throat dried up.

'I asked you how many,' he insisted.

Sarah swigged the last of her Coke and managed to say, 'That'd be up to you, John, wouldn't it?'

He nodded in an approving way. 'I see that they chose you well.' John sat on the side of the bed, facing the mirror doors of the closet. He patted his left knee and turned his right leg out sideways. 'Come here then.'

A thousand hummingbirds fluttered their tiny cold wings inside Sarah's tummy. Dragging her feet, and having no problem looking scared, she rounded the bed and bent over his left knee. His right knee clamped hers. He'd done this before. His hand pushed down between her shoulder blades.

What was she supposed to do with her hands? Veronica should have given her lessons.

Sarah felt her skirt being lifted. Christ, here it comes. Any moment now . . . A hand smoothed over her bum, which might as well have been bare for all the protection her thong gave her. Maybe the thong had been a mistake. If there'd been some sort of fabric covering her cheeks, it might have helped.

'Very nice,' he said.

That was her bottom he was talking about. One cheek was compressed gently. Perhaps he wasn't actually going to spank her. Perhaps it would be pretend, not for real. He was stroking her skin now, as if he was admiring it, not at all as if he . . .

Ouch! So much for the 'pretend'. That really hurt. His palm came down again, on the other cheek, then on the first one again. Now he was caressing her once more. Was that it? Had he finished with . . .

'Ow!' No, he hadn't finished. Sarah took a deep breath. 'Ow!'

Was that OK, to yelp like that?

'Uh, uh, uh!' She had no choice but to make noises. Her entire bottom was stinging. It had to be crimson by now. She could feel it burning. And some women liked this?

Her legs flailed, or tried to. His right leg was clamping her thighs, making her struggles impotent. His blows came fast, staccato, then slow again. It felt as if he was striking obliquely, clipping her rounded bum cheeks rather than slapping straight down on them.

And she was enduring the abuse. That was something to be proud of, wasn't it? To be able to take it without . . . Funny, it didn't hurt so much any more, no, that wasn't right, it did hurt, but in a different way. Her bum had to be swollen and glowing and the heat was spreading and . . . She was wet, between her legs. Sarah realised that her clit was tingling and had been for some time. Her face was wet as well, so she'd been crying without realising it. What did she look like? Oh – the mirror.

She turned her head. His face was intent on what he was doing to her. Her bottom was fiery. It was very sexy, watching him spanking her. It occurred to Sarah that a lot of people would be turned on if they could watch her bottom getting slapped.

And it continued. It should have been unbearable by now but somehow it wasn't. Out of nowhere, Sarah felt a sudden rush of absolute bliss. Her clit, even though he hadn't touched it, felt incredibly sensitive. Yes, she was getting off on what he was doing to her. Amazing!

The slaps stopped. Sarah pushed her bum up at him.

'That's enough,' he told her. His voice was hoarse with lust.

Sarah slithered off his thigh to kneel on the floor between his feet. Looking up at him, and in her best Oliver Twist imitation, she asked, 'Please, sir, may I have some more?'

There was admiration in his coal-black eyes. He said, 'You little hussy! What a pain-slut you are.'

'Please? I was – I think I could have – you know.'

'Climaxed? Do you usually climax from a spanking?'

Sarah shook her head. 'I was telling you the truth when I told you that I'd never been spanked before. This was my very first time, honest. I do think I could have got there, though, if you'd gone on a little longer.'

He pulled her up to sit her tender bottom on his lap and cuddled her close. 'I believe you. You're quite incredible, young lady. I've never known a girl take her first spanking so well. You are as brave as you are beautiful.'

Sarah whispered, 'Thank you,' against his chest. 'Are you going to spank me again?'

'Let me see.' He flipped her over, belly down, across his knees again, and pulled her skirt up. A hand stroked her bum gently. 'You're burning hot, young lady. What is your name, by the way?'

'Sarah.'

'Well, Sarah, I pride myself on the care with which I spank, but your cute little derrière is showing some blue through the crimson and pink. It's a pretty effect. Take a look.'

He stood her with her back to the mirror. Sarah peered over her shoulder. Jesus Christ! Her entire bum, from the backs of her upper thighs up, was mottled with livid bruises.

'If I spanked you any more right now, you'd be very stiff afterwards. I wouldn't want that. I like my lovers to be flexible. Still, we have the rest of today and all of tomorrow. When and if your bruises have faded, ask me again and we'll see.'

Sarah said, 'Thank you,' but she could feel that her face was pouting.

'Are you very horny?'

'Yes, John.'

'I like that. I like you, Sarah. We'll have fun, I promise. Meanwhile, take your thong off.'

'Yes, sir.' Sarah reached up under her kilt and pulled her thong down. It tugged from between the lips of her pussy as if reluctant to leave it.

'And lose the kilt.'

'Yes, sir.' She unbuttoned its waistband and let it fall.

'Did you watch yourself in the mirror when I spanked you?'

She nodded, suddenly shy at being stark naked between her flimsy see-through shirt and her hose.

'You enjoyed watching yourself?'

'Yes,' she admitted.

He hitched himself further back on the bed and patted the duvet between his spread thighs. 'Sit here, Sarah.'

Sarah sat. His chest was a warm padded wall behind her. She leant into its comforting bulk. He reached over to take hold of her thighs, lifted and spread them, so that they overlapped his. His fingers untied the knot that secured her shirt.

'Isn't she lovely?' he whispered into her ear, smiling into their reflections in the mirror. 'The picture of depraved innocence.'

'And he's handsome.'

'Thanks, but let's concentrate on her for now. The poor girl is so horny, it hurts, right?'

Sarah nodded.

'We can see it in the little slut's lovely eyes. She looks so young and innocent but, deep down inside, she's depraved. She's going to play with her pussy now, Sarah. She knows that we're watching but that just makes it better for her, doesn't it?'

'Yes.' The Sarah in the mirror spread her sex with two fingers.

John's lips brushed Sarah's nape. His breath was hot. 'Today, she had her first ever spanking and she almost came. What a naughty girl she is.'

Sarah's reflection worked the index finger of her other hand into the glistening pinkness of her sex.

John cupped Sarah's breasts, her nipples held between his thumbs and index fingers. 'She's ashamed to be watched, that little hussy, but that just makes it better for her. Right?'

Sarah nodded. There was something about this man that made it impossible for her to deny her own depravity.

'There's so much she wants to try, that bad girl. She loves sex. She loves to be fucked, but there is so much more that she's curious about. Tell me, Sarah. Tell me what that wicked little girl would like to try.'

'I ...' Sarah's voice left her. There were things, things she hadn't admitted even to herself.

His right hand left her breast to hold her throat, not tightly, but letting her feel his strength. 'Tell me about Sarah,' he insisted. 'Tell me her deepest and darkest fantasies.'

'She ... She enjoyed that movie – the woman tied up while the man tormented her.'

'And she'd like that, to be bound and helpless with a man teasing her?'

'Yes.' It crossed Sarah's mind that John had hypnotised her, but she knew he hadn't. It was just that he had somehow given her permission to reveal her wildest self. He was so much in control of her, more so than even Peter the Masseur had been, and feeling totally subjugated somehow freed her.

What Peter had done to her body, making it his toy, John was now doing to her mind. The thought was simultaneously exhilarating and terrifying.

'What else?' he continued. 'Tell me what she hasn't done yet, the degrading things, the humiliating ones, the things that something dark and secret inside her craves.' His thumb and finger were teasing her nipple. Sarah could feel a pulse in her throat, beating against his palm. Part of her wanted to flee; another part wanted to grovel at John's feet.

The mirror Sarah was fingering her clit. The captive Sarah whispered, 'I've never ...'

'Never what?'

'Um, Greek?'

'You've never been buggered?'

'No, never.'

'Would you like to be?'

How could she answer that? It would hurt, for sure. It would be degrading. Somehow, she croaked, 'I'm not sure, but . . .'

'I understand,' he whispered. 'She's thinking about what it'd feel like. Look at her.'

The girl in the mirror had made a fan of her fingers and was frotting it across her clit frantically. And that was her. And the thought of being sodomised was exciting the mirror Sarah into a frenzy.

John released Sarah's nipple. His hand dropped into her lap, where she was masturbating herself shamelessly. Hooked fingers went up into her, sure and strong, taking her sex as if they had every right to use it anyway they wished, and they pumped while she played with her clit until Sarah yipped and . . .

A deep convulsion ejected a sudden gush of fluids from her sex.

John chuckled. 'A squirter, eh? Is that the first time you've ejaculated?'

'No. It's happened a couple of times before.'

'There's a good girl. I want you to be honest with me. Honesty frees you.'

'Thank you.'

'Sarah, now we've taken the edge off your lust, we'll take a break. I'm going to order supper from room service. For the next little while, I want you to think about what you've confessed to me, and to yourself. If you want to take any of it back, tell me. If you don't, I'm going to make some of your fantasies come true. I'll enjoy teaching you. Would you like me to be your sexual tutor?'

'I think so, sir. But what about . . .?' She twisted round in his arms and worked a hand down between their bodies, to where his erection strained against his fly.

'That'll wait,' he said. 'Anticipation is at least half the pleasure, don't you agree?'

She nodded.

'And don't make me tell you again. Lose the "sir".'

12

John ordered Bento boxes from Sakura, the hotel's Japanese restaurant, and a bottle of Mumm. Sarah thought that the Dom Perignon Jack had bought her was better, but the Mumm was still delicious.

Wow! Some of her girlfriends liked Coke; some preferred Pepsi. She, however, had champagne preferences, Dom Perignon over Mumm. How sophisticated was that!

She'd eaten a lot of Thai and Indian food over the years but never Japanese. John warned her about wasabi, thank goodness, just before she got the portion she'd scooped up on her chopsticks to her mouth. The tempura was crunchy-yummy but she wasn't so sure about the sushi. Perhaps it was an acquired taste.

A good escort makes interesting or witty conversation but all Sarah could think to ask was, 'Have you known a lot of escorts, John?' As soon as the words left her mouth, she regretted them, but he didn't seem offended.

'I had a friend who was in your business, once, but you'll be the first girl I've made love to who was paid for it.'

'A friend who was a professional escort?'

'Why not? In her case, it was her vocation. It's an ancient and honest trade. My friend loved sex and was very skilled at it. Isn't that the best sort of career, getting paid for doing what you'd do for nothing but the pleasure of it?'

'I guess it is.'

'Don't you enjoy your work?'

Sarah thought about that for a moment. Every paid date she'd been on, so far, had been fun. She was honestly able to reply, 'Yes, I do enjoy this work, very much.'

'That's good. If you didn't, it'd be a hard life, I imagine.' He dipped a tiger shrimp into pineapple sauce and popped it into his mouth. 'Why did you ask about my experience with escorts, Sarah?'

'You seem to know so much about women. I guessed you'd had a lot of experience.'

'Sarah, I'm close to forty. I've never married but I've lived with several women, not to mention casual encounters or "friends with benefits". I adore women. It'd be a sad reflection on me if I hadn't learnt a thing or two about them.'

'And you don't mind teaching me?'

'Teaching an apt pupil is a distinct pleasure for me, I assure you.'

'Then tell me what men like.'

He almost spluttered. 'Surely you know.'

'I want to know more. From you.'

'That's a tough one. There are men who don't like women at all, as you probably know, and there are some who have extreme tastes. I take it that you're asking me what most men, average men, like?'

'Please?'

'About the only universal I can think of, not counting those men with extreme tastes, is enthusiasm. We like women to ask for what they want. Men like women to show that they're horny and to express it openly; also to show that they enjoy whatever activity they're engaged in, whether it be giving or taking.'

'What about faking orgasms?'

'In your business, I image that's not unusual.'

'I've never had to, not yet.'

'That's wonderful! Either you are that paragon among women, not only hot but easily satisfied, or you've been very fortunate with your clients.'

'Talking dirty is good, right?' Sarah asked.

'Usually, but not always. There are men who'd find it offensive. With those, non-verbal communication would be better.'

'Like screaming when I come and such?'

'Exactly.'

'But most men like sexy talk?'

'Yes, the franker the better.'

Sarah grinned. 'So, if I told you that I'm really looking forward to wrapping my talented lips around your beautiful big cock, you'd like that?'

'Both the words and the deed.'

'Well, I am – looking forward to it.' Sarah stood up, shrugged out of her shirt-blouse, and rounded the table towards John.

A broad grin took ten years off his age. He said, 'I'm very attracted to you, Sarah, but let's wait for just a little while. I flew in early this morning and haven't had time to freshen up properly. Give me half an hour to shower and shave and then my cock will be at your disposal, I promise, and we'll continue with Sarah's education.'

'I'll try to be a straight A student, John.'

'And I'll be a strict tutor.'

Giving him her coyest look, Sarah asked, 'An oral exam first, please?'

'Oral first,' he agreed.

As soon as he disappeared into the bathroom, Sarah checked her bum in the mirror again. It was still mottled. When she touched it, it was still hot. He'd said he liked girls to be flexible. Sarah touched her toes; tried a back bend and did a couple of jumping jacks. She was no contortionist but she could kiss her own knees with her legs straight and together. Hopefully that'd do.

Being naked but for her hose and tie was sexy. She kicked off her shoes and tried strutting on tiptoe. It did nice things for her legs. Back at the mirror again, she flexed the cheeks of her bottom.

Poor little bottom. It was going to be violated for the very first time, and soon. She sucked a fingertip and managed to work it up her rear passage. When she concentrated on the sensations and put her shame aside, it didn't feel bad at all. Of course, her finger was nowhere near the size of . . .

'Preparing yourself?'

Sarah whirled. His hair was still wet. John was wearing pyjama pants and nothing else. It suited him. He had the shoulders for it, and a broad chest that tapered nicely to his waist.

'Just wondering what it'll feel like,' she explained.

'The thought scares you?'

'Some, but I still want to try it. As long as it's safe.'

'Of course. If you change your mind . . .?'

'It's not up to me, is it. I have to submit to you, sir, I mean, John, no matter what.'

'You like that idea, don't you?'

Sarah nodded, suddenly shy.

'Can you divide your mind into compartments, Sarah?'

'Absolutely.'

'Make a compartment where you know that you are safe in my hands and can stop anything I do to you or demand of you with a simple request, "Please stop." Make another compartment where you consider yourself totally at my mercy, no matter what. Can you do that?'

Sarah bit her lower lip and considered. 'Yes.'

'Excellent. How do you stop me?'

'Please stop.'

'Good. Remember that, in that compartment.' He sat on the end of the bed. 'And now, I promised you the chance to show off your oral skills.' His voice deepened and became commanding. 'Give me your tie.'

Puzzled, Sarah obeyed.

'Turn around, wrists crossed behind your back.'

Ah, right. She'd told him she fancied trying bondage. It would be different, giving him head without having the use of her hands. The woman in the movie had done it. She should have paid more attention.

When her wrists were secured, he turned her to face him. His hands on her shoulders pushed her down onto her knees. He reached into his fly and pulled his shaft out. Nice! Really nice! It mightn't have been quite as thick as Luigi's, but it was longer, with smooth skin that was all one colour. He was fully erect already, as far as she could tell, which was a nice compliment.

John's left hand made a fist that gathered both of her bunches, tugging at her hair but not painfully. His right hand took hold of her throat. She was a toy to him. It was scary how vulnerable she felt. Her safety depended on his skills and gentleness. Sarah felt that she'd come to a crossroads. She could use, 'Please stop,' and trust that he'd release her, or she could put herself into his hands totally. Absolute surrender. Absolute.

Her clit was tingling. Part of her wished that the hand that held her hair was more cruel. That same part wanted the hand that held her throat to tighten, not to choke her – that'd be crazy – but enough that her breathing would be restricted, just a little bit. Sarah licked her lips.

John's hands moved her head. It brought her lips to within an inch of his cock's moist head. Its aroma filled her mouth.

She looked up into his eyes. 'Please?'

'You want it?'

'Please.'

'Tell me.'

'I want your cock, please. I want it in my mouth. I want to taste it, lick it and suck it. Please let me show you how much I need it.'

'Tongue first,' he ordered her.

She lapped out. The dome was smooth and hot and wet. It tasted sweet but tart at the same time, with musky undertones. The tip of her tongue explored its glossy circumference. The most sensitive part, she'd learnt, was its knot, just beneath its dome. She found that perfect imperfection and caressed it with tiny wet laps.

'Good girl.'

He approved!

John allowed her mouth to come an inch closer. Sarah pursed her lips as if to bestow a baby kiss on his knot but sucked air in as hard as she could instead.

He shivered and murmured, 'Nice!'

Score one for Sarah.

She strained forwards against his grip. He allowed her to get another inch closer, close enough that her lips could gloss over his plum. How different he was from the other men she'd given oral sex. They had all been keen to get their cocks' heads into her mouth as quickly as they could. She suspected that John was no less eager than the others but he was controlling his urges. That was comforting. If he could keep that much of a tight rein on himself, he'd be much less likely to get carried away by lust and accidentally hurt her. She could trust him.

Her lips mumbled over smooth hard flesh. Her tongue lashed at it. A fraction at a time, he allowed her to take him deeper until the flare at the base of his glans passed between her lips. Sarah could feel his thighs flex, even though he didn't thrust. She moaned softly, encouragingly. If he wanted to ram into the depths of her mouth, she was ready for it. He didn't.

Did she want him to be a little more demanding? Sarah wasn't sure. As if he sensed her unspoken question, his hands gripped her harder, really pulling on her hair and definitely restricting her breathing. Sarah gurgled. If he didn't feel that, he had to be able to hear it. Her mouth was too full for her to form words. The sounds she was making were as close as she could come to 'talking dirty'.

He said, 'There's a good girl. I think I'm as hard as I'm going to get, Sarah.' He pushed her head back so that her lips lost their treat. 'Fetch me the butter off the trolley.'

'I – How?' She twisted to remind him that her wrists were bound.

'You'll find a way.'

Sarah lurched to her feet. John was giving her a physically challenging task to perform. How did she feel about that? Unsure, she shelved the question for later, when she wasn't in the peculiar mental state that he'd somehow put her into. With her back to the trolley, she groped around until she got a two-handed grip on the silver butter dish. It was vital that she didn't tip it and let the butter drop to the floor. To do so would be to fail him. On the Web, she'd learnt about girls who were styled 'brats'. A brat would drop the butter deliberately, hoping to get punished for it. Sarah would hate to be considered one of those dishonest girls. She resolved to always be honest about what she wanted and never try to provoke a man into ...

Into what? Brats craved corporal punishment. Did she? Spanking certainly turned her on. Was it just the physical pain or was it something more complicated? More questions to consider, but later.

John took the butter dish from behind her back and set it on a bedside table. There was a mound of pillows at the head of the bed. He moved it down and to one side. It had to be something to do with what he planned to do to her. Oh – of course! Sarah crossed to the bed and bent over the pile of pillows.

'No, not like that,' John said. He took her nape in one hand, slid his other arm under her knees and flipped her over, the back of her head on the bed, her hips high on the soft pile, her body titled up at forty-five degrees.

'Oh?'

'Your first time is important, Sarah. It'll be a very intimate and emotional moment for both of us. We should be able to see each other's faces. I especially want to watch your eyes.'

She and Jack had been face to face when he'd taken her maidenhead, if her memory was accurate. They hadn't made much eye contact though. Was her first time 'up her bum' going to be more romantic than when she'd given her virginity away? That was a weird thought.

John's big fist wrapped both of her ankles. He pressed her legs back until her knees bracketed her breasts. Sarah felt fingers spread the cheeks of her bottom. He bent closer to that forbidden valley. Christ! He was inspecting her there, looking directly at her bum hole. She felt herself flush.

'Absolutely gorgeous,' he said. 'You look as if you'll be very tight but looks can be deceptive.' His face went even closer.

Sarah felt the cheeks of his face press against the cheeks of her bottom. Something wet and warm ... Fuck! He was licking her there. Her culture decreed that this was a dirty place, forbidden. Taboo. Now a man's tongue was circling and circling and spiralling in and . . . probing at the tiny hole in the centre. Sarah knew that she could have, and should have, refused to allow that obscene caress. The words, 'Please stop,' filled her mouth but somehow refused to come out. She clenched her sphincter. John's tongue insisted. If he really wanted to do that thing, it'd be rude to refuse, wouldn't it? It wouldn't do to offend a client, particularly one she found so attractive.

Little by little, she made her sphincter relax. His tongue couldn't actually get inside but her relaxation exposed an area that was incredibly sensitive. It felt . . . It felt delicious, in a deeply depraved sort of way.

After this, after his doing this incredibly intimate thing to her, for her, she wouldn't be able to deny him anything at all, no matter how shameful.

He stood. His arm reached out to the side table. His fingers scooped butter. It felt cold on her bottom, particularly on her anus. John smeared around and around, probing at her hole each time his fingers passed over it. He straightened. Sarah peered up her body at him. His shaft reared up beyond and between her feet. He was rolling on a condom.

'Now,' he said. He released her ankles but she held them up close to her chest. His hand took hold of her sex, four fingers splayed across her mound, his thumb up inside her, so that he was grasping her by her pubic bone. With that iron grip, he had total control over her body. A twist of his wrist could have turned her over, painfully, irresistibly. He could have raised her up or pressed her down. But that didn't seem to be his intention. He held her simply to steady her.

His other hand bent his shaft down, out of her sight. She felt its cool slipperiness nestle against the knot of her anus. John leant forwards at an angle. His jet-black eyes gazed down into hers.

'Are you ready?'

Sarah nodded.

'You can still change your mind. We don't have to do this if you've qualms.'

She shook her head. 'I want it, please.'

'Very well.' The pressure increased.

There was no way that thing was going to fit in there. It was far too big. Involuntarily, she clenched. The pressure continued. Sarah felt her flesh indenting. She wasn't opening to him. He was just pushing a deep dimple into her.

Ah! That tight little ring of muscle surrendered to his male power and sighed open. The great hard bulb of his cock was forcing its way in, stretching her every bit of the way.

'It's happening,' he told her. 'I'm doing it. Your naughty little bum is opening up for me nicely. Does it hurt?'

'Yes – don't stop. Do it, please. I want it.' She was being forced to dilate and the surrender was so incredibly sweet.

His tip was gripped by her sphincter. Gazing into her eyes, a sardonic grin on his face, John pulled back a fraction of an inch, then eased forwards again.

'Please?' she begged.

'All the way?'

'All the way.'

'This far?' His knob passed just beyond her muscular ring.

Sarah's rubbery flesh closed around John's shaft, immediately behind its head. 'More please?' she asked. 'All the way in.'

He rocked. Each little push forwards buried his cock a fraction of an inch deeper into the tight sleeve. If she could have, Sarah would have thrust up at him, but his grip on her pubic bone held her immobile. She had to accept whatever he granted her, at whatever speed he allowed.

John's free hand took hold of her hair. She was totally helpless. His bulk pressed her thighs back. Her arms were bound behind her. His double grip kept her immobile. There wasn't a muscle in her body that she still had control over.

Or was there?

She concentrated. Even though she was distended, she still managed to compress her rear passage on his shaft, once, twice, then in a steady rhythm.

'You little bitch!' he told her. 'This is the first time you've ever had a cock up your bum and you're squeezing on it? I am impressed.'

'Thank you. More? Please?'

'Get your feet flat on my chest.' He allowed her a little room to manoeuvre. With Sarah taking some of his weight, John rocked forwards, pressing her knees down to bracket her throat. He let gravity pull him down, drive his shaft vertically into her, until his pubes were squashed against the lips of her sex. 'Take it,' he said, and jerked. The thumb inside her worked the sensitive area behind her bone. His splayed fingers rotated hard on her, grinding her clit. His cock was deep, so deep, and yet it seemed to strive for even greater depth with each convulsive movement of his body.

His eyes blazed into hers. The fingers of his free hand moved to force her lips apart and thrust between them, into her slavering mouth. Sanity left Sarah. The sensations overwhelmed her. She moaned and twitched. Her internal muscles in both her front and rear passages spasmed. There was wetness. She was spilling. Had she climaxed? How strange, not to be sure. If she had, she wanted more, and more.

He was thudding on her now. She wasn't certain, but she thought his feet had come up off the floor. She was being crushed beneath him, impaled by him, distorted, destroyed, annihilated.

And it stopped. He rolled aside, carrying her with him to topple off the pile of pillows. Utter calm washed over her.

After a few moments, she said, 'I've been folded, spindled and mutilated, right?'

Through his laughter, John got out, 'Thoroughly, I think. Sarah, you are something else. I can't recall ever having such a good time in, or on, or out of a bed. You're beautiful, bad to the bone, charming and funny.' He gave her a strangely soft look. 'I could almost wish that we'd met under different circumstances.' His face cleared. 'And now for something completely different, I think.'

'Did you come?' she asked.

'Yes, I did, thanks.'

Sarah felt proud. She'd been gurgling and grunting, feet up and nether parts, fore and aft, exposed, and it had made him come. 'So, what kind of different? I'm at your command, John.'

'A shower together, and then we shall see, but something less strenuous, I think.' He released her wrists. Being freed almost felt as if she'd lost something.

Sarah had never showered with anyone before, not counting the showers at school. She'd thought about having a man with her in the stall, usually when she was having a shower in the morning, but her fantasies had been all about two wet and soapy bodies, sliding on each other, leading to fucking standing up. Her shower with John was nothing like that. It was part romp, part meticulous cleansing. Of course her soaping his cock and balls, and his using a facecloth to wash inside her pussy and then twisting it into a spiral to cleanse her up inside her bum, were sexual acts, but in a relaxed way. That wasn't surprising, considering the furious activity that preceded their mutual washing.

The most intense moment that they shared under the shower, Sarah thought, was when she drank the water that was cascading down his chest. She considered giving him head with her mouth full of warm water but somehow she never got round to it.

He patted her dry as carefully as if she were a delicate porcelain statuette. That was funny. Twenty minutes earlier he'd been handling her as if she'd been a rubber toy.

They returned to the bedroom hand in hand. Sarah almost felt like skipping. 'How do you want me?' she asked.

'On the bed.' He scooped her up and tossed her onto it, on her side. It seemed that porcelain statuette time was over. John threw himself after her, head towards her feet. He swivelled in closer, took hold of her right knee and lifted it. His cheek snuggled on her left thigh. 'I want to get to know you better, physically.' He added, 'Not that you aren't a fascinating creature in many other ways.'

His eyes were inches from her sex. Gentle fingers parted her naked nether lips. He'd been serious. He was actually studying her, inside her pussy. 'Lovely. Such delicate colours. Such intricacy.'

Sarah felt his tongue, tasting her. It was different than if he'd been licking her for her pleasure. She sensed he was savouring the flavour of her and approving, thoroughly.

'I can guess, from your taste, what you've eaten lately,' he said.

'Oh?' She couldn't help but giggle. Was it possible? Until this moment she'd never have imagined it but now, with him, she half believed it was true.

'Absolutely. You're not a vegetarian, but you don't eat a lot of red meat. Chicken, I think.'

'Hmm.' Incredible.

'You like foreign food: Indian, Chinese, Thai. Yes?'

'Yes.'

'And you eat a fair bit of takeout. Salads, yes, but also –' He flicked his tongue up and down her slit – 'hamburgers?'

'Oh my God! How did you know?'

'I can tell, from the way you taste. I can taste that famous secret sauce.'

'Get out!'

'OK.' He pulled back. Their eyes met. 'Well, it also has to do with what little information I was given about you.'

'I'm relieved, frankly.' Sarah grinned. 'Tell me more!'

He leant into her again, tasting her with his tongue and lips.

'Let me see if I can guess what you like to eat,' she said.

His shaft was limp on his thigh, a foot away. Sarah reached for it but pulled her fingers back before she touched it. What he was doing, tasting her, fingering her gently, was thickening his cock. It lifted a fraction. She watched in fascination as its slight relaxed curve straightened and it raised up, its head moving in an arc. In under a minute, stimulated only by what his tongue was doing to her, his cock was a rigid column that reached up his belly to just above his navel.

That was about as sincere a compliment as a girl's pussy could be paid, she thought.

Now that he was fully erect, she was facing his scrotum. Sarah curled her body to bring her face closer. With two delicate fingertips, she moved his heavy sac aside to expose the sensitive area beneath it. Her tongue touched it.

John grunted.

So, he liked that, did he? Very well. Her tongue tickled and laved, working back and to the side, to trace the crease of his groin. He buried his face between the lips of her sex and lapped deep into her. The game had changed, or she'd changed it. She no longer wanted to joke about their eating habits. Her palm cupped his balls. She burrowed, lips mumbling. His cock twitched. Could she get one of his beautiful big balls into her mouth? Sarah stretched her lips wide. How strange, that something so wrinkled could be so lovely. She managed to encompass the bulk of one testicle. Funny, in a way, she had his semen in her mouth, even though he hadn't ejaculated yet. The thought made her laugh.

'What?' he asked.

Sarah released his testicle and explained.

'Which is best?' he asked her.

'I like the taste and I can't very well swallow it, not while it's still in your balls.'

'Then you shall have some to swallow, I promise. To make it fair, Sarah, I'd like you to squirt for me.'

'I'll do my best.'

'I'll help.'

It felt as if two of his fingers entered her, hooked up and homed in on her G-spot. He pressed his face closer and slid his tongue between the outer lips of her sex, up high, near where they joined. When he licked, it was along the left side of her clit, half on its sheath, half on its head. How did he know that was the way she liked it best? John was taking his time, tantalising her, not driving her.

To match him, she took the head of his cock into her mouth and idly stroked his shaft between her fingers and her thumb. It was a different sort of sex, for her. There was no urgency, though she knew that urgency would come. Was this what it was like for long-married couples – warm, affectionate, leisurely? Being swamped by lust, getting desperate, was great, but this sort of loving certainly had its charms.

And they'd only met a matter of hours before. Was it that he was so skilled a lover, or was there something deeper developing between them?

Dammit, Sarah, don't keep falling for your clients!

The pads of his fingers were rotating. She tightened her fingers' grip a fraction and gently drew on his shaft. A little sigh escaped her. If only this could go on forever.

You lick me; I suck you. We both stroke. Quiet bliss.

Sarah tried something new. She used the head of his cock to draw tiny circles on the flat of her tongue.

John said, 'Nice.' Praise from Caesar.

His other hand was on her left breast, just holding it, not moving. In her head, she told him that it was his to hold for as long as he wished. If holding turned to squeezing, to rolling her nipple, that'd be fine, too. Sarah's lust was there, deep inside her, but calm. Either of them could have stirred it up at any moment. When one of them did, it would become a tropical storm, a hurricane of desire. Meanwhile, she'd wallow in its calm warmth.

Sarah felt incredibly relaxed. Not all of her muscles were limp though. Now that she was thinking about it, her thighs were quite tense. The fingers of the hand she was moving John's shaft with gripped him tighter. Inside – inside her sex – although she hadn't felt her clit tingle yet, she felt as if the walls of her vagina were seeping. Yes, her lust was rising, but in a different way than she'd ever felt before. She was melting into it, except for her thighs, which had now begun to tremble uncontrollably.

John's tongue deserted her clit. He sucked one lip of her sex into his mouth and closed his teeth on it, not biting but threatening to.

Sarah lifted his cock off her tongue for long enough to ask, 'More licking, please, John.'

He chuckled. 'Good girl.' His tongue went back to her clit but with more pressure.

Sarah took his knob between her lips and let it rest on the flat of her tongue. Her hand pumped in long, strong strokes.

She decided that, unless he told her otherwise, she'd mastur-bate him into his climax while she kept her lips and tongue relaxed. Her mouth would be a receptacle, nothing more, not until he'd filled it.

Her thighs were vibrating. Tension had crept up on her. She was rigid from her waist down. A climax was on its way, but a different sort of climax. Her clit was engorged and extra sensitive, but her orgasm wasn't going to come from there. It was going to come from deep inside, maybe one of those vaginal climaxes that she'd read about and dismissed as mere fantasy.

She was a knot, paralysed with lust except for her one hand and arm that were urging the man to give her the essence that made him male. Her greedy mouth and tongue were waiting, waiting . . .

It was like a cough of joy that convulsed Sarah's entire body. Her vagina clenched tight. As if it had been full of fluid, it ejaculated a great gush of liquid ecstasy.

Perhaps that triggered John, because he flooded her mouth. She swallowed. He, and she, spurted again and again. At last it stopped.

Sarah said, 'You were right. That *was* something different.'

'I'm drained,' he admitted. 'Snack time? A nibble and a glass of champagne?'

'Nibble what?' she asked.

'Food, I promise.'

'You know something?' she said.

'What?'

'We haven't fucked yet, not in the usual way, I mean.'

'You're insatiable. We'll get to it, I promise.'

Sarah got up and walked towards the bathroom door where two fluffy white robes hung, and reached for one.

John said, 'No. Stay naked.'

'May I go fix my face?'

'Do you have any lipstick that doesn't taste like candy?'

'Yes.'

'Then use that.' He rolled over to the bedside phone.

His request, that she paint her lips with more mature lipstick, seemed to say that she'd graduated, in his eyes, from the role of a 'naughty schoolgirl', to a toy to play with, to a woman to make love to. It felt good.

13

Sarah had heard of a book called *The Naked Lunch*. Though she'd never read it she understood it to be mainly about drug addiction and sex. Here she was, having a 'Naked Supper', and although she hadn't taken any drugs or smoked anything and had only drunk a little champagne, she felt she was high. Infatuation can be intoxicating.

She'd discovered that with Jack. This time, she resolved, she'd enjoy the trip but wouldn't confuse it with love. It was hard though, sitting, bare, across a small table from the broad strong chest of a man who'd already taught her so much and who would, she was sure, teach her much more. They still had twenty-four hours of their date left. That was a long time for a tryst. Even so, it was far too short.

She could excuse herself for feeling so emotional towards John. He had everything a girl could want in a man. Maybe he wasn't movie-star handsome but his face appealed to her. He had a fine physique, a powerful personality and he was an incredible lover. John was very intelligent, as well. That was important. She could never really love a man who wasn't bright, brighter than she was.

Had Jack been bright? She hadn't thought about that with him.

John reached across the table to offer her mouth another of the lobster puffs. Beyond him, on a side table, stood a pink plastic shopping bag marked 'Intimates' in gold script. It had been delivered along with their supper. He hadn't offered to tell her what was in it and she hadn't asked. Intimates, she knew, was the name of a chichi boutique in the hotel's concourse. Had he ordered a gift for her, or was it for him to take home to his girlfriend? She could only hope it was for her – maybe lingerie?

John dabbed his lips with a napkin and asked her, 'Enough?'

'Plenty, thanks.'

'More champagne?'

'Later.'

'Want to watch a movie?'

Sarah looked at the bed then straight into his eyes. 'You know damned well what it is that I want, John.'

'Tell me.'

'I want you to fuck me, or something.'

'Be more specific.'

'How can I be? You're the teacher. I want to learn. What's on the curriculum, teach?'

'In general terms?'

Right – he liked her to talk dirty. She could do that. 'You could bugger me again, if you liked. You could fuck my face. Do anything you like to me, just so you make me be your . . . bitch. You know I'm horny for you, John. Use me.' She cocked her head in thought. 'What I really want, I've just realised, is to be defiled. Would you defile me, please? Just don't make me wait for it.'

'Waiting can be fun.'

'Please?'

'That movie I caught you watching.'

'Yes?'

'You liked it – the woman tied to the bed, being teased.'

'Yes,' she admitted. 'That was hot.' Sarah glanced around the room. 'Do you have some rope hidden somewhere?'

'Not rope, exactly. Onto the bed with you, Sarah, spreadeagled, just like in the movie. I'm going to make that fantasy of yours come true.'

Sarah obeyed, quivering with anticipation. John brought the pink Intimates bag to the bed. From it, he took four sets of manacles, white leather bands that were lined with imitation ocelot fur, that buckled and were joined in pairs by chains. He held one pair up.

'You want to try this?'

'Please.'

'Some women get panicky the first time they're fully restrained.'

'I won't. I didn't when you tied my wrists behind my back, did I?'

'No, you didn't. Very well.' He pulled her ankles far apart and fastened each to a brass scroll at the foot of the bed. Next, her arms were extended high and wide, and secured to the bedhead. He was strong, strong enough to stretch her body achingly taut.

'Comfy?'

'I'm fine. "Comfy" wouldn't work, would it?'

'Of course, you're a pain slut. I was forgetting.'

It thrilled her to be so matter-of-factly referred to in such a way. Sarah let her eyelids droop and deepened her voice. 'Please remember, John. I need it.' She was very aware that her strained position narrowed her waist, spread the fans of her ribs and made her breasts more prominent. How could any man resist?

'I won't, I promise.' His hand went back into the bag. 'How's your bottom healing, Sarah?'

'It's all better, thanks. Ready for you.'

'Hmm. Last time I looked – a couple of minutes ago – it was still bruised. Perhaps come morning?' He took something out of the bag but he was turned away from her so she couldn't see what it was.

John picked two pillows up from the floor and wedged them under her bum, lifting it. 'Feeling stretched enough now?' he asked.

'Please?'

'Please what?'

'Do it to me, whatever it is you're going to do.'

'The woman in the movie – she was begging.'

'I'm begging.'

'You think? I have some things that'll make your pleading more sincere.'

'Show me, please?'

'Ever use this stuff?' John held up a small glass bottle with a pump top.

'Lubricant? Don't need it. I lubricate just fine, naturally.'

'Yes and no. It's a sensitising gel, made in the UK, called Play O. A lady friend of mine recommended it, but I've never tried it on anyone. It'll be a first for both of us.'

'How does it work?'

He half sat, half lay next to Sarah. 'First,' he announced, 'we expose that cute little clit of yours.'

Concerned, Sarah asked, 'Is it little? Too little?'

'Silly girl! Of course not. It *is* cute, though.' He rested his palm on her mound. One finger curled down and between her pussy lips. 'You horny little thing! Its head is exposed already, before I touched you.'

'John,' she said, 'you've been touching me one way or another ever since you got back from your meeting. You've kept that little button of mine swollen non-stop, except maybe for a little while just after you made me climax.'

'I'm flattered.' He took the bottle in one hand and pumped a pea-sized blob onto the index finger of his other hand.

'Is that enough?' Sarah asked.

'That's the recommended quantity. We'll see if you need more.' His hand returned to her mound.

Sarah felt a slight chill as he deposited the gel onto her clit. 'Now what?' she asked.

'We wait and see.' John leant over her, his hand still resting lightly on her sex, and kissed her for the first time.

His tongue was playful with hers. The kiss was gentle, questing, nowhere near the demanding force she'd expected. She melted into it.

That ghost of a tingle started in her clit but that was no wonder; erotic expectations did that to her, but the ghost became a real tingle in less time than it took her to suck in a deep breath and the tingle got warmer until, just as it began to feel uncomfortably hot, hot became cold, as cold as an exposed nose on a prairie February, and then the tingle turned ferocious.

The pad of his fingertip was making gentle circles on her clit's head.

A 'Mmmph!' burst from Sarah's mouth.

John pulled back from their kiss. 'How does it feel?'

'Good. Fuck me!'

He raised an eyebrow. 'That good, huh?'

'Please, *please*?'

'But I've only just begun to tease you, Sarah.'

She jerked at her manacles. 'I can't stand it!'

'You have no choice but to endure it for as long as I decide that you shall.'

'Hurt me, then, please, John. I'm sure I could come from pain.'

'You asked me to tease you. Remember what Oscar Wilde said, "Be careful what you wish for; you might get it"?'

'Fuck Oscar Wilde!'

That made John laugh out loud. 'I'd rather fuck you, thanks, and I will, but not just yet. Perhaps this will help?' He showed her a vibrator, a ten-inch ivory-coloured cylinder with fluted sides and a slightly lopsided smooth head.

'You're going to fuck me with that?'

'Perhaps, later.'

'*Now!*'

The sadistic bastard leant over her on one elbow and sucked her tongue into his mouth. Sarah wanted to keep kissing him for hours. He was as enthusiastic and artful as she in that department, but . . . Cool plastic touched the tip of her hip bone and began to tremble. The tremble became intense vibrations. She could feel it through her pelvic bone. His tongue pushed hers back into her mouth and followed it. Her lips closed on it softly, imitating the lips of her sex for his tongue-cock to fuck.

Sarah tried to twist her hips sideways to get the vibrator closer to where she desperately needed it but an inch was all the play her bonds allowed her. As John tongue-fucked her wet and yielding mouth, he trailed the instrument of torture slowly down the crease of her groin. It reached the plumpness of her pussy's left lip. There it rested, vibrating her pussy, not penetrating her, not making contact with her aching clit.

Sarah mumbled, 'John, John,' and broke the kiss.

He drew back and trailed the squirmy wet tip of his tongue down the side of her neck, lapped its hollow, then across the smooth skin of her breast to her nipple. He took that engorged nub between his pursed lips and suckled on it like a baby, drawing it in and out, sending threads of pulsating sensation deep into her flesh.

'On my clit, John. Please? Let me come, John. Do my clit and I promise to worship you forever. I'll suck you, fuck you, you can fuck me up the ass – anything you fucking well want, just so you let me climax.'

'You'd crawl for me?'

'Yes, yes!'

'On your hands and knees?'

'Yes!'

'You want to be my slave?'

'Yes, please let me be your slave, please, John. Use me, abuse me, do whatever you fucking well like to me, just so you let me come.'

He told her nipple, 'Now you're begging.'

'Begging enough? Enough that you'll do it for me?'

'Soon, or pretty soon, anyway.' He ran the vibrator's head along the crinkled crease where her pussy lips met and paused with it a fraction of an inch away from the shaft of her straining clit.

'You bastard! You fucking bastard. You're killing me!'

He chuckled and moved the tip of the vibrator to rest beside her clit, pressing into the crease between it and fleshiness that bracketed it. 'Sarah, is that nice? Calling me names?'

'Sorry, sorry. I didn't mean it.'

'I'm partial to dirty talk in bed, though I prefer to be the one doing the name calling.'

'Sorry. It's just that I'm going mad!'

'You really want me to make you climax?'

'Yes, yes, yes.'

'Scriously?'

'Oh fuck!' Sarah babbled, unable to form words, terrified of

149

blurting out the wrong ones. She'd promised him everything she could think of and still he was showing her no mercy. Much more of this and she'd burst into tears of frustration. How could a man be so cruel?

His mouth descended onto hers again, this time ravishing her, demanding that she yield. He was the best kisser ever. She wished she could relax into his kisses but her need was far too sharp. The vibrator lifted. She heard its song change, becoming even higher pitched. It touched her, moved a fraction, then pressed down. He held it parallel to her clit's shaft, snug against it, where its divine vibrations shivered through her pubic bone and trembled into her core.

Sarah twisted her face desperately away from John's voraciously demanding mouth so that the 'yips' could stream out from between her lips in one long ecstatic stream.

When she finally fell silent, he asked her, 'How was it?'

Sarah lay panting, her chest heaving, looking up with glazed blue eyes into his amused black ones. Eventually, she managed a carefully controlled, 'Good, John. Very good, thanks.'

'The gel works then?'

She giggled. 'Yes, I think you could say that.'

'More?'

The thought of enduring what she'd just been subjected to again terrified her, and was totally irresistible. She asked, 'I'm dry. Drink first?'

He fetched a flute of champagne, held her head up and tipped it to her lips. Sarah let the liquid gold flow down her throat.

'More wine?' he asked.

'No, not yet. Are you going to do it to me again, John?'

'Not exactly.' He cupped her mound and squeezed.

Sarah squelched, and she wasn't ashamed. 'I can take it, I promise,' she said. 'No matter how much I beg or curse, I can take it. John, I admit, it's torture, but, please, tease me and tease me until I scream.'

He reached to her right wrist and worked the buckle.

'You aren't releasing me yet, are you?'

'Only partly. You want more teasing? Very well, but I'm not going to be the one who does it.'

'Who will?' she asked, suddenly alarmed. Sarah looked from side to side. Had he brought a friend to share her with? That woman who'd recommended the gel? If so, how did she feel about that possibility?

'Silly. There's no one else here. I meant that you are going to tease yourself.'

'I don't understand.'

'You don't have to, not yet.' He picked up the gel container. 'Ready?'

Sarah lowered her eyes. 'I'm still . . . There's still a tingle left, just a ghost of one, so yes, I'm very, very ready.'

'*Incroyable!*'

Did he really speak French? It wouldn't surprise her; he was obviously a well-educated man.

This time he pumped the droplet of gel directly onto her clit's head. Sarah wriggled. The tingle started.

John walked around the foot of the bed to sit back on it to her left. He told her, 'Play with yourself, Sarah. Diddle yourself, but slowly. Show me just how long you can make it last.'

'Vibrator?'

'No, use just your fingers. I want to see how you play with yourself when you're alone.'

The tingling in her clit had become an erotic itch that screamed to be rubbed, but he wanted her to show him how long she could make it last. Sarah bit her lower lip. She was desperate for another orgasm but he was testing her to see how well she could control her own lust. Her needs were in direct conflict. Delay her own release, or disappoint John? Cater to her physical needs, or her emotional ones? She was tortured, and it was all his doing.

She'd show him!

Sarah turned her head, glanced at his rigid erection, then lifted her eyes to gaze directly into his. Despite her clit's desperate craving, she cupped her right breast on her palm and gently compressed it. John's eyes followed her movement.

Pupils dilate when they see something they like, don't they? It was hard to tell with John because his irises were almost the colour of his pupils, but if she watched carefully ... She made her grip relax, then tighten, sending ripples through the firm flesh of her breast. Did his eyes widen? When she let her index finger flip across the nub of her nipple, did they open even further? How about if she rolled her nipple between her thumb and index finger? Yes, he definitely reacted. Sarah dropped her eyes to his lap. His cock looked as hard as a candy cane. As a girl, she'd loved to suck on candy canes. She used her eyes to direct his to his own rigid shaft and pursed her lips.

John grinned. 'Bitch!' There was warm admiration in his voice.

She wasn't at all insulted, quite the opposite. It excited her. So he liked her to tease him back, did he? Very well ... Sarah took her nipple by its very tip and pulled it away from her chest, elongating her breast obscenely. John's face became intent. Good! She shook her flesh by her grip on her nipple. Jags of sweet sensation crackled from her nipple to her clit, stoking its need. Her clit sparkled with desire.

John's left fist closed around the column of flesh that jutted from his lap. He wanted to watch her toy with herself, did he? What's sauce for the gander is sauce for the goose! She'd get extra kicks from watching him as he jerked off, if she could persuade him to, and the best way to persuade him would be to tell him so, as he so loved her to talk dirty.

Sarah made her voice go husky. 'Stroke it, John. Show me how much I turn you on. Stroke that lovely long cock of yours for me, please?'

'You want to make this a contest?' he asked. 'Who can outlast the other?'

Sarah nodded and licked her lips. 'But I've got that gel on my clit, so it wouldn't be fair.'

'Very well, though it's intended for women.' He picked up the little glass container and pumped a generous blob of the gel directly onto the eye of his cock. 'Fair now?'

'Almost fair,' she agreed. 'But aren't you going to rub it in?'

'You haven't,' he pointed out, 'but OK.' His palm glossed over his dome, spreading the gel.

Sarah watched his face. The corners of his mouth twitched. The gel had to be starting to work but he was exercising control, which was what this little game was all about.

Sarah twisted her nipple. John gave his shaft a long slow stroke. They stared into each other's eyes. Sarah smoothed her only free hand down her own body, over the dimple of her navel, until her fingertips reached the smooth pillow of her mound. She pressed down hard, depressing and tilting her clit's shaft, pulling its sheath further back. Exposing its pink head more completely.

Yes, he liked to look at her clit's head, swollen and glistening from its coat of gel. His pleasure showed in his face and in the slight tightening of his grip on his own flesh.

'Does it tingle, John?'

He nodded.

'Me too.' She smoothed a fingertip over the head of her clit, just once, even though inside she was screaming for more.

John changed his grip on himself to two fingers and his thumb.

'I like to watch you do it to yourself, John,' she told him. 'I want to see you climax. I want to watch your face as you shoot your jism. I want to see it spurt out of you. Will you cream on me, John? On my breasts? On my belly? I want to see it.'

He retaliated with, 'You'll see it, but not until I watch you squirt from your pussy. You come wetter than any woman I've ever known, Sarah. Did you know that? It's a rare gift. If I had my camera here, I'd record it and play it back late at night, when I'm alone.'

'You wouldn't show anyone else?'

'Not unless you'd like me to.'

'To that girlfriend of yours?'

'Friend with benefits, not girlfriend.'

'You could show her if you liked, John. I wouldn't mind.'

He chuckled. 'Wouldn't mind? You'd love to have your climax recorded and shown off, you kinky little exhibitionist.'

'You have a cellphone?'

'Yes.'

'Doesn't it take movies?'

'Why yes, it does. Not good ones, but it would do. Hold on a minute.'

Sarah cringed inside from her need to touch herself but she managed to resist for the thirty seconds it took him to fetch his phone and prop it on a pillow between her thighs, aimed up at her pussy.

'There,' he said. 'Shall we continue our little game?'

'Not yet.'

'Why not?'

'In my purse, I've got a BlackBerry that takes movies.'

'But so does my phone.'

'Record you, just your hand and cock, for my evenings alone.'

'You really want to?'

'Really.'

'OK.' He found her purse and her phone and propped it up against her left breast. 'Right, it's recording.' He sat beside her, turned towards her, so that both she and her phone could see what he did.

Knowing she was being recorded added spice to Sarah's self-fondling and made it even harder for her to restrain herself. She parted her pussy lips with two fingers and dabbled between them with a third while her thumb's ball smoothed over her clit.

'Beautiful,' John sighed. 'You personify pure lust, Sarah. You're a remarkable young woman. Whoever gets you to keep will be a lucky man.' His hips rocked backwards and forwards, counterpoint to his slow masturbation.

'Come for me, John?' she asked. Her thumb squished down on her clit and rubbed it.

'You first.'

'Do we have a bet on this?'

'If you like. What stakes?'

'A regular fuck? We haven't done that yet.'

'Missionary?' His fingers tightened on his shaft, and accelerated their strokes.

'Please.'

'If who wins?'

'Me.'

'Very well. If you win, we'll fuck missionary style. And if I win?'

'Anything you like, John.'

'No matter what?'

'No matter what.'

He grinned. 'You're hoping it'll be something really kinky, aren't you?'

'Perhaps.'

'You're so much fun, Sarah.'

'Mmm.' She made her thumb slow down. 'You too.'

Still stroking himself, John picked the vibrator up again and turned its base one-handed, like he'd done it before.

'What?' she asked.

'This.' He reached over with the trembling toy and touched it to the left lip of her sex.

'Cheat!'

'No. Teasing you turns me on, so it's fair.'

'Fuck!'

'We will, later.' The smooth buzzing head slipped between her pussy lips and traced a line up from the bottom of her slit to push into her and press up behind her pubic bone.

'I can't stand that,' she whined. 'You'll make me . . .' Her hand became a fan that frotted across her clit furiously.

In turn, John stroked himself hard and fast. 'Come for me, Sarah,' he demanded.

'Yip, yip, yip, yip . . .' She convulsed inside. Her essences jetted from her pussy.

John stood, still stroking, then leant over Sarah and ejected a great foaming ivory spurt of jism across her chest. Two lesser jets followed, one aimed at each of her nipples.

'You cheated!' she accused.

'True. I concede. Give me half an hour to recover, Sarah, and you shall have your missionary fuck.'

14

John showered first, and alone. After her own leisurely shower, Sarah changed her hairstyle from twin bunches to a short ponytail. Bunches had been for the 'naughty schoolgirl' look. She felt she'd graduated from that and deserved a more stylish look. The schoolgirl thing hadn't been John's idea, anyway, though it had amused him. She made her face up to be more sophisticated as well, heavy on the mascara, eye shadow and deep-pink lipstick. She hadn't brought a change of clothes, unfortunately, so she settled for tying one of the hotel's enormous bath towels around her like a sarong.

No, that wasn't right. He liked her to be bold, outrageous, even. Sarah changed the big towel for a smaller one that she knotted very low around her hips. There! Lots of torso on show, pert breasts, narrow waist, sweetly curved belly, bare down well below her navel to within an inch of her mound, and one long leg exposed to her hip.

When she went into the other room John was in a hotel robe and holding two flutes of champagne. His eyebrows lifted when he saw her. 'Nice!'

She sketched a little curtsey and almost lost her towel. John handed her a flute and sat in the room's only armchair. He patted his thigh.

'Another spanking?' she asked.

'Not right now. Come sit on my lap.'

He really was a remarkable man. They'd had debauched, depraved, illegal-in-some-states sex, and now he was being romantic. She perched on his knee. He pulled her deeper into his lap and wrapped her in his strong arms. Champagne slopped from her flute onto the outer curve of her left breast. John lapped it off but didn't lick any further, though her nipple would have welcomed his tongue. He seemed content to simply cuddle for now. Sarah was sure that would change but meanwhile, she would enjoy the sweetness of the moment.

'John,' she said, 'you're obviously very bright. What sort of work do you do? I'm sure it's fascinating.'

'I'm contemplating a career change,' he told her. 'In fact, I committed myself to that, this very afternoon.'

'Doing?'

'Sarah, I'm not going to discuss it. How about you? Do you have a life outside of being an escort?'

Hmm! She couldn't very well tell him she was a student, could she? He'd be able to guess which university she was at, and that'd never do. Would it? She said, 'I'm a student of life. Let's talk about something else.'

'Good idea. Such as?'

The only topics she knew really well were her major and minor courses, so she said, 'Philosophy?'

He chuckled. 'Of the boudoir?'

'Is there such a thing?'

'A man wrote extensively on the topic. You might have heard of him – the Marquis de Sade?'

She shivered. 'Yes, I've heard of him. He's the man that "sadism" is named for. From what I've heard, he went far too far and he liked some pretty icky stuff.'

'Agreed. Carefully and lovingly administered pain is one thing, whipping someone's flesh to bloody shreds is quite another.'

'We think alike,' Sarah ventured.

'On that topic, from opposite sides of the fence, but yes, our tastes seem to match beautifully.'

Sarah snuggled closer. 'He hurt women for his own pleasure, with no consideration of theirs. You give pain-sluts what, um, what we want and no more, right?'

'Not even that much sometimes.'

'I get excited by being spanked and so on, but I wouldn't want a lover to actually harm me.'

'In the BDSM world, the rule is "Safe, Sane and Consensual".'

'That sounds like a good rule.'

'It's the one I follow, assiduously.'

'You're an expert, aren't you, when it comes to giving loving pain but doing no damage?'

'I try to be.'

'Show me?' she challenged.

'I thought we'd agreed we'd try some good old-fashioned missionary sex next.'

'But until then?'

'What did you have in mind? Remember, I told you no more spanking until tomorrow.'

Sarah turned her face up towards his. 'Kiss me, please, John, and torment my nipples as we kiss. I think that'd get me very, very hot.'

'You've never experienced nipple torture?'

'You're my first . . . my first . . . master . . . is it? The first man to spank me or to really understand what I need. Or to care, come to that. I didn't really understand it myself, before today. I suspected I'd enjoy pain and submission but I think I denied it because it seemed perverse, unnatural.'

'It's perfectly natural, if what animals do is your standard of natural behaviour. A bitch wolf won't give herself to a dog wolf until he's shown his mastery, usually by holding her throat between his jaws. A vixen won't lift her tail for a dog fox until he grips the scruff of her neck between his teeth.'

Sarah snuggled closer. The way the conversation was heading was giving her that ghost of a tingle. 'Which am I, John?' she asked. 'A bitch or a vixen?'

'Let's see, shall we?' He took hold of her ponytail and pulled her head back to expose her throat. His jaws descended until he had her larynx gripped lightly between them.

Sarah purred, knowing that his lips would feel her words vibrate in her throat. 'You can mount me, anytime, Mr Wolf.'

John released her, bent her head forwards and nipped her nape somewhat harder than he had her throat. It was the first time Sarah had been bitten there, and she liked it. She shivered. No wonder geishas showed the backs of their necks off as erogenous zones. 'Oh, Mr Fox, I'd be honoured to lift my bushy little tail for you. Your choice of which entrance you decide to use.'

'Vixen wins, by a shiver,' John declared.

'And this vixen made a request. Please?'

'Of course.' He moved her head by her hair, which was something else she was discovering she liked.

With her face tilted up towards his, at the exact angle and position that suited him, he lowered his lips to hers. At first they brushed, gently, just lip on lip, though hers were soft and parted in invitation. He mumbled on her lower lip. Sarah was very aware that his big warm palm was resting on her ribcage, an inch below her left breast. John pulled her hair slightly, tipping her head back further. His tongue ran across her lower lip. She was so glad she'd changed her lipstick from the candy-flavoured one. She didn't want to be the schoolgirl he was debauching any more. She needed to feel like a sophisticated but submissive real woman – one who knew exactly what she was doing, not one who was innocent and being seduced into depravity.

His tongue accepted her open mouth's invitation. As it passed between her lips, his hand slid upwards to hold her entire breast in its grasp. Sarah sucked a deep breath, lifting her breast, reminding him of her need for pain.

A finger and a thumb closed on her nipple. It was rolled, too gently, as his tongue explored the sweet wetness of her mouth. Sarah wriggled. Yes, he had an erection. It lay along his leg, under her thigh. She shifted her weight, rolling his shaft beneath her.

His tongue thrust into her mouth, pulled back, then thrust again. His fingers tightened on her nipple. Tiny pangs radiated from her breast's nub. Sarah pushed a hand down her belly, dislodging her towel. She need skin on skin, more than she had. Her hand beneath her parted John's robe. She hitched towards his knees, allowing his shaft to slap up against his flat belly. A hitch back again trapped it between him and her naked hip.

John kept kissing her, at the same time twisting and pinching her nipple. The pangs became white-hot streaks of pleasure/pain that bordered on the unbearable. Her fingers worked between her own thighs, found her button and pinch-pulled its sheath back.

She was panting, panting into his mouth. Somehow, she managed a mangled, 'Other nipple, please?'

John released her tongue, and her hair. One big hand clamped over her mouth and pushed her back, and back, until she was bent straining over the broad arm of the chair, her hair dangling almost to the floor. She could breathe. Her nose was uncovered. Even so, it felt like she could only suck in as much air as he allowed.

His free hand gave her left nipple one last vicious twist before darting to her right breast, to crush it between his fingers, squeezing so hard that her nipple extruded between his knuckles, which clamped on it. Sarah wanted to beg, though she didn't know what for. The way he was abusing her was exactly what she craved but somehow it seemed right that she should plead with him, either for mercy or for more intense torment. It was the act of pleading that she needed. Perhaps, later, he'd make her crawl to him on her hands and knees, make her grovel.

She had a vision of his foot on the back of her neck that made her moan. She adored him and desperately needed to tell him so. He was the primal male, elemental, controlling. She was the essential female, totally under his control and loving it.

What could she do to show the depth of her surrender when he'd already overpowered her? Sarah threw her thighs wide apart and lifted her hips, presenting her sex, her womanhood, her sacred profanity, offering it to him to use or abuse, or just to amuse himself with. The way he was mauling her breast was agonising; the pain intoxicating. Sarah forgot to breathe. Doubled backwards and splayed across his lap, she was open to his every whim. Her arms were free but they couldn't defend her. She could have been beyond his reach and she'd still have been defenceless. His will bound her more surely than the power of his arms and hands.

Then he was lifting her up and carrying her to the bed. She was tossed onto it, on her back. Instinctively, she raised her arms above her head and spread her legs wide.

He knelt between her thighs and leant over her on one elbow. She looked up into his eyes, pleading for it. He sheathed his cock with latex and directed it with his hand until its bulbous head nudged the slick lips of her sex.

Right. He'd promised he'd fuck her missionary style, and John was a man of his word. That hot hard plum slithered upwards between her pussy lips until it found the tiny engorged nub of her clit. He rubbed it there, round and round, up and down, as if trying to insert her tiny pink pearl into the eye of his cock.

'Fuck me,' she begged. 'I need it, John.'

He grinned down at her, the teasing bastard. No, she shouldn't think that. If he wanted to tease her, that was his right.

He moved his cock lower. It parted her outer lips, then her inner ones, and paused in the quivering softness of her vestibule. John smiled and asked, 'Now?'

She wanted to lift herself up to him, to take his cock, but he was in charge. Sarah nodded, biting her lip.

He eased an inch deeper, then thrust. His magnificence dilated her, filling her, forcing her inner convolutions to straighten and conform to its shape. John paused once more, buried deep inside her. He hitched forwards as if trying to bend his shaft but only succeeded in pressing it hard against her clit. There, watching her eyes with amusement, he rocked slowly, then fast, then slowly. His hips swivelled, aiming his column into her at a different angle, then rocked again. He changed angles a dozen times, always slowing his thrusts as she felt herself rising towards a climax.

Gazing up into his eyes, Sarah told him, 'I really need an orgasm, please, John.'

'Do you now?'

'I said "Please".'

'I know you did, but "please" isn't enough, is it?' He dipped his head and sucked her nipple into his mouth without breaking the rhythm of his thrusts.

'What do you want me to say?'

He released her nipple. 'What do you *need* to say?'

'Need?'

'I know your needs, sweet little Sarah. You need the right sort of pain. You need to submit. Then there's the other thing. Confess, Sarah. Tell me what the other thing is.'

'To be fucked?'

'Apart from that.'

'I ...' Not long before she'd fantasised about his foot pressing on her neck. That was submission, but more. A submissive obeys her master and that's one level of descent. She'd never so much as considered it before today, before John, but now that she realised that there was something lower than submission, she also understood that she craved those depths.

'I think I need to be humiliated and degraded, John.'

'Good girl. Or should I say, bad girl? Now humiliate yourself, Sarah. Beg me to let you come. Acknowledge the reality. You can't climax until I give you my permission, can you?'

And she couldn't have. Now that he'd explained it, it was obvious. With other men, she'd probably be able to get there normally, but John had somehow taken control of her lust and it wouldn't be assuaged until he said it might.

Although lust confused her mind, Sarah ordered her thoughts, composing her words carefully. 'John, my master, my climaxes are yours to give me or deny me. Your humble slave is begging you, pleading, please, *please*, have mercy on your little bitch, your sex slave. Grant my wish as only you can do; let me fucking well come!'

'As you ask so nicely. On ten, then. One, two ...'

The arrogant bastard! He thought he had that much control over her, did he? He actually thought that he could launch her orgasm like some fucking rocket? Still, she found his arrogance exciting. He ground into her, crushing her clit with each deep and deliberate stroke. She was so fucking close to coming. So goddam fucking close . . .

'Eight, nine, *ten!*'

The climax hit hard. Her eyes opened wide as her hot tunnel gripped and released his cock, squeezing a surprised 'yip' from her lips. It kept coming, rolling through her from the paroxysms in her pussy up the back of her spine, blowing her mind and making her yelp over and over again. 'Yip, yip, yip, yip.'

He thrust hard and stayed buried inside her, his moan building to a great leonine roar.

15

It was ten in the morning when Sarah woke. John was still asleep, with his arm a welcome but heavy weight across her body. She eased out from under it and out of bed. In the bathroom, she checked her bum. It was fully healed, or almost. There was just a faint trace of deeper pink on the underside of its left cheek.

She showered on 'gentle' to minimise the noise. Once she was dry, she padded softly back into the bedroom. He slept on. Kilt or no kilt? No kilt. Wearing it would be a return to her 'schoolgirl' persona.

His flannels had been discarded, tossed across the back of a straight chair. Moving carefully so as not to jingle any change in its pockets, Sarah eased his belt from its loops. His right hand was still flung out. She sat on the bed, lifted his wrist gently onto her lap, and pressed the buckle end of his belt into his palm. John snuffled and shifted. Sarah froze until he settled down once more. With infinite care, she wrapped the leather strap round his hand until just eighteen inches dangled free.

How to wake him? How else? She lifted the bedclothes and exposed his naked body. His left leg was forwards of his right. The soft length of his shaft lay along his thigh. Sarah moved lower down the bed, curled up and rested her cheek on his leg. A tender finger lifted his cock. Her head moved forwards, mouth wide open. With the head of John's cock in her mouth, Sarah settled down to wait, but not for long. Her lips felt a pulse. The head of his cock lifted off her tongue a fraction. She closed her lips around its shaft in case it tried to escape.

John yawned and said, 'Good morning, slut Sarah.'

Sarah gurgled a, 'Good morning,' around his shaft.

'By what you've done with my belt, I guess you're after something harder than a spanking.'

She nodded.

'Show me your bottom.'

Sarah swivelled round without losing his cock.

His palm smoothed over her cheeks. 'You heal well.'

''hank 'ou.'

'Do you have a date for tomorrow?'

She shook her head, moving his cock head from inside one cheek to inside the other.

'So if you were marked for a day or two, it wouldn't be awkward for you?'

Sarah shook her head again.

'You do understand that a beating with a belt is far more severe than a spanking by hand, don't you?'

She nodded.

'But you're ready for that?'

Sarah took his cock from her mouth but held onto it. 'I'm ready, John. I'd be able to stop you if it was more than I could stand, wouldn't I?' She took his cock back between her lips and gave it a long suck.

'Of course you would.'

Once more, she released him to the open air. 'I'm going to get strapped someday, John. I'd rather it was by you than by some amateur.'

'Good point. Very well, you shall have your beating, but after breakfast. What would you like? Better keep it light.'

'A fruit salad, please, John, and maybe some toast?'

'Good choices.' He ordered a small steak with a fried egg on top for himself, with a side of hash browns, a pot of Blue Mountain coffee and a carafe of Buck's Fizz.

'What's Buck's Fizz?' Sarah asked.

'Champagne and orange juice, sometimes served with a float of grenadine.'

Sarah grinned. 'That sounds lovely and decadent, for a breakfast drink.'

His face took on a concerned look. 'You're obsessing about "decadence", Sarah.'

'Is that bad?'

'Not with the right people, but not everyone follows the "Safe, Sane, Consensual" rule. You will be careful who you submit to in future, won't you?'

Sarah's heart lifted. He cared, really cared, what became of her after their date.

They wore their robes for the benefit of room service. Sarah shed hers the moment the boy left their suite. Being stark naked while John was still at least partly dressed somehow seemed appropriate for a good little sex slave.

John ate a little awkwardly, with his belt still wrapped around his fist. As Sarah picked at her salad, every sway of the free-hanging end drew her eyes, like a rabbit following the movements of a cobra. But this rabbit couldn't wait to feel the cobra's bite. Or could she? It was going to hurt, really hurt. She could beg off. John would allow that, she knew. But if she did, she'd be showing cowardice, and she needed his respect. Undecided, Sarah did what she always did when in a serious quandary, she made her mind go blank and let whatever was going to happen, happen.

Her mind still in a fog, she was led to the bed and spreadeagled once more. John secured her wrists to the brass scrolls. Seemingly without effort, he lifted her bottom off the bed, lifted it high, right over her head, and manacled her ankles, wide apart, to the top of the bedhead. A pile of pillows under her shoulders made the awkward position more comfortable. Nice man. Sarah gazed up at her delta from only a foot beneath it. Pretty pussy.

John made a few adjustments to her bonds and her legs, so that her thighs were perfectly horizontal, parallel to the bed. 'Ready?' he asked.

'Hmm?'

'Are you ready?'

She couldn't really nod, not folded like that, so Sarah was forced to vocalise her affirmative, though not in articulate words, even though she wasn't sure what he was asking her. When you don't quite understand what's going on, 'yes' is best, or at least, easiest.

John stroked the undersides of her thighs. Nice. That wasn't why she was contorted like that, though, was it? He rested the loose end of his belt across her legs, halfway between her knees and her upturned bottom, then moved it a little higher.

'This is above where the hem of your skirts usually come to, isn't it?'

Why was that significant? Whatever, she made another 'yes' sound.

The leather strap lifted. That meant something, something frightening but thrilling, she didn't think about what. The belt came down, hard. Sarah yelped involuntarily. A line of fire burnt across the backs of her thighs.

'You still want it? You can still change your mind.'

'Um, want, yes.'

Leather cracked down again, an inch higher. Sarah emerged from her fog. Oh fuck! It was really happening. What had she let herself in for? Was she crazy?

The third and fourth and fifth blows landed, each closer to her bottom. Pain seared into her. Tears were streaming from her eyes and she'd almost decided that she was ready to face the humiliation of begging him to stop when the sixth whacked down on the lower curves of her bum cheeks, and she was suddenly in absolute bliss.

The belt progressed from low on her bottom to halfway up it, where her cheeks were fullest, then made their way down towards her thighs again. Her flesh was glowing embers. Each blow reignited the skin it landed on. The pain was hellish and heavenly. It was as if she'd taken some powerful euphoriant that had set her spirit free to soar through and to pure delight. Her thighs and her bottom had been transformed by ecstatic agony. Deep inside, she was starting to clench.

Something dripped onto her chin. Of course! Her sex was weeping with joy. The internal convulsions accelerated and became stronger. She was so fucking close! Sarah knew she could take the belt forever, yet when it fell to the bed she moaned with relief.

Something – his fingers? – forced entrance to her sex and drove deeply into her pussy. The invader pistoned. Other fingers manipulated her clit.

Sarah heard herself shouting, 'Love it! Love it!' The fingers forced their way even further into her, into where she was clamping rhythmically, and triggered – 'Yip, yip, yip, yip!' – erotic bliss.

Things were white and fuzzy for a bit. When Sarah opened her weary eyes, John had released her and covered her with bedclothes.

'How was it?' he asked.

'Paradise. Devastating paradise.'

'I'm glad. Now you should rest.'

'But you?'

'We can take care of me later.'

'No, I want to . . . Only fair . . .' And she fell asleep.

When she opened her eyes again he was at the little table, reading a book. There was a platter of tiny triangular sandwiches, some of them eaten. She could smell fresh coffee.

'Coffee?' she asked.

He poured a cup, added cream and brought it to her. Rolling onto one side to drink hurt, but in a nice way.

'You were very brave,' he said.

'Thank you.' He likely wouldn't understand if she tried to explain that courage had nothing to do with it. When she'd submitted and endured, she hadn't been herself. She'd been some sort of automaton. 'I'm feeling fine now,' she said. 'I don't think I could lie on my back, not with you on top of me, but I'd really like to do something nice for you, if you'd let me?'

'Have a sandwich. Then let's talk. Tell me all about yourself, nothing that you wouldn't want to, but I'd really like to get to know Sarah, outside of her obvious skills and gorgeous attributes.'

Sarah lay on her tummy, John beside her, and they chatted the afternoon away. She discovered that he was quite knowledgeable about philosophy, for a layman. When it came to her second area of expertise, he claimed to know very little about drama, but revealed snippets that made her doubt that. He had attended a lecture on acting that Michael Caine had given, and had been so impressed he was able to recite parts of it verbatim. He knew of the works of various dramatists, from Marlowe and Kyd through Sheridan and Feydeau, to Joe Orton and Edward Albee. She concluded that he was a real Renaissance man, complete with a knowledge of Italian, French and German. She practised her Italian on him, including her favourite phrase, 'Fottere mia bocca, per favore'.

That made him laugh out loud. 'I don't think you're up for that, not yet,' he told her, 'but perhaps a little slow and gentle fellatio, if you don't mind?'

Sarah reversed on the bed, gingerly, and took him into her mouth with some sadness. Their date was almost over. Chances were, she'd never see this marvellous man again.

He let her mumble and lick and suck for a while before he began to fondle her pussy, very gently. She sucked a little harder and nodded an inch or two. Neither of them was in a hurry, thank goodness. She was too stiff and sore for any frantic activity. Eventually, she climaxed, just a soft little clench and release. A little later he emptied into her mouth. They dozed for a while until he touched her shoulder.

'Time for you to go, I'm afraid, sweet Sarah.'

'You have me till ten and that's another hour yet.'

'I have a plane to catch. It's time for me to start getting packed and ready.'

'Take a later plane?'

'I must return to my real life. I'm sorry.' The kiss he gave her, though sweet, stifled her protests, definitely signalling farewell.

When Sarah got down to her Volvo she sat in it for a while before starting its engine. She hardly cried at all.

16

'What are you and David planning for New Year's Eve, Sarah?' Mr Meadows took another bite of turkey leg and chewed, open-mouthed. 'Delishush', he told his wife.

Sarah dropped her eyes to avoid grimacing at his poor table manners. She'd never realised, until this trip home, how lacking in etiquette he was. No wonder her sister habitually ate with one hand up to her face, like a blinkered horse.

'We'll probably go to a dinner party at the university. Unless something better comes up.' She toyed with a Brussels sprout. The very mention of David made her stomach queasy. She hadn't managed to break up with him before leaving Toledo for the Christmas holidays. 'What about you, Donna?'

Donna shrugged. 'I'll probably go clubbing.'

Mrs Meadows clucked her tongue impatiently. 'And spend the first day of the new year in bed with a hangover,' she said sharply.

'Yeah,' Donna replied cheerfully. 'Probably.'

Sarah sipped her wine. She'd been playing peacemaker between her menopausal mother and her self-proclaimed Asperger's sister ever since her arrival in St Paul. It was getting tiresome. She glanced at her father. He grinned good-naturedly and gestured to the box of wine on the table. Sarah shook her head. Much as she agreed with his unspoken suggestion that alcohol always helped, she was too much of a snob to drink any more boxed wine than was necessary to be polite.

'What schools have you applied to for graduate work, lovey?' Mrs Meadows was speaking to Sarah, but her eyes were on Donna.

'I haven't decided what I want to do next year. I have a new part-time job, with a catering company that I like a lot. It pays really well. So I might take some time off school and concentrate on making money.'

She saw the glances exchanged between her parents. Was that relief? Why had it never occurred to her, until now, that the cost of her education, even with her student loan, was a weight on them?

'Anyway, Professor Braun's final exam was way out there. There was only one question on it. "Write everything you know about the meaning of life." A friend of mine, Christopher, wrote, "I know nothing about the meaning of life," and walked out.'

'Brilliant!' Mr Meadows laughed heartily.

'We'll see. I think he'd like to fail us all, in which case we won't have the credits to take his second semester class on ethics. It's a problem for all the Phil. Honours students.'

'Braun. He's the professor you think is losing his mind?' Mr Meadows tapped his forehead with his fork, leaving a little mashed potato at his brow.

'Yes,' said Sarah. 'So all I can tell you, Mom, is that right now I'm considering staying in Toledo.'

'Wonderful!' Mrs Meadows clapped her hands. 'David must be thrilled. I'm so glad you're taking my advice. Stand by your man, Sarah, that's what I say.'

Donna choked on a mouthful of wine. 'What happened to, "Never get married, never have children"? God, Mom, you've really changed your tune.'

'Well, Germaine Greer says –'

'Germaine Greer is a traitor to feminism,' said Donna. She waved her glass impatiently under her father's nose. He took it and busied himself filling it from the box.

Mrs Meadows glared at her youngest daughter. 'It astounds me that a high-school dropout imagines herself so well-informed on every single issue that –'

'I don't need a piece of paper to be informed. Or to have an opinion.'

'Pass the peas!' Mr Meadows bellowed. He handed Donna her glass, full almost to the brim, and gave her a glowering frown.

Christ. In an instant Donna and Mrs Meadows could and would veer from chit-chat to attack. Sarah was weary of it. She could only imagine how much it exhausted her dad. She handed him the peas.

'What are you two doing for New Year's Eve?' Sarah glanced from her dad to her mom.

'Nothing much,' muttered Mr Meadows.

'If you were staying over New Year's we'd likely have a dinner party,' said Mrs Meadows. 'Invite all your old school chums.'

Donna snorted. 'Sarah only has one, and Alice didn't come home for Christmas.'

'Don't be cruel,' said Mrs Meadows.

'She can't help being a loner. That's the way Asperger's people are,' said Donna.

'Here we go,' sighed Mrs Meadows. 'Doctor Meadows and her internet diagnoses.'

'She fits the profile. Brilliant, strange, lousy communicator. She's even a picky eater.'

Sarah quit toying with her food.

'Oh, you're just jealous of your sister, always have been,' grumbled Mrs Meadows.

'I am not! Jesus fucking Christ, Mom –'

'Quiet, you.' Mr Meadows pointed his fork at Donna. Turning his head, he asked, 'What do you think, Sarah?'

'About being high-functioning autistic? I . . . I think I'd like more wine, please, Dad.'

Sarah retired to the room she shared with her sister as soon as she could. She lay in her twin bed, in the flannel pyjamas she'd received from Santa that morning, and yearned for sleep. She'd been in St Paul for four days and four nights. After this one, there'd be only one more day and night before she flew back to Toledo. If only she could will herself to fall asleep, right now. But of course the harder she tried, the wider awake she became. Her fingers drifted to the waistband of her pyjama bottoms. Masturbation was one way to find relaxation, but she didn't think she could do it, not with her family, her dysfunctional family, lurking about the house.

Donna flounced into the room. She switched on the bedside lamp. 'I fucking hate her.'

'I don't know,' said Sarah wearily. She didn't know how much more peacekeeping she'd be able to do without a break. 'She's just Mom.'

'Easy for you to say. You're the good one.' Donna stripped off and started pulling on her new pyjamas. 'What the fuck are these things supposed to be?' She gestured to the pattern on the pyjama bottoms.

Sarah peered at Donna. 'Come closer,' she ordered. Donna complied, bending over so her bum was inches from her sister's face. 'I think they're kitties,' Sarah said. She threw back her covers. 'What're mine?'

Donna perched on Sarah's bed and scrutinised Sarah's flannel-clad body. 'Some weird sort of bunnies?'

They giggled.

'Space bunnies?' Sarah asked, giving her sister an exaggerated look of confusion.

'Kitties from hell?' Donna bit her lip quizzically.

They erupted in a full-blown fit of laughter.

'Shut up. They'll hear us,' said Sarah. She slapped her hand over her sister's mouth.

'Mmph,' mumbled Donna. She clapped her hand over Sarah's mouth.

They'd almost stopped laughing when they heard their parents' footsteps in the hallway. Sarah and Donna gave each other identical horrified looks and the hysteria bubbled up again.

Once they heard the door to their parents' room close they finally collapsed, weak from silliness. Donna crawled under Sarah's covers.

'I miss you sometimes,' whispered Donna, 'even though you're a pain in the ass.'

'Thanks,' whispered Sarah. 'Ditto, I'm sure.'

'It totally sucks here.'

'I know,' Sarah whispered back.

Donna sat up. 'Wanna go clubbing?'

'Now? Here? Christmas Day in St Paul? You're kidding.'

'I know a "speak" that's always open. Want to? You might just like a taste of the underworld.'

'I'm not as much of a goody-goody as everyone thinks,' said Sarah.

'Prove it,' challenged Donna. She jumped out of bed. 'We'll go like this.'

'In our pyjamas?'

'Yeah. It'll be fun. C'mon, Sarah.'

Sarah paused for a moment, remembering all the nights she'd lain in her bed, half envious, half pitying, and listened to her little sister quietly escaping this buttoned-down suburban house. What was out there, she'd wondered, that was so enticing it beckoned Donna away from warmth and safety, propelling her into darkness and danger? She jumped out of bed. 'I'm in.'

The streets of St Paul were silent; even downtown seemed deserted. Once they were on the other side of the core, Donna drove slowly, peering intently through the windshield. 'It's here somewhere,' she muttered. 'I haven't been in a while.'

Sarah sat in the passenger seat, holding a shoe bag with their fuzzy slippers in it.

They'd donned their coats and boots over pyjamas and bare feet and had silently left the house. Once they were strapped in, Donna had released the parking break and put the car in neutral. The driveway was on an incline, so the car simply rolled backwards onto the street. Only then did she turn the key in the ignition and flick on the lights.

'So that's how you always got away with stealing the car. I never could figure it out.'

'I'm an evil genius,' Donna had replied.

'There it is!' Donna's expression was triumphant.

Sarah peered through the windshield. She saw nothing but dark, seemingly abandoned warehouses. 'Are you sure?'

Donna parked the car. 'Trust me. Things are not always what they seem.'

Sure enough, Donna's knock at an alleyway door was answered by a big man in black leather. 'Sweetie!' he cried in a surprisingly shrill voice. 'Long time no see!'

He and Donna air-kissed.

'Come in, come in. How's my favourite fag hag?'

'Peachy,' said Donna.

The sisters climbed a seemingly endless flight of steel stairs.

'Fag hag?' Sarah whispered to her sister's back. 'Is this a gay bar?'

'Yeah. You got a problem with that?'

'Well, no, not exactly. I was hoping for a little action is all.'

Donna paused on the stairs to glance back at Sarah. 'Really? My, how you've changed.'

Sarah shrugged.

'I gotta meet this David guy some day. I want to meet the man who deflowered my big sister.' Donna resumed climbing.

Sarah chuckled. Let Donna think what she liked. Sarah thought about all the men she'd been with. Except for three – David, Christopher and Luigi – they'd all paid for the pleasure of her company. She allowed her thoughts to linger on her last assignation, the weekend she'd spent with John, then resolutely pushed him from her thoughts. Just another john, albeit one who had touched her in a way no one had since Jack, the man who had really taken her virginity. In between the two she'd had, she realised, a lot of men.

As they approached the top floor they could hear the boom boom boom of synthesised dance music. Two big guys swung open the double steel doors and the girls were assaulted with such a noise that Sarah felt she might be pushed back down the stairs by it.

They entered a dark cavernous space, alive with the writhing bodies of men in heat and lit with swirling coloured spotlights. Donna grinned at her sister as she shucked off her coat and boots. She grabbed her slippers from Sarah and slid them on her feet. 'Come on!' She dragged Sarah through a packed crowd of mostly male bodies, towards the bar.

Sarah had never seen anything like it. The place was vibrating with the combined energy of music and dancing men. Everywhere she looked she saw men pressed against other men, dancing or making out or both at once. The bar was crowded but Donna managed to worm her way to the front and returned with two plastic cups of beer. Sarah took one and tipped it to her sister. 'Merry Christmas,' she mouthed, and took a long draught.

They danced. Sometimes together, sometimes with guys, sometimes alone. They danced for hours, until the flannel stuck to their skin and their hair was slick with sweat. They danced with guys in jeans and shirts and guys in nothing more than thongs and running shoes. They danced until the music stopped and the floor show began.

Two men, one at each end of the stage, danced solo in a spotlight. One was young, fit but skinny, with a flop of black hair. The other, big and bald, was incredibly muscular. His body gleamed with oil. Both wore thongs and nothing else.

There were a few catcalls from the audience, which had gathered on the dance floor to watch. But when the bald man raised his head, as if from a trance, and stared menacingly into the crowd, the heckling ended. He spotted the other man, apparently oblivious to everything but the music, writhing sensuously. The bald man approached, his spotlight following him, until he was behind the young man. He paused, then pounced.

The young man feigned shock. He struggled to break the iron grip the bald man had on him, and was rewarded with a slap across the face. He fell to his knees and his well-oiled aggressor raised his fists in triumph, like some hairless King Kong.

'I don't know about this,' Sarah muttered to her sister.

'Silly. It's all for show.'

'Yes but –'

On the stage, the young man's head was pushed down and his hips tugged up. He was being arranged by his aggressor, handled like he was nothing more than a bendable sex toy. He glanced up at the audience. His eyes were wild, full of fear. The bald man put his foot to the younger man's shaggy head and pushed it back down.

'He's afraid, Donna!'

'Shh. Don't be silly. They're lovers.'

'In real life?'

'Yes. This is what they do. Don't you study drama?'

'Yeah.' Sarah wanted to look away, but she couldn't, she was riveted by the passion play taking place on the stage.

'So. It's a play. A sex play. OK?'

Sarah nodded. She realised she'd been holding her breath. She exhaled, just as the bald man bent to tear the string of his victim's thong apart with his teeth. The young man raised his head. Sarah caught a glimpse of his cock. She was gratified to see that it was hard. God, he liked being on display like this. Again the bigger man put his foot to the back of his prey's head and pushed it down.

Sarah could only imagine what it must feel like to be the focus of such a powerful man's abuse. A foot to the head like that must make the submissive feel like the lowest of the low. She was tingling all over. She glanced at her sister. Donna's cheeks were bright with colour. Her own face felt hot, too. Her blood was rushing, her pulse pounding. She wanted it, just like that, her nose to the floor and John's foot on the back of her head. Depraved. She was hopelessly depraved. Fuck.

Now the muscular, oiled man spit into his hand and rubbed it carelessly up the crack of the other man's bum. He pointed to his bulging thong and grinned at the crowd.

'Take if off!' The cry was quickly taken up by the mesmerised crowd. 'Take it off!'

'He won't,' muttered Donna, not taking her eyes from the stage.

But he did. His cock was massive, by far the biggest Sarah had ever seen. Her mouth fell open in amazement. Was it even real?

The muscleman thrust out his hips, showing off his meat. It

rose from his hairless pelvis like a great one-eyed monster, a heat-seeking beast of prey. He strode back and forth across the front of the stage, his wagging cock leading the way.

Any doubts Sarah had about the authenticity of it were dispelled. She'd like to try that thing. She couldn't take it in her mouth and wouldn't take it up her ass but what would it feel like, a cock that size, shoved deep inside her pussy? She moaned.

'Gives me a new appreciation of size queens,' muttered Donna.

Sarah nodded.

The young man, noticing that his aggressor was busy showing off his manhood, tried to crawl out of the spotlight.

'He's getting away!' someone in the crowd piped up.

The bald man spun to see his prey crawling on all fours towards the back of the stage. With a roar, the big man crossed the stage and grabbed his victim by the hips. He hauled the pliable young man up, so that his toes and fingertips were all that touched the ground.

'He won't,' Donna muttered again.

Holding his partner by one hand, the big man used his free hand to guide the tip of his fat shaft between the other man's ass cheeks. With a roar, he thrust himself fully into his victim's bum.

'Oh. My. God.' Donna's eyes were as wide as saucers. 'He really did it.'

The crowd roared, the aggressor howled, the young man shrieked, and the sudden sound of sirens pierced the din.

'Ho, ho, ho,' yelled the big man. He waved to the crowd with one hand, using the other to move the young man back and forth on his cock, as if he were masturbating and the man impaled on his pole were nothing more than an extension of his own hand. 'Merry Christmas!'

The stage went black.

17

Donna drove like a lunatic. They had managed to grab their coats and boots and make good their escape, but neither had taken the time to put them on. Both girls' teeth were chattering by the time they'd leapt into the car and taken off, the car wheezing its displeasure at being driven cold.

'Did you fucking see that?' Donna was incapable of more than the one sentence, repeated at frequent intervals. She didn't take her eyes from the tiny spot in the middle of the icy windshield that was her only view of the road.

'I fucking saw it, but I still don't fucking believe it,' said Sarah. She glanced over her shoulder to see if they were being followed. The rear windshield, like the front, was iced over. 'Were those real sirens?'

'I don't know. I thought so but I didn't see any cops. Fuck. I hope the club doesn't get closed.'

'A live sex show in St Paul,' marvelled Sarah. 'What next?'

Donna pulled the car over on a deserted downtown street. 'I have to warm this thing up,' she said. She exchanged her slippers for her boots and reached into the back seat for her coat and a windshield scraper. 'Be right back.'

Sarah sat in the car and watched as her sister scraped the windshield clear of ice. The heat was up full but set to defrost. Her feet, in their sodden slippers, tingled with cold. She removed her slippers and donned her boots and coat, shivering on the outside, boiling on the inside. She wanted sex. Hot, sordid sex. Her thoughts flew to John, then reluctantly past him to David, and then to Christopher. Christopher would do her like that, she imagined, but only if she told him to.

'That's better,' said Donna as she climbed back into the car. 'At least I can see the road now.'

'Do you really think the club will get shut down?' Sarah watched the road with Donna. Dawn was breaking. One more day, one more night, and she'd be back where she belonged.

'I hope not. Because if it's not, that's where I'll be every Christmas night till I die.'

'Thanks for taking me there. I never would've thought . . .'

'That gay clubs could be such a turn-on?'

'Yeah,' confessed Sarah.

'You should have a look at their porn. It's fabulous.'

'I guess I just imagined that guys who are into guys wouldn't do much for me. You know, that there'd be no place for me in the picture.'

'That's Asperger's for you. Concrete, literal thinking.'

'I don't know.' Sarah didn't want to talk about autism. She wanted to talk about what they'd just seen. She wanted to keep the camaraderie she'd shared with her sister. They hadn't been joined together in secrecy since . . . since she could remember.

'I wish you'd think about it,' said Donna. 'It answers a lot of questions I've had, about how I am, how you are, even how Mom and Dad are. Asperger's syndrome.'

'OK, I will,' said Sarah. 'But I don't really see what difference it makes now.' She shrugged. 'I am who and what I am, and so are you, and so are Mom and Dad.'

'It just explains –'

'But I don't need an explanation,' said Sarah. Exasperation was creeping into her voice. Damn. She affected a tone of insouciance. 'I don't really care.'

'Do you love David?'

'I dunno.'

'See, here you are practically engaged to someone and you don't even know if you love him. Doesn't that tell you something?'

'I suppose it tells me he's probably not the one for me.'

'What about your other relationships? Other men? Friends? Even family? Do you love anyone? Because it's hard for A.S.

people to really experience love. Either they behave inappropriately or they're just ... detached.'

'Hmm.' This interested Sarah. The beginnings of an idea slithered around the fog in her brain. 'I'll consider it, Donna. I promise.'

'Thanks.' Donna pulled into their driveway. 'Thanks for coming with me, Sarah. I liked hanging out with you. I wish we'd done more of it when we lived together.'

'Me too,' said Sarah. She met her sister's eyes. They were, she realised, the exact same shade of blue as her own. As if on cue, both sisters' eyes welled up.

'What the fuck,' said Donna.

'Yeah, what the fuck,' said Sarah.

'Too late now,' said Donna.

'Is it?' Sarah grinned. 'Don't be so sure.'

The next day, when Sarah's flight left St Paul, it left with both Meadows sisters on board. Sarah had made a few calls on Boxing Day, one to her landlady to arrange the rental of the room across the hall from her, which had been empty since her hip-hop neighbour had been evicted. The other had been to the airline; she'd been able to wangle another seat on the plane by booking first class. She'd upgraded her own seat as well.

Only when she'd accomplished all that did she sit down with her family and announce her plan. She was taking Donna with her to Toledo. The plan had met with more resistance than she'd anticipated, from her parents of course. Her sister had been so excited she'd actually screamed, as if she'd picked the right briefcase on a game show.

'What about your studies? Donna's a handful, honey,' said Mrs Meadows.

'It'll be fine,' replied Sarah.

'Yeah, Mom,' said Donna, rolling her eyes. 'What do you think I'm gonna do? Seduce her into a life of crime?'

'We can't afford to pay for her room and board,' said Mr Meadows. 'I'm sorry.'

'Yeah, but I'm making money, like I told you. This catering gig is a good one,' said Sarah.

'Maybe I could work for them too,' piped Donna.

'No.' Sarah had anticipated this. 'You're not old enough to serve alcohol and, anyway, they have no openings. But until you get a job I can manage both our living costs. Really. And just think, Mom and Dad, the two of you will be kid free, for the first time in decades. Won't that be good?'

Mr and Mrs Meadows exchanged pleased glances. 'Yes,' they'd replied in unison.

The flight was a short one but Donna was taking full advantage of the free booze. Was that her second drink or her third? The kid was damn lucky she never got carded, although she probably had fake ID. Donna, Sarah was beginning to understand, knew all the angles.

Sarah closed her eyes and willed herself to relax. Here she was, finally heading back to Toledo, and she'd arranged to have her badass little sister in tow. Christ. She was now covering the costs of not one but two other people.

She really needed to get back to work.

18

'Classique, how can I help you?'

'Veronica?'

'Yes? Sarah! Welcome back!' Veronica's voice on the phone was delightfully warm.

'Thanks. I wanted to let you know I've decided to stay on with the agency after I graduate. I'd like to work full-time.' Somehow, saying it out loud made it breathtakingly real.

'Are you sure?'

'Yes. Will you have me?'

'Of course! You're becoming one of our most popular escorts. In fact –'

Sarah rushed to say all of it, before she lost her nerve. 'I like the fetish stuff, Veronica. Of course I'll date whoever you like but the normal guys ... it's just not as much fun with them as with the kinky ones.'

'You're sure?'

'Yes. I mean, so far. That is, I don't know if I'd be much good as a ... a dominant, but I like to play submissive. Anal is good, too. Anything offbeat but not ... not too bizarre. Anyway, when those sorts of things come up I hope you'll think of me.'

'Noted. I'm glad you called, Sarah. One of my girls cancelled on me this morning and I'm having a devil of a time filling her spot. Interested?'

'Absolutely. Christmas turned out to be way more expensive than I'd anticipated.'

'Isn't that always the case? There's a New Year's Eve party tonight that's looking for a lot of girls. It's a costume ball. You'd be eye candy, more than anything, but it pays double the usual rate, and it could get a little cosy, later. Interested?'

'Yes.' Sarah resolutely pushed the thought of her New Year's Eve dinner date with David out of her mind.

'Wonderful. There goes my other line. I let Debra have the holidays off so I'm answering my own phones. Listen, I'll have something suitable sent over to you. A car will pick you up just before nine. Got it?'

'Yup. Thanks, Veronica.'

'Bye.'

Sarah snapped her phone shut. She'd have to rush to get everything arranged by tonight, but then she'd been rushing since she'd returned from St Paul. First she'd checked her marks, which had finally been posted online, and had been relieved to find she'd passed the existentialism course with flying colours. Then she'd helped Donna settle into the room across the hall. The next day had been devoted to David.

Sarah had hoped meeting Donna would be enough of a diversion to keep David from groping her but, although the three of them enjoyed a nice dinner out, her sister had excused herself early so the 'lovebirds' could spend some time alone. Another bout of barely adequate sex had ensued, resulting in a tepid orgasm for her and a gusher for David.

Damn. Her goal, a break-up with David, was going nowhere, and she had only herself to blame. She was just too much of a professional to deliver anything less than her best in bed. Speaking of which, she'd yet to connect with Christopher, who she considered her antidote to David, and as a result she'd caught herself mooning over her weekend with John more than once. It had to stop.

Sarah crossed the hall and knocked at Donna's door. A sleepy voice beckoned her into the messy room. Her sister, she'd quickly discovered, displayed many of the characteristics of the house cat. When not amused (which was easily accomplished) and not hungry (for takeout) she slept.

'Donna, wake up.'

'Mmph. What time is it?'

'Time for little sis to do big sis a favour.'

'OK.' Donna sat up, rubbing her eyes. 'I must've fallen asleep.'

'Something's come up. I have a gig with the catering company tonight. I need you to fill in for me, with David.'

'Dinner at the Faculty Club? I don't know ... I thought I'd go bar hopping ...' Donna scrunched up her nose, looking even younger than her nineteen years. 'I don't have anything to wear.'

'I'll lend you something.' Sarah tried to keep the impatience from her voice. 'If you like it you can keep it. Everyone needs a little black dress.'

Donna's face brightened. 'OK. But won't David be disappointed?'

'It can't be helped. Besides, he seemed to enjoy your company.'

'Oh, I'm just Sarah's little sister to that big old historian.'

'That'll have to do. Just don't drink your face off, OK? Be on your best behaviour. It's important.'

'I'll be *très* genteel, Sarah. I promise.'

'And watch your fuckin' mouth.'

'I will, I'll be good as fuckin' gold. C'mon, let's go plunder your fuckin' closet. Got any fuckin' heels?'

The afternoon was almost gone by the time Donna made her selection. She twirled in front of the full-length mirror in Sarah's room. 'God, I love silk,' she proclaimed. 'It breathes so beautifully, don't you think?'

'Yeah,' grumbled Sarah. Her sister had an eye for quality, she'd give her that. Donna had picked through everything Sarah had offered, rejecting all of it, before discovering Sarah's best little black dress. Naturally, it fitted her perfectly. Sarah was sorry to see it go.

'Such a pretty neckline,' cooed Donna. 'Got any jewellery?'

'No,' Sarah replied shortly. 'You don't need it with that dress,' she quickly added.

Donna grinned mischievously at Sarah. 'I don't know. Maybe pearls? After all, I have to fit in with the faculty wives, right?'

'David's not faculty, not yet. And you are not his wife. But I get your point.' Reluctantly, Sarah reached for her jewellery box.

There was a knock at the door. It swung open to reveal Nancy, loaded down with plastic-protected clothing. She barked, 'Where do you want these?'

'How did you get in without buzzing me?' Sarah's voice was shrill with dismay. She hurried to grab the garments but Donna was closer. Donna hung them on a hook on the door and stripped them of their plastic.

'What kind of uniform is this?' She held up a blue-checked pinafore.

'We're working a costume ball,' said Sarah. 'Thanks,' she said to Nancy, trying to edge her back out the door. 'See you later.'

Nancy ignored her. She sat down and yanked off her boots. 'Christ, it's cold out there. Got anything to drink?'

'No.'

'There's rum,' said Donna. She opened the cupboard above Sarah's desk. 'Oh! And gin and vodka, too. There's even some vermouth. Would you like a Martini?'

'That'd be great,' Nancy replied. She grinned slyly at Sarah. 'Aren't you going to introduce me to your friend?'

'I'm Donna, Sarah's sister,' Donna called over her shoulder as she assembled the Martini-makings on Sarah's desk.

'I'm Nancy. Your sister and I work for the same agency. Has she told you she's a ca–'

'Caterer!' Sarah was shouting but she didn't care. 'We're caterers.'

'*Classy* caterers,' said Nancy. 'You look nice,' she said to Donna. 'Special date tonight?'

'Sort of. Since Sarah's working tonight I'm taking her place as David's date. We're going to the Faculty Club for dinner.'

'You didn't tell me David was a professor, Sarah,' said Nancy.

'He's not.' In fact, Sarah hadn't told Nancy anything about her private life. 'Donna, don't spill that booze on my laptop for God's sake.'

'I'm being careful,' said Donna. She gave Sarah a quizzical look. 'Relax.'

Relax? Sarah almost laughed out loud. She felt herself growing bigger, like Alice in Wonderland after she took the wrong pill, or perhaps more accurately, like the Incredible Hulk, becoming huge and green with rage.

'How did you get in?' Sarah repeated the question she'd first asked when Nancy appeared.

'What's the big deal? Veronica didn't give me a suite number and I don't know your last name –'

'Meadows,' offered Donna.

'– so I knocked and a nice lady let me in and directed me up here. You do want your costume for tonight, right?'

Sarah nodded. She took the glass her sister offered and swigged. 'What's the theme?'

'*The Wizard of Oz*,' replied Nancy. 'Oh. You'll need these.' She rooted around in her bag and withdrew a pair of adorable red sequined flats. 'You're Dorothy,' she said.

'The ruby slippers! They're so cute,' squealed Donna. 'Who are you going to be, Nancy?'

'The witch,' said Nancy. She sipped her Martini.

'That's going to take a lot of green paint,' commented Sarah.

Nancy sputtered. 'The good witch, Glenda, of course,' she said.

'It sounds like so much fun,' said Donna. 'I wish I could work there.'

'There's always room for a pretty girl,' said Nancy.

'She's not old enough to ... serve liquor,' said Sarah. 'Finished?' She grabbed Nancy's glass. 'I'm sure you have a lot to do to get ready for tonight.'

'Yeah, well, now that I've done Veronica the favour of dropping off your duds, I'll be on my way.' Nancy rose.

'Thank you,' said Sarah. 'I appreciate it.'

'You should,' said Nancy. 'Nice to meet you, Donna Meadows. Have fun at the Faculty Club with David. Where will you be sitting?'

'With the history department of course,' said Donna. 'I can pretend I'm Mrs Caruthers, faculty wife.' A puzzled look crossed her face at Sarah's groan. 'Oh come on, Sarah, I'm kidding.'

Nancy grinned at Sarah. 'Well, I hope David Caruthers, historian, doesn't mind you working tonight, Sarah. I'll have to remember, next time I see him, to be 'specially sweet to him for letting us have you on New Year's Eve.'

Christ. Nancy was as good as promising to contact David.

'And I'll be sure to be sweet to your family,' Sarah said. She gave Nancy a warning look as she opened her door.

Nancy paused. 'I don't have any family,' she said. Then she was gone.

Two hours later, Sarah was the one pirouetting before the full-length mirror. Her costume was authentic down to the last detail. Little white shirt with puffy short sleeves, detailed in the same blue gingham as her pinafore. Her hair was styled in two short braids with long tails, tied with blue ribbons. She wore matching blue ankle socks. And the shoes. They were a tad tight, but still, shoes to die for! She'd already practised clicking the heels together three times. Now she did it again.

So cute. And she was lucky not to be wearing high heels. It was likely to be a long night. Nancy had neglected to bring Sarah a basket but she had one that would do, and a little stuffed dog that would stand in for Toto. Fun!

Sarah had sent Donna off to meet David for drinks before dinner. Happily, he hadn't called to complain, yet, and, as soon as she was tucked inside the car that was coming for her, she'd turn her phone off.

This was going to be a great night – making double her usual pay for partying with the wealthy in a private mansion, hobnobbing with Toledo's elite – dressed to thrill as little Dorothy from *The Wizard of Oz*. The men were going to eat her up. The very last thing she needed was David whining in her ear about obligations and broken promises.

Sarah applied one more barely there coat of lipstick and batted her lashes at her reflection. She shrugged, dropping any vestiges of guilt as easily as she might once have dropped a cardigan from her shoulders. She slid her ruby slippers off her feet and tucked them into the basket beside Toto, pausing to pat the stuffed toy's head. 'Fun, fun, fun, here we come!'

The private home at the end of the winding driveway was more fortress than mansion. Sarah tried not to gawk as she got out of the limo and ascended the stone steps. Before she could knock, the double doors swung wide open. Men in chitons stood on each side, beckoning her into the massive hallway. They bowed as she entered, then relieved her of her coat and boots and ushered her towards more double doors, these, no doubt, leading to the party room.

These doors were also manned by guys, but in togas. Sarah didn't recall any such characters in *The Wizard of Oz* story, but then, she hadn't read the book, just seen the movie. One of the men touched her arm. 'How would you like to be announced, *mademoiselle*?'

'Dorothy, thank you,' she replied, quelling the '*duh*' that sprang to her lips.

The doors opened, revealing a costume-clad crowd of Roman soldiers, Greek gods and goddesses, gladiators and pharaohs. The music and chatter stopped as Sarah made her entrance.

'Ladies and gentlemen, may I present Dorothy,' announced Sarah's companion.

There was stunned silence as Sarah was regarded by what seemed like a thousand pair of astonished eyes. She felt her face flush scarlet. She scanned the crowd and picked out a few Classique girls, resplendent in the garb of ancient citizens of Rome and Greece. Yes, there was Nancy, a fat smirk on her pug face, dressed in a glittering Cleopatra costume. She pointed and laughed.

'I – uh –' Sarah felt big and stupid and ridiculous. No. She was none of those things. Sarah popped open her basket and tugged the stuffed dog into view. 'Gosh, Toto,' she squeaked as loud as she could, 'I've a feeling we're not in Kansas any more.'

It brought the house down. Sarah grinned at the laughing, applauding crowd, curtseyed prettily, clicked her heels three times and proceeded into the ballroom.

She decided against killing Nancy immediately. First she

downed a glass of *Veuve Clicquot* champagne and chatted up her host and hostess, Mr and Mrs Pettifer. They were a handsome couple, old Toledo money in the hands of a new generation. The woman's bright green eyes, in particular, seemed to linger on her as Sarah introduced herself and apologised for her inappropriate costume.

'Nonsense, you're adorable. And we hardly need another Cleopatra traipsing about the place,' said her hostess.

Sarah asked if there were any particular men they'd like her to entertain and, armed with their answer, set about dancing with one single man after another, flirting and laughing her way through the band's first set. Earning her pay.

It wasn't until close to midnight that Sarah found herself face to face with Nancy.

'Dorothy,' said an older man with a balding pate, an impressive moustache and a curling beard, 'come entertain me with a story.' He patted his knee.

Sarah knew the man was an international tax lawyer, someone her host was particularly intent on impressing. She perched herself on the old man's knee and playfully tugged the laurel wreath that adorned his balding head. 'I think you have the best stories to tell, sir.'

'What makes you say that?'

'I've heard rumours about you, Socrates.'

'Ah, you recognise me?'

'But of course.'

'Aren't you the clever little poppet?' He jiggled her on his knee.

Nancy must have noticed the two of them, circled by the old man's sycophants, just as Socrates had been in his time, and wormed her way into the group.

'I'm a clever poppet, too, Socrates,' she said, pouting. 'I know you ask questions as a way of teaching.'

'True, true,' admitted the old man, nodding his head.

'I wonder about the Socratic Method, actually,' said Sarah. 'I know Socrates used questions as a teaching method but perhaps he was also seeking to refine the contours of his own hypotheses.'

'What do you think?' The old man looked at Nancy.

'Well, I disagree.' Nancy faltered but stood her ground.

'Have you studied him, Nancy?' Sarah gave her nemesis a wide-eyed look.

'I've read everything he ever wrote,' said Nancy. She tilted her chin defiantly.

'That's quite a feat,' commented Sarah, 'since he never actually *wrote* anything.'

'He did so.'

'Nope. He talked. Xenophon and Plato wrote.' Sarah batted her lashes at the old man upon whose knee she sat. 'Isn't that so, sir?'

'Quite right,' said the old man, beaming at her. 'I think, little miss,' he said, glowering sternly at Nancy, 'Socrates would suggest you not feign knowledge when you are ignorant.'

Nancy blushed beet red. Sarah would've felt sorry for her if she hadn't been a thorn in Sarah's side for so long. As it was, she sat on the old man's knee and giggled.

Nancy attacked!

Bright costumes and shocked faces kaleidoscoped as Sarah flew in an arc off the man's lap. When she landed on the floor, Nancy still had hold of one of her braids.

'Bitch!' Sarah struggled to break Nancy's grasp as Nancy slapped her face repeatedly with her free hand. 'Let go!' Sarah punched wildly and was gratified when her fist connected with Nancy's pug nose. Nancy shrieked and dragged her nails along the length of Sarah's arm as she was pulled off her prey. Sarah sat up, stunned.

Nancy was being firmly escorted from the ballroom by Mr Pettifer. The stupid, stupid bitch! Sarah could only guess how Veronica would react to news of the way they'd represented Classique on New Year's Eve. Damn. They could get canned for this.

She burst into tears, as much from humiliation as pain, although her scalp ached and her arm was bleeding. Mrs Pettifer helped her to her feet.

'I'm so sorry,' wailed Sarah. 'Please –'

'Come on,' said the older woman grimly. She propelled Sarah through the crowd and out the ballroom doors. There was no evidence of her husband or Nancy in the hallway, much to Sarah's relief. She fully expected to be tossed out of the front doors, but instead she was climbing the Scarlett O'Hara staircase to the second floor.

Mrs Pettifer led her to the lush en suite bathroom off the outrageously opulent master bedroom. Sarah sat, mute and miserable, on a white cane bench while Mrs Pettifer washed her bloody arm and then, with a fresh washcloth, mopped her tear-streaked face and hands as if she were a toddler.

'I think you got the worst of it,' said Mrs Pettifer.

'Only because she surprised me,' grumbled Sarah. 'I punched her though, and she only hit me and pulled my hair.' She brightened at the thought then, remembering who was tending to her wounds, darkened again. 'She must be insane. We'll get the sack for this,' she added, hoping for a hint from her hostess that it might not be so. 'I'm really, really sorry, Mrs Pettifer.'

'Call me Caroline. I'm no more than ten years older than you.' She squeezed cream onto a swab and daintily dabbed at the long scratch marks on Sarah's arm. Somehow, she managed to do it elegantly.

'I'm sorry, Caroline.'

'That girl had a real hate-on for you. Why?'

'We had a misunderstanding. I stole her date by mistake. She's convinced I did it on purpose, but I didn't. I mean I didn't even know what was going on until the next day when I found the envelope. Full of money. On the pillow in the hotel room.'

'You picked up a john by mistake?' Caroline laughed. She tilted her head to look at Sarah with her sly green eyes. 'That's pretty funny.'

'I wish Nancy could see the humour in it. Ouch.' She flinched as Caroline started winding gauze around her wound. 'Will it scar?'

'No.'

'I don't look for trouble. It's just the way I think. I misunderstand what's going on, or what people are talking about, like I'm on a slightly different plain than everyone else.'

'Like Superman's Bizzaro World?'

'No. Not that bad. More like Unusual-o World,' Sarah rattled on, oblivious to the amusement in Caroline's expression. 'My sister thinks I have Asperger's syndrome.'

'What do you think?'

'I think she's crazy. It's like I either think big thoughts or I don't think at all. I mean I get distracted or whatever and I just latch on to what I perceive is happening and go with the flow. Sometimes I make mistakes.'

'That must be dangerous in your line of work.' Caroline sat on the bench beside Sarah to fasten the gauze.

'I've been lucky. This is the only bad thing that's ever happened to me since I started at Classique. Most of the time people are good.'

'Perhaps because your heart is pure? Or, as pure as it can be, given what you do for a living.'

'Oh, I'm not a real –' Sarah bit her lip. She'd been about to say she wasn't a real call girl, but that would be a lie. She glanced at her neatly bandaged arm. 'Thank you for taking care of me,' she said instead.

'You're welcome, little Dorothy.'

A roar sounded below them, counting down. 'Ten ... nine ... eight ... seven ...'

'Oh my God, now you've missed midnight!'

'No I haven't. I'm celebrating with you.'

'Four ... three ... two ... one ... Happy New Year!' A cacophony of noisemakers and voices rumbled in the ballroom below.

But Sarah didn't hear it. She was focused on the feel of a woman's lips on hers, soft, plump and as red as cherries, as delicate as rose petals. Caroline drew her closer with a slender hand at the base of her neck. Sarah could smell her perfume and beneath it, her light natural scent. Caroline's tongue tasted sweet as it flicked her lips in a teasing manner, urging her to open her mouth, which she did. The teasing turned into something else, something sensual and sexy. Caroline touched Sarah's face. Sarah mimicked her, stroking Caroline's cheek, so smooth, and sliding down Caroline's elegant ivory neck to feel her clavicle, like bird bones under Sarah's hand.

Sarah's eyes opened when her hand felt the swell of the other woman's breast. But Caroline lured her back in, her mouth insistent on hers, her gaze gentle for all its intensity. She touched Sarah's breast, above the pinafore, and kissed Sarah throughout the initial shock of a woman's touch. Sarah didn't know her buttons were open until Caroline's hand slid inside her blouse and bra to cup her bare breast.

Sarah closed her eyes again.

19

The notice on the bulletin board said that the ethics course had been moved to the Grand Auditorium.

'That's crazy,' Sarah said. 'How many philo-nuts are we, a dozen? In a hall that seats a hundred and forty?'

Penny giggled and nudged her. 'There'll be more than a dozen of us this semester. Haven't you heard? Doc Braun's been sent to the funny farm. It seems that he's gone totally gaga. For real.'

'Poor guy,' said Sarah. 'But what's that got to do with enrolment?'

Christopher grinned at her. 'It's not who's gone, but who's taking over, that's drawing the crowd.'

'I still don't understand.'

'We have a celebrity lecturer now – Professor Jonathon Trelawney.'

'Is he good?'

'Supposed to be, but it isn't just that.' Penny wrapped an arm around her friend's waist and gave her a squeeze. 'Ever have a crush on an older man, Sarah?'

Of course she had, but she wasn't going to admit it. 'Not really, why?'

'If you had, he'd likely be something like our new prof. He's tall, good-looking in a rumpled sort of way, very strict, I hear, absolutely brilliant and has an air of danger about him. Shame he's so old, but that won't stop some of the girls from throwing themselves at his feet.'

Whispering, Christopher confided, 'As I hear it, at his last post, a lady teacher and a townie got into a fight over him – a real catfight, with hair pulling and everything.'

'It happens,' said Sarah. She was wearing a long-sleeved T-shirt to cover the souvenir she had from her own catfight. 'You'd be surprised.'

'Why do you think he's come here, when Harvard or Yale'd be glad to take him?' Penny wrinkled her brow.

'Their loss, our gain.' Sarah shrugged.

'He's English,' Christopher supplied. 'That means he's gay. Maybe Harvard and Yale have filled their quota of gay profs.'

'Just because he's English doesn't mean he's gay.' Penny shook her head at Christopher. 'He could be kinky, though,' Penny added. 'All Englishmen are kinky.'

'Cut it out you two,' said Sarah, giggling. 'Show some respect.'

Christopher said, 'Maybe he's gay and kinky. A gay, kinky ethics professor would be cool, don't you think?'

Penny got to the Grand Auditorium early and saved seats in the front row for Christopher and Sarah. By the time they arrived the hall was half-filled.

'Look who's at the back,' Penny hissed.

Sarah twisted in her seat. At the very highest tier there were half a dozen profs, four women and two men. 'They're curious to see the new guy perform,' she said.

'Fans, I bet,' Penny whispered. 'Hoover's gay and old Loretta's after anything in pants. That's two of them at least who are interested in more than Professor Trelawney's style of lecturing.'

The auditorium fell quiet. A tall figure in a tweed jacket with leather patches at its elbows strode to the centre of the stage. He wrote on the board, 'Ontology recapitulates phylogeny. *Post hoc, ergo propter hoc.*

Sarah sank down in her seat. John – Jonathon. Her John, her dream john, had really been a 'Jon' and here he was, her prof, the man whose marking she was relying on to get her degree; the man she'd been fantasizing about in her dreams. The man who'd . . .

Thank goodness she was dressed in jeans and a T-shirt, with

no make-up. Maybe he wouldn't recognise her? For an entire semester? Who was she kidding!

He turned to face his audience. Sarah lifted her notebook to half obscure her crimson face.

He started, 'First, I would like to thank my learned colleagues at the back for showing up to support me during my first lecture at Seneca.'

Christopher nudged Sarah. 'Gay, def-in-ite-ly gay.'

She elbowed him back, harder than was necessary.

Penny whispered, 'Doesn't that accent simply make you tingle?'

Professor Trelawney continued, 'For the rest of you, I have good news and bad news. The good news is, I don't give a damn about attendance. Many renowned scholars achieved academic success without ever attending a lecture. Can anyone name one?'

Christopher's hand shot up, drawing Jonathon's unwelcome attention to the area that Sarah sat in.

'Yes, young man?'

'You, sir?'

Jonathon grinned. 'Thank you for that unsubtle sycophancy, but I was thinking of such luminaries as T E Lawrence – Lawrence of Arabia – and Sir Richard Francis Burton – translator of *The Arabian Nights*, among other things.'

Christopher muttered, 'Gay, like I said.'

'The bad news is,' Jonathon went on, 'that I expect my students to think, to use their intelligence. Bear with me while I explain what I mean by "intelligence".'

At the end of his first lecture, most of which failed to penetrate Sarah's funk, Jonathon drew their attention back to the words he'd written on the board. 'I'd like you to consider these statements,' he said. 'How do they relate to each other? Do they have a relationship? Does either contradict the other? Think about those questions and write your thoughts down for me, perhaps two thousand words? By Friday at noon?'

The students saluted him with the traditional groan, applauded and filed out. Sarah scurried to the door, bent over as if in pain which, in a way, she was.

* * *

That night in her bed, in the misty zone between fantasising and dreaming, Sarah imagined that she'd been summoned to Jonathon's study. She wasn't the least surprised to find that he'd had two whipping posts set up. He did have a reputation as something of a disciplinarian, after all. Without any transition, she was tied, spreadeagled, between the posts. The dress she was wearing was gauzy, white, flowing and virtually transparent. Beneath it, she was nude.

Jonathon took an old-fashioned crook-handled schoolmaster's cane from a rack. He circled Sarah, describing her many shortcomings in humiliating detail. He paused behind her but she could still see him clearly from some out-of-body viewpoint. He slashed the cane down, ripping the fabric of her dress from just below her bottom to its hem. She flinched even though the cane hadn't touched her skin. He resumed pacing, then slashed again. The tip of his cane tore her dress from side to side, just below the swell of her breasts. She pushed her chest out in an effort to seduce him away from punishing her further, but in vain. The cane whipped again and again, reducing her dress to shreds and then slicing the tatters away to leave her totally naked but completely unmarked.

Dream-Jon tossed his cane aside and was instantly nude, or perhaps he'd been naked all along and she just hadn't noticed. He embraced Sarah. She had just enough time to be aware of his burning shaft, pressed against her cool belly, before she experienced a hard little climax and woke up with her fists clenched between her thighs.

The next morning there was a note for Sarah, asking her to drop by Jonathon's study at four-thirty, if it wasn't inconvenient. Was her dream about to come true?

She didn't have the chance to get home and change but she did touch up her make-up before reporting as 'invited'. She knocked.

He called, 'Come in.'

Jonathon was seated behind his desk so she didn't have to decide whether or not to run into his arms. He said, 'Take a seat, please, Sarah.'

She sat, hands in her lap, twiddling her thumbs.

He smiled. 'We have a slightly uncomfortable situation here.'

'Yes, Jon.'

'Best call me "sir" or "Professor Trelawney", like the other students do.'

'Yes, Professor Trelawney.'

'Our past relationship, brief as it was – it'd be unfortunate for both of us if it became public knowledge.'

'But the proctors already know. I was a gift to you from Seneca, wasn't I?'

'No.'

'Then who –'

'It's none of your business, Sarah.'

'Of course.' She flushed. 'I'd never tell a soul.'

'Nor would I. We are agreed then? It never happened? You're a student; I'm your professor. We met for the first time, yesterday, in the auditorium.'

'I can keep secrets.' She gave him a conspiratorial grin. 'In my "other life" I have to.'

'I understand. So, no secret looks, no innuendos between us, just our professional relationship from now on? I give you my word that my assessment of your work will not be affected one little bit, neither positively nor negatively.'

She looked up at him through her lashes and purred, 'I was hoping . . .'

He shook his head. 'Delightful as our encounter was, Sarah, and even if things were different, on a professor's salary, I couldn't possibly afford you.'

'That's not what I meant.'

'Explain then.'

'We – I know I was paid, but I felt, um, there was a connection, wasn't there? You and me? A fit? Something more?'

'I won't deny that I felt more emotional involvement with you than the circumstances of our meeting warranted. Had we met some other way – but no – that wouldn't have worked, either. You're my student, so off-limits.'

'I'm twenty-one, an adult, and you know I'm no little innocent.'

'Sarah, I'm incredibly flattered. Our encounter was great, but we can't possibly resume our relationship.'

'Why not? You want me, don't you? I want you.' She pressed on. 'Jesus, Jon, you made me come to the count of ten! Don't tell me we weren't connected then.'

He smiled. 'That was a matter of pain and Play-O and, more than anything, luck.'

'I see.' Her voice wavered. 'Strange. This is the first time you've truly humiliated me.' Tears welled in her eyes.

'Sarah. Please. It's a matter of ethics. We "fit" as you say, because of our natures: me dominant, you submissive. No ethical dominant will take advantage of a dependent relationship. That means no doctor and patient; boss and employee.' He smiled. ' No Scout master and Boy Scout, priest and parishioner, and especially, no tutor and pupil. Can you understand that?'

'It would be against your morals?'

'I have no morals, just ethics, which are much more binding.'

Sarah blinked back a tear. 'But I think, I lo –'

'Don't say it. In any case, at the most, what you feel is infatuation.'

'Is not!'

'Don't sulk.'

'Or you'll spank me?'

Jonathon sighed. 'Sarah, is this the way it is going to be? Are you going to be coming on to me every time I lecture? If so, you're going to make my life very difficult.'

Sarah dropped her eyes. 'Sorry. No, I won't come on to you, I promise, not overtly. I can't make the same promise about covertly.' She raised her eyes again and gazed directly into his. 'Just remember, Professor Trelawney, every minute I spend in your class I'll be wanting you. Any time you change your mind about your ethics, all you have to do is crook your finger and I'll be yours, any way you want me.'

His face was stone. 'Then, the situation is this, we keep our past secret, but you intend to torment me in any unobtrusive way that you can. I'll treat you as just another student and will be impervious to your subtle seductions.' He sighed. 'The unfortunate thing is, this conflict that you insist on will inevitably sour us against each other. We're going to end up detesting each other, and that's sad. It'll sully some very happy memories, on my part, if not on yours.'

Sarah made fists. 'You . . . You . . . You man you!' She got up and ran from the room before she broke down in tears.

20

'Sarah. Nancy. Come in.' Veronica's voice was carefully neutral.

The two girls, who had been left in the waiting room for what seemed like an eternity, rose as one. They shuffled into Veronica's office. Craig was already inside, seated on an armless chair. He was holding a crop. Veronica closed the door behind them.

'I think you know why I've asked you both to come in. I've just been informed that your behaviour on New Year's Eve was a shockingly poor representation of Classique.' Veronica slowly circled the girls as she spoke.

'That bastard said he wasn't gonna tell,' griped Nancy. 'What a jerk.'

'I thought Mrs Pettifer was a satisfied customer, too.' Sarah flushed as she remembered the brief but intense make-out session she'd spent with Caroline.

'The Pettifers did not complain, happily. Nonetheless your dreadful behaviour has been drawn to my attention. Comments?'

'Who was it, then? Mimi? Andrea? Those bitches.' Nancy's voice rose. 'Or was it Naomi – I saw her there and she's a vicious gossip –'

'Not gossip. Fact. My girls, rolling on the floor, clawing and scratching at each other. Classique girls.' Veronica shuddered. 'The image is seared into my brain.'

'I'm sorry,' said Sarah. 'It won't happen again.'

'No, it won't,' said Veronica. 'Have you any guesses about the identity of my informant, Sarah?'

Sarah shrugged. 'Not really. Does it matter?'

'You have no guesses because you don't know any of my girls. Isn't that right?'

'Um, well, I'm an independent worker –' Sarah faltered.

'Not a team player,' stated Veronica. 'That may be fine in your other life, but here at Classique I expect my girls to back each other up. Understand?'

'Yes, ma'am.' Sarah hung her head. 'I shouldn't have made Nancy look stupid. But how do you think I felt, showing up dressed as Dorothy?'

'Nancy? Any ideas on how Sarah ended up with such an inappropriate costume?'

'I was rushing around and I guess I grabbed the wrong one.' Nancy jutted out her jaw. 'I was just trying to do you a favour, Veronica, and –'

The swish of the crop slicing air cut short her explanation. Nancy glanced at Craig, flushing furiously.

'I'm sorely tempted to let you both go, but I'll give you one more chance. No more back-stabbing. No more idiocy. Understood?'

'Yes, Veronica,' whispered Nancy. She couldn't seem to take her eyes off the crop, which was once again settled across Craig's knees.

'Yes, Veronica. Understood.' Sarah was also mesmerised by the lethal-looking instrument.

Craig grinned at the girls. 'Right then, who's first?'

'Not the crop, please, I can't stand it –'

'Stop snivelling, Nancy. It's the only way I know to get through to you,' said Veronica. 'You've only yourself to blame.'

'I'll go first,' said Sarah.

Craig lifted his hands from his knees and gestured, inviting her to lie in his lap. Sarah complied. Her limbs felt heavy, as if she were moving through water. Her mind was fogging up. Probably a good thing. Did she have nice panties on? Yes. Always flimsy bikinis or thongs, now that she was a call girl. Pretty, but no protection from the crop.

Craig lifted her skirt and tucked the hem into the waistband. He placed his palm on her bum. She flinched instinctively. He laughed. Sarah chuckled too but the sound caught in her throat as he delivered half a dozen firm slaps to her ass.

It hurt! She wriggled in a pointless attempt to escape his hand. Craig slung one leg over her thighs, trapping her with her bum up and helplessly exposed. He raised the crop and brought it down across the fullness of her cheeks.

God! It stung! It stung horribly. Wriggle as she might, there was nothing she could do to escape it. Again, and it stung just as bad, worse even. She had to protect herself somehow.

Sarah tried to cover her bum with her hands but Craig simply grabbed both of her wrists with his free hand. Helpless, totally helpless, she willed herself to relax and receive. Impossible! The terrible crop sang its terrible song repeatedly, whistling through the air to a staccato stop, one bar, one beat at a time.

She'd been clenching her teeth but as the punishment continued Sarah's mouth fell open. Inarticulate pleas for mercy mixed with groans and sobs. Tears coursed down her cheeks. Would it never, ever end? What would happen if she shouted 'red', or at least, God help her, 'yellow'? But she did not. This was punishment, real punishment. It frightened her, though whether that was because of the pain or because of the deep yearning that pain sparked within her, she didn't know.

Suddenly she was riding the pain, with it and then above it, like a surfer struggling for position on a board in a storm-tossed sea. Up, up, and yes! Free! And then the inevitable tumble, submerged in an ocean of agony.

'Stop!' Sarah screamed. 'Stop! I'll be good!'

Craig ignored her. The crop bit into her for what seemed the hundredth time.

'Enough,' said Veronica.

Craig stood. Sarah tumbled to the floor. 'Next,' Craig said cheerfully.

Nancy burst into tears.

That night, Sarah was trying to study in bed, an icepack to her bum, when her intercom buzzed. In response to her hello,

Christopher's cheery voice greeted her. Ah, Chris, her balm for all things weird and scary. She let him into the building and a moment later, into her room.

'Your study partner's here!' Christopher spoke loudly in case Donna was listening at her door. Sarah had told her sister that she tutored him on Wednesdays, which he'd found hilarious, as his marks were every bit as high as hers. He dumped his knapsack by the door and jumped onto her bed. 'What's tonight's topic?'

'Donna's not home,' said Sarah. She closed the door and locked it.

'She get a job?'

'Not yet.'

Christopher picked up each text on the bed, considered its title with a mock-quizzical frown, and dropped it on the floor. 'Autism? Socrates? Zen? What? You think old Socs was autistic? Or the Buddha?'

'Maybe both,' she replied enigmatically. Sarah stretched out on the bed beside him and rucked up her nightie. 'Eat me, baby, I want to feel those cold cheeks between my burning thighs.'

'Say no more, mistress.'

'Mmm,' Sarah moaned with delight. Christopher's mouth on her mound was a godsend. Just what she needed. She wriggled and moaned again. She was already on the cusp of a climax that'd been hovering since she'd been cropped hours ago. 'Ouch.' He'd cupped her ass in his hands and although his cool touch was welcome on the hot cheeks, pressure was not. 'Careful.'

'Holy shit. Who did this to you?'

'Behave. No questions. Just be careful.'

'Are you kidding? Is this – did you – are you?'

'It's OK, I did, I am. C'mon, Christopher, I need to come.'

'You're a strange one, Sarah.'

'I know, baby,' she whispered. She pushed his head down between her legs. 'I know.'

21

Veronica asked, 'Can you smoke, Sarah?'

'Smoke? No, I don't smoke.' Sarah crossed her ankles and tucked her knees to one side. As Sarah watched Veronica's appraising eye follow the line she'd created – from the top of her straight-cut highlighted chestnut hair down past her wide blue eyes and scarlet lips to the tip of her jaw to a hint of cleavage to her tightly belted waist to her curvy hip and down her legs to the slender, crossed ankles and so off the tips of her black stilettos, she congratulated herself. She'd gone for sexy and sophisticated with a clear but understated hint of kink. Gorgeous and depraved. Eager. Open. Fun. Experienced but unsullied. Unique.

It was the first time she'd talked to Veronica since their meeting with Nancy and Craig. Happily, neither were present and Veronica made no mention of the New Year's fiasco. If the cropping from Craig had truly been her punishment, it seemed to have released everyone, including her, from dwelling on the past. In which case it had been well worth it.

'That wasn't what I asked. I asked, "*Can* you smoke?" Have you ever tried it? If you did, did you choke or throw up?'

'I tried it once, Veronica, back when I was a kid. My sister and I swiped half a pack a visitor had left at our folks'. We snuck out behind the house and lit up.'

'And? How was it?'

'As I remember, she smoked three and I smoked two. We threw the pack away after that.' Sarah peered at her boss. 'Why do you ask?'

'It didn't make you sick or anything?'

'No.'

Veronica pulled her desk drawer open and took out a plain cedar box. 'Our client has these custom made in Vietnam.' She lifted the lid to show that it was full of incredibly long, perhaps ten-inch, ivory cigarettes with golden filter tips. 'He's a smoking fetishist.'

'A what?'

'Women smoking turns him on.'

'That's weird.'

Veronica's eyes narrowed. 'Perhaps, but we don't judge, do we, Sarah?'

'No, of course not, sorry.'

'He pays double.'

'Oh? That's interesting.'

'Yes, isn't it?'

'He'll pay double just to watch a girl smoke?'

'Not "just". He wants sex as well, but with cigarettes as important accessories.'

'I'm not sure I follow. Does he want the girl to masturbate with a cigarette?'

'Very likely. Sarah, the smoking fetish, like most fetishes, is very structured. There are looks, styles and so on that go with it. There are smoking fetishists who prefer the woman to smoke cigars, for instance.'

'You mean there are lots of these – "gentlemen"?'

'Thousands. Tens of thousands. There are websites devoted to their kink, and magazines. There are even smoking porno flicks with the girls fully clothed, just puffing away, nothing else.'

'You're joking.'

Veronica shook her head. 'No I'm not. This is about money, and I never joke about money.'

Sarah took one of the cigarettes from its box and sniffed it. 'Just tobacco? These don't contain any illegal substances, do they? I'd hate to wake up in a Vietnamese brothel.'

'They're safe, as safe as cigarettes can be. I'm not suggesting you take up the habit. This'd be for the date, nothing more.'

'Tell me more, please.'

'When it comes to fetishes, a girl has to understand the nuances. With smoking fetish, the fetishists are very particular. It's not just the smoking that they want, but the style of smoking, what they smoke, what they wear, how they act and so on.'

'Poor devils.'

'Why do you say that?'

'If a guy wants someone who smokes, and smokes a particular brand, and she has to dress and look and act ... What're his chances of bumping into the right, and willing, girl?'

Veronica smiled the smile of a predator. 'Exactly. That's why the rich ones will pay handsomely for dates with their impossible dreams. Do you think you could play the part, Sarah?'

'Double pay? Give me time to research the kink, and I'm sure I can.' Sarah paused for thought. 'Veronica, if I'm going to spend time on research, and if the date is so obsessed, why don't you tell him that for three times our usual rates we promise him the smoking sex experience of his life?'

'You think you could deliver on that guarantee?'

'I bet I can.'

Veronica pulled half a dozen magazines and a couple of DVDs from her desk drawer. 'Very well, here's a start to your research. The magazines are his. He wants them back. He's marked the pictures that turn him on the most. That should help you.' She pushed the box of cigarettes towards Sarah. 'These are what he'll want you to smoke. A warning, though.'

'What?'

'If you research online, have your virus filters and so on in place and up-to-date. Some smoking fetish sites are contaminated.'

'I'll be careful, I promise.'

That night, Sarah pulled her little desk over to one of her two small windows, opened it wide, slid a DVD into her laptop, lit one of the long cigarettes and picked up her pen. There was a yellow pad beside the stack of magazines. She was prepared for total immersion in her research. By the end of the week, she'd decided, she was going to be the smoking fetishist's ideal woman. For the very first time, she was being chosen for a date for her sophistication, not for her innocence. That was very satisfying.

Two days later, she spent eight solid hours in front of her mirror, practising. Three days after that, she scoured the better hotels, looking for exactly the right setting. At the end of the week she delivered a typed sheet of paper to Veronica.

'Tell him that he has to follow these instructions, to the letter.'

Veronica scanned the page. 'You think he'll play along?'

'He's a fetishist. He won't be able to resist. His cock won't let him.'

'I like your attitude, Sarah. Anything else I can do to help?'

'Costume is important. So is hair and make-up. May I borrow from wardrobe?'

'Craig will take care of you there. I'll book you with Carlo for the make-up and hair.'

'I'll need a wig, a long straight blonde one.'

'Carlo has wigs. Anything else?'

'You'll bill the client for the hotel room?'

'Of course.'

An hour before her date was due, Sarah let herself into the room she'd booked. It had no bed. There were two oversized leather club chairs and a matching four-seater sofa, each with its own side table. Sarah drew on her stagecraft to arrange the furniture and lighting.

In the en suite bathroom, she checked her appearance. Her hair glistened halfway down to her waist. Her eyes were theatrical, with heavy silver lids, impossibly long artificial lashes and tip-tilted corners. Her lips were wet and scarlet. Carlo had exaggerated her cheekbones for her while leaving her face very pale. She looked wicked.

The bodice of her smoke-grey silk dress was an 'M' held up

by spaghetti straps. The points of the 'M' just, only just, covered her nipples. The skirt of her dress was slit to her waist but rendered barely decent by press studs from the top of her thigh to her hip. She kicked her loafers off and stepped into pumps that had impossible heels.

Setting the scene so elaborately, in a way that was designed to delight a man, was fun. What sort of scene would Jon have liked? It was a shame that she didn't know. The schoolgirl thing hadn't been his idea, so she had no clues as to his secret fantasies, except that they included bondage and corporal punishment.

Sarah set what was left of her box of cigarettes on the sofa's side table, in easy reach, with two books of matches and an oversized ashtray. One cigarette she held, with a third match-book. She arranged herself carefully, back arched over the sofa's rounded arm, one leg extended along the seat, the other foot dangling over the edge, with its shoe hanging from her toes. That's what he'd see first, when he entered the almost dark room, an elegant ankle and foot with a hanging stiletto pump, carefully positioned so as to show 'toe cleavage'. By the pictures he'd marked, foot fetish, including heels and hose, was his secondary kink.

There was a diffident knock at the door. Sarah said nothing. His instructions were to let himself in. She ignored a second knock. The lock clicked. Her client slipped into the room, opening the door just wide enough to pass through. All Sarah saw of him was his silhouette, tall and slim, in the light that leaked in before the door closed. His shadowy shape settled into the armchair opposite her and ten feet away. She hadn't put an ashtray on his side table. Like many smoking fetishists, he didn't smoke. It was sinful, which made it exciting.

Sarah gave him a minute to admire her ankle, foot and dangling pump. She put her cigarette between her lips and struck a match. The client sucked in a deep breath. For him, the sight of a woman lighting a cigarette was the equivalent of one baring a breast to a tit freak. Sarah had learnt a lot in the course of surfing fetish sites. Slowly, she closed the distance between the flame and the end of her cigarette. Nonchalantly, she reached out to the chain of the standard lamp and pulled it. Now her face was spotlit – the face, to him, of an excitingly depraved woman.

She drew deeply, held the smoke in her lungs, then let it trickle from between her lips to be sucked back in through her nostrils – the classic French inhale. Sarah was rewarded by a dramatic sigh. As far as she could see, without letting it show that she was looking, he had his hand in his lap already.

She dropped her head back, took another drag, and exhaled a long plume of smoke. The wall behind her was dark. The way she'd arranged the lamps, her smoke would be backlit, pale grey.

Yes, he definitely had his hand in his lap, and his cock in it.

Ignoring him, she French-inhaled, blew plumes, tried a smoke ring and, when she was sure his attention was on the smoke, surreptitiously popped the press stud at her thigh. A movement of her leg hissed the silk of her dress on her nylon, drawing his attention down to the length of slender thigh she'd exposed. Her cigarette was half burned. She stubbed it and lit another. In the course of consuming her second cigarette, she popped another stud and shifted to part her dress to the top of her thigh. A movement of her foot swayed her dangling pump. Her client gurgled his appreciation.

Sarah managed to rub herself against the arm of the sofa, dislodging one strap of her dress to dangle halfway down her upper arm, almost baring one breast. After all, he did want actual sex, as well as to watch her smoke.

Once more, she stubbed half of an extremely expensive cigarette. At last, she turned her gaze in his direction and husked, 'Light me.'

He stood as fast as he could while tucking in and zipping up and strode to her. In the indirect lighting from the floor, he looked to be in his late forties, ginger-haired, with a broad high brow, aquiline nose and thin lips. His hands shook as he fumbled with the matchbook and held a quivering flame to the end of her cigarette. She drew deeply and aimed a stream of smoke at his face.

'I . . .' he said.

'Stay there, beside me,' she told him, still keeping her voice husky, like that of a heavy smoker. Keeping her eyes hooded, she treated him to two more plumes of smoke to his face. For the first time, she let him see that she was looking directly at him. A shrug slithered the loose strap to her elbow, baring her right breast. His eyes darted from her nipple to her mouth and back again. Sarah bent her head and aimed a stream of smoke at her own nipple. In the still air of the room, wreaths of smoke circled her breast. That focused his attention.

Sarah took her cigarette from between her lips and held it low, letting its smoke rise in a rippling veil over her breast. Her fingers reversed her cigarette, bringing its glowing tip close enough below her nipple that she could feel its heat. His eyes widened.

'Ashtray,' she said.

He took it from the table and held it for her. After she'd flicked her ash, she brought the filter end of her cigarette to her nipple and caressed herself with it. He spluttered in a most satisfactory way. While his eyes were riveted to what she was doing, she popped the last stud on her skirt's slit. Cool air caressed her tummy.

'Take it out,' she told him.

'Wha–?'

'Your cock. Take it out.'

'Yes, of course.' He unzipped and pulled out a very slender, very white, shaft. It was cute rather than impressive and might have been a rather thick king-sized cigarette. Could the similarity be the origin of his sexual preference, or just coincidental? The way he stood there with his cock hanging out half-erect, it looked as if he was unsure what he should do with it. Sarah let him wonder and smoked some more, ignoring his discomfort. It felt a little strange for her, taking the dominant role, but she let herself be guided by what she'd learnt from her research.

When she stubbed again, he snatched up the matches and held them ready. Very slowly, Sarah selected another from the box of identical smokes, inspected it and put it to her lips with, 'You may.'

'Thank you.' Once more, his hands trembled as he lit her cigarette. Seeming to gather his courage, he asked her, 'What may I call you?'

Sarah let her eyes narrow before replying, 'Lady Nicotine, of course.'

'Of course.'

Her next smoke ring circled his cock. It leapt in response. She directed a plume directly at its head. It twitched. Sarah filled her lungs, French-inhaled, and opened her mouth into a smoke-filled 'O'. Holding the smoke there, she brushed her dress aside, exposing her pubes and slit, reached down and inserted the filter tip between her pussy lips.

Her client buckled at his knees.

Sarah slowly masturbated herself with the cigarette. His cock strained and quivered. She plucked the cigarette out and held it up to his mouth.

'I don't,' he said.

'Do it!' she commanded.

His lips closed on the pussy-juice soaked end. He sucked. She returned the cigarette to her pussy.

He gasped, 'Oh God!'

She gave him another drag with the order, 'Hold it!'

He obeyed.

She pulled his face down to hers and told him, 'Kiss me.' As he did so, she sucked the smoke from his mouth, blew it back, sucked it again and then released it, their mouths an inch apart, to swirl about both of their faces. When she took his shaft into her free hand it was rigid.

With an aloof look on her face, she slowly pumped his cock while blowing smoke at it. He had to clutch the arm of the sofa to stay upright. By the way his thighs were flexing inside his trousers, she had him close to a climax but it was far too soon for that. The poor man was paying dearly for the smoking fetish experience of his life. She owed it to him to prolong his pleasure.

She said, 'There are drinks in the minibar. Pour me one.'

'Oh – of course. What would you like?'

Somehow, champagne didn't seem appropriate. 'Whiskey.'

'Should I get ice?'

'No, pour it straight up, for both of us.' Instinctively, she knew that he'd rather drink what she told him to drink than whatever he usually did.

When he returned with a drink in each hand, Sarah had another cigarette waiting to be lit. She made no move to take a glass from him. Looking confused, her client clunked both glasses down on the side table and hurriedly fumbled a light from the matchbook. Sarah arched back to take a glass. She took a long drag from her cigarette, drank half the whiskey in her glass, looked him in the eye and exhaled the smoke she'd been holding in her lungs while she'd swallowed. He seemed to like that so she did it again, draining her glass.

'You may drink,' she said.

'Thank you, Lady Nicotine.' He made the last word of her pseudonym three distinct and savoured syllables.

Sarah twitched her extended foot. Her pump fell to the floor. He glanced down at it, uncertain how to react.

'Put it back on for me,' she told him.

He stooped. His fumbling fingers obeyed her command, inserting just her toes and leaving the pump dangling once more. When he touched her stockinged foot, his face contorted with lust.

'Kiss it,' she said.

He pressed his lips reverently to her instep.

'Stand now.' Her cigarette was halfway burnt so she put it out and had him light her a fresh one, which she held in her left hand instead of her right. The first two fingers of her right hand took hold of his stem in the same way that she was holding the cigarette. She looked from one to the other, as if comparing. Sarah held her next drag in her lungs, applied her lips to his cock, sucked on it, withdrew and exhaled a plume, as if his cock had been a cigarette. He clutched the sofa's arm again.

Sarah repeated, cigarette, cock, French-inhale, cigarette, cock, plume, over and over. He was trembling from head to foot. Very subtly, she moved the fingers that held his shaft, gently masturbating him. His face turned purple. His legs stiffened, pushing his hips forwards. When Sarah judged that he was on the very brink, she stubbed her cigarette and moved the ashtray closer, just in time for him to grunt and ejaculate into the tray, on top of the ashes and crushed butts.

He staggered backwards. 'Oh! Oh!' The backs of his calves hit the armchair. He fell into it with a groan.

Sarah lit up again and waited. She was heartily sick of the smoke but she didn't let it show. Would he want to go again?

Her client recovered, stood and zipped himself. 'Thank you. That was . . . Most marvellous. Thank you.' He left the room.

Sarah butted out. The entire date, not counting her research and preparation time, had taken an hour and a half. Usually, she earned about a hundred bucks an hour plus tips. This time, she'd made twenty times that. When next she spoke to Veronica she'd remind her that she wanted any kinky fetishistic clients, provided they weren't dangerous or icky.

Those upmarket whores she'd seen in Veronica's waiting room – she bet that they never made $3,000 an hour by attending their silly parties.

22

'God I love this class.' Penny moved the books she'd used to save Sarah a front row seat so Sarah could sit down. 'Professor Trelawney really makes you think, doesn't he?'

Sarah nodded. Christopher, seated on Penny's other side, leant forwards and tapped his temple. 'I love to think, don't you?'

'Yes!' Penny hugged him. 'I'm going to miss you next year. Why don't you come to Berkeley with me?'

'Perhaps. It all depends on which fine institution of higher learning offers me the biggest scholarship. In the meantime we could spend the summer together, baking in the blazing Bajan sun,' said Christopher. He grinned at Sarah. 'You too, babe. It's time for some midnight love ...'

Sarah smiled. She'd given up trying to engage in playful banter with her friends in the moments before Jon entered the lecture hall. It was pointless. They'd figured out she had a mad crush on the teacher. Perhaps it was because every time she saw him Sarah blushed beet red. She could not help herself. Apparently, her sympathetic nervous system went into hyperdrive at the very scent of Jon.

'Sympathetic to what,' Penny had wondered when Sarah'd offered her clinical explanation for her flushed face.

'Her pudenda,' Christopher had suggested.

No, better to just sit quietly and let them amuse each other while she arranged her notebook and pen and tugged her short skirt down so her friends couldn't see the lacy tops of her fancy stayups.

'My love,' whispered Christopher, 'is like a red, red rose.' He grinned, then suddenly gaped at Sarah. 'Hey!'

Jon strode to the podium. Sarah dropped her pen. She leant down to pick it up and knocked over Penny's stack of notes.

'Shit!' Sarah almost never swore out loud. Why now? 'Sorry,' she said in response to Jon's raised eyebrow.

'Everybody ready? Let's begin,' he said.

Sarah tried to concentrate. Jon was, as Penny had opined, a terrific teacher and the material was nothing short of mind-blowing. Yet all she could do in his class was compulsively play their weekend together in her mind. He was the one. Why didn't he see that?

Or was she destined to fall in love with her clients, over and over again, mistaking business transactions for something much more. Something she might never have, if she continued in her present profession. The sound of the bell shook her from her reverie.

She glanced around, startled that an hour had passed. Sarah was gratified to see that she wasn't the only blank-eyed student. Boys and girls alike were transfixed by Trelawney's lectures.

As this was their last class of the day the three friends usually repaired to the student pub before heading home. Christopher had something to attend to so Penny and Sarah started off together.

'Come to Berkeley with me,' said Penny. She was on a crusade to get Sarah to at least apply to a few universities for the fall and the one she was heading to was top of the list. 'We could have a blast. Fun, sun and philosophy. I bet you could still get in.'

'Nah.' Sarah kicked the loose snow along the path to the pub. She always felt a little blue after her ethics class. She couldn't seem to shake Jon from her system the way she'd eventually managed to shake Jack. 'I'm sick of school.'

'I never thought I'd hear you say that,' said Penny. 'I thought you were going all the way, sister. Dr Sarah Meadows.'

'We'll see. Maybe later,' said Sarah.

'What's going on?'

'Nothin', why?'

'Lately you've become aloof again. I thought we'd really become friends.'

'We have.'

'So talk to me. I can keep a secret. If there's something going on between –'

'Between?'

'I don't know. Between you and Professor Trelawney. Or maybe you and Christopher?'

Sarah froze in her tracks. Trelawney? Christopher? 'Oh my God! I have to stop Christopher!'

'Stop him from what?' Penny called after her as Sarah took off at a dead run back towards the philosophy department. 'OK so I'll save us a table!'

Why, why, why can't I connect the dots? Sarah stabbed the button repeatedly even though she knew it wouldn't summon the elevator any quicker. 'Why do we do that?' she wondered as she gave up and headed for the stairs.

She'd seen the look on Christopher's face when Jon had entered the auditorium. But she'd been so flummoxed by the presence of her true love she'd failed to recognise what had happened. Her only hope now was to get to Jon's office before Christopher and . . .

As soon as she opened the door to the fifth floor she heard the sound of men arguing. Her heart sank, although if they were arguing it meant they hadn't come to blows – yet.

'Don't play cute with me, you pervert.'

'Get out or I'll call security.'

'Big baby teacher is afraid of the black kid from the Islands?'

'You're making no sense, Christopher.'

'You think it makes sense to mark my friend, your student's, ass the way you did?'

Fuck.

Sarah slipped in the open door and closed it behind her. 'Christopher, it wasn't him.'

She was just in time. Both men were standing. Christopher was rolling up his sleeves, something he never did because he was always cold. He obviously meant business. Jon's fists were clenched at his sides. He glared at her.

'I'm sorry Jon – Professor Trelawney.' Sarah glared at Christopher. 'It wasn't him. Got that through your thick skull?'

'But –'

'But nothing. Not him.'

'But –' The expression on Christopher's face would've been comical if the situation hadn't been so dire. 'He didn't . . . Those welts aren't from . . . I just assumed . . .'

Jon spoke. 'You assumed because I'm English that I'm responsible for the marks I've come to understand that my student, Ms Meadows, bears on her bottom?'

Christopher nodded miserably. 'That sums it up, sir. Very nicely, may I add.'

'From one island man to another, Christopher, I'd call that stereotyping.'

'Sorry, sir.'

'I never fuck with my students. Never.' Jon's tone was even, his volume low, but the look on his face was terrible to see. Still, Sarah noticed that he'd unclenched his fists.

'I understand, sir. I just wanted –'

'– to protect your girl?'

'I'm not his girl,' interjected Sarah.

'Then who –' Christopher gestured to her bum.

'Jesus Christ, Christopher,' she hissed. 'None of your business.'

'Right. OK then. I'm glad we cleared that up.' Christopher tried a friendly smile. 'Do you like chicken wings, sir? I'd be honoured if you'd join us, my treat, of course.'

'Go!' Sarah threw the door open.

'Again, my apologies, Professor Trelawney,' said Christopher. 'Should I wait for you?' He smiled sheepishly at Sarah.

'I'll be along in a minute. Get out.'

Christopher shuffled off down the hall, his head hung low.

Sarah shut the door. 'I'm sorry. He jumped to conclusions. I've never breathed a word about us. Not to anyone.'

'Nor have I, Sarah. But I applaud his desire to protect his friend.'

'OK, fine, we're friends with benefits.'

'Are they as bad as he says?' He tilted his head towards her rear, his face expressing nothing but a somewhat fatherly concern.

'You tell me.' Sarah turned her back to him and leant forwards, pressing her face to the wall and jutting out her bum. Somewhat to her surprise, Jon lifted her skirt.

He cleared his throat. 'I can see how the uninitiated might think this constitutes abuse. It is a rather severe set of marks. Quite professional. The crop?'

Sarah nodded. She glanced over her shoulder. His cheeks were tinged with pink. She already knew hers were blazing scarlet, she could feel the heat radiating from her face. But Jon, blushing? Surely he wasn't embarrassed. Envious? Excited?

He met her eyes with an even look. 'They'll fade,' he said. He let her skirt drop.

'They always do,' she said. Sarah turned to face him once more. 'Why the concern?'

'I'm concerned about the well-being of all my students.'

That stung. One more reminder of how little she meant to him. 'Right. Well, it's nothing. Business as usual.'

She opened the door and stepped out into the hallway.

'Sarah?' Jon hesitated in the doorway.

'Yes?'

'Be careful out there.'

'You bet,' she said, heading off to kill Christopher.

23

Sarah tapped the nipple on the baby's bottle against her wrist. The milk was warm but not hot. Perfect. Little Bengie had had his lunch and playtime. He should be ready for stories and a nap by now. She carried the bottle and the storybook she'd selected and returned to the pale blue and yellow painted nursery.

He seemed intent on his building blocks but when she entered he looked up with a beatific smile. One swipe of his fist and the tower he'd built was gone. He giggled with delight.

'Funny Bengie,' said Sarah. She settled in the oversized beanbag chair and tapped her knees. 'Come sit with Mommy and we'll have a story and a baba.'

'Baba!' Bengie lumbered on all fours across the room, gazing at her with the stunned delight of babies everywhere.

Veronica hadn't been kidding when she'd told Sarah this would be her strangest date yet. No sex, no discipline, no dirty talk. Just mommy and baby at home. Kisses and cuddles and pampering and playtime. Nonetheless, Sarah would've turned it down had Veronica not assured her that, pre-verbal though this baby might be, the precocious tot was fully potty trained.

So far, so good. She'd improvised madly for the first hour or so, thankful for the weeks her improvisation class had spent discovering the inner clown. That at least helped her be playful. The rest she'd tapped from TV and movie moms she'd liked as a kid: a little of the mom in *E.T.*, a smidgeon of Mrs Potts and a whole lot of Bambi's mother. As time passed and she became more comfortable in her role, she'd been able to relax into the scene and play an exaggerated version of herself.

It hadn't been easy, getting used to this big baby. He was about thirty, chubby enough to keep his baby face and little belly, but not fat. Still young, in the grand scheme of things, young enough to get past this and have a real relationship.

Sarah returned his affection with an adoring gaze of her own, doing her best to convey maternal love to this jumbo bundle of joy. 'Come up.' She tapped her knees. Bengie scrambled onto the beanbag chair and lay with his head in the crook of her elbow. It was a good thing her arm was supported by beans. The rest of him stretched from the end of the chair onto a futon on the floor. All in all, this nap area was surprisingly comfortable for both of them. Cosy even. She drew his blankie up over the sailor suit she'd changed him into after his messy lunch, and propped the storybook on his chest.

'Once upon a time . . .' she began.

'Baba!' Bengie frowned mightily.

'Poor baby!' Sarah covered his chubby cheeks with kisses. He beamed. She teased the nipple into his mouth. He gripped his baba with both big hands and sucked contentedly.

'Once upon a time . . .' she began again. She couldn't actually recall her mother ever reading her a story. It must've happened, although her parents had been busy, her dad with work and her mom with the National Organization of Women and their various causes. Her childhood had been similar to the one portrayed in the movie *Mary Poppins* – without, of course, the magical Ms Poppins herself.

It was easy enough to read aloud and allow her thoughts to wander, she discovered. She'd grown up in institutions of learning. A highly structured nursery school, then day care, then elementary school and so on to the present day. Until she'd moved out she'd been home for supper, homework and bed. Much of that time had been spent with her father as her mom was always on the phone or on the road.

What must it have been like when her mom had discovered that while she fought for the rights of the women her daughters would become she'd missed their childhoods? No wonder she wanted grandchildren now. Another chance to cuddle a baby. Who wouldn't want that?

She glanced at Bengie. His eyes were half-closed, but he was watching her. She jiggled her elbow a little, letting his head settle more deeply into the crook of her arm. It was mesmerising, this job of cuddling Junior.

Her instructions had been very clear. Once he fell asleep she was to hold him for at least fifteen minutes, then turn on the CD player so he'd have music to sleep by and let herself out. This funny day was almost over.

'. . . and they lived happily ever after.' Sarah closed the book and gently set it aside.

She stroked Bengie's cheek. 'Good little baby boy. Mommy loves her baby,' she said. Bengie cooed his delight.

'Hush, little baby, don't say a word . . .' Sarah began to sing the only lullaby she knew all the words to. It was a good one though. She rocked from side to side, lulling him to sleep.

What motivated him? Why did he want this so badly he'd turned one bedroom of his home into a nursery and hired someone to come play mommy to his baby? Was he healing some awful wound from his youth or just getting in touch with his inner child? Would he get better? Did he even need to get better?

She muddled the words to the song and focused all her attention on it. It was nice, anyway, to still her thoughts and lose herself in the moment. If Bengie wasn't genuinely sleeping he was very good at pretending to be. The nipple hung loose in his open mouth, the bottle almost empty. She tilted it up so he could finish it if he was so inclined. His lips sucked instinctively, then stopped. She tugged the bottle free and set it aside.

'Dear little Bengie,' she whispered. She brushed a soft lock of his hair free of his closed eyes. She rocked sideways, humming, being with baby for as long as possible. When her arm grew numb she slid out from under him as carefully as she could. She tucked the blanket up to his chin and turned on the music. A classical lullaby played.

When he awoke he'd tidy up everything and change into his

adult clothes, ready to face the adult world. But for now, Baby Bengie was sleeping like a cherub. Sarah felt tears prickling the backs of her eyes. He really was a dear little thing. She wasn't sure she was ready for the adult world, but ready or not it was clearly time to go.

24

The letters on the screen blurred. Sarah rubbed her eyes. These footnotes were killing her. But her final paper for her ethics class was due tomorrow and there was no way she'd be late with it. Sarah was deeply satisfied with the actual essay. She'd had to do a lot of medical research in order to link the indications of Asperger's syndrome with the prophets and philosophers of old. Much more research would be required to bolster her hypothesis in any true academic manner but she'd managed to present it with confidence and a certain amount of elegance.

She hoped it would blast right to the marrow of Trelawney's teacherly bones. Nothing but top marks would suffice. However, since a one-on-one interview with the professor regarding the final paper was one of the requirements of the course and she had no intention of fulfilling it, she needed a perfect paper to manage a top grade.

As she wasn't going on to do a master's, the mark didn't matter as much as it might have, but she was damned if she'd bring her brilliant grade point average down now. In a few weeks she'd be graduating and she fully intended to do so at the top of her class. She would have a Bachelor Degree in Philosophy, with Honours.

After she'd blown Jon's mind with her perfect paper and her perfectly presented bibliography and pages and pages of flawless finicky footnotes, she promised herself, she'd be free to blow her brains out. Which was what she felt like doing every time she relived the last time she'd seen him, his blushing student and one time bedmate, the one with the striped ass and the avenging suitor. Oh God. Oh Jesus. Don't go there.

Laboriously crediting Plato's works made Sarah think of Nancy and the New Year's party. Another fiasco, though they'd managed to salvage their clients: Nancy with the mister and Sarah with the missus. More than salvage them in fact; they'd requested a repeat visit from both girls. Her first double date was with the one escort Sarah loathed.

Still, it was time do a double and she'd decided to see girl on girl as just another kink. She'd give it her best college try. Not with Nancy, of course, she'd made that clear to Veronica, but if Caroline Pettifer wanted to play she wouldn't object. A frisson ran through her at the thought of their New Year's Eve make-out session. She wouldn't object in the least.

Her intercom buzzed. She hoped it was Christopher; she hadn't seen much of him in the last few weeks, her preference, not his, but she couldn't stay mad at him for ever. Not when it was possible that soon she might never see him again. She felt another frisson at the thought of her FWB. The voice on the other end disappointingly belonged to David 'no frisson 'cause he's fusty' Caruthers.

'It's me. Open the door.'

Sarah did as she was bid, albeit reluctantly. She had no time to waste. Sarah stayed at her desk, only swivelling away from her work when the door opened. She asked, as if she cared, 'How are the allergies?'

David looked terrible, like he'd just witnessed a fatal accident or a vicious crime. He dropped his jacket on the floor and stalked towards her. 'Is it true?'

'What?' Sarah paled. Her pulse thudded in her ears.

'Are you a hooker?' He grabbed her by the shoulders. 'Are you a whore? Tell me the truth.'

'Let me go.'

'Why? I'm told you like it rough.'

'And stop yelling at me.'

'Why? Should I be afraid you won't love me any more? You never loved me.' He released her with a shove, sending her chair crashing into her desk.

'I did!'

'Not since your goddam birthday. Look!' He pulled a ring box from his coat pocket and threw it onto her desk. 'I had it all planned. A surprise party for your birthday, your parents here to see me propose, a congratulatory glass of champagne, your first drink a toast to our engagement. How perfect is that? Your parents go to their hotel and I make love to you.'

'David, I'm sorry.'

'You're supposed to make the person you're trying to surprise think you forgot. That's supposed to work in the party giver's favour. Goddam it.' David banged his fist on the cupboard above her desk. It opened, revealing several bottles of hard liquor. 'Hah! Just what I need. Whiskey!'

'Be careful –'

'You shut up.' David unscrewed the bottle and tipped it to his lips. He gulped without gagging. 'You haven't answered my question.'

'I'm an escort. You saw the kind of work I do. Car conventions and –'

He shook his head. 'No. See, now you're just lying to me.' He leant over the back of her chair and grabbed a fistful of her hair. Sarah tried to shake him off but he was strong, surprisingly so. Slowly he turned her head up until he could see her eyes. 'Say it. "Yes, David, I'm a whore."'

'I can't,' she whimpered.

He put his free hand to her neck, holding her without constricting her breathing. 'How much are you worth?'

'It's not like that! I –'

'It's *exactly* like that.' The hand at her throat dropped to the buttons of her pyjama top. He flicked them open, exposing her breasts.

'Don't –' Sarah started pleading but his response was to shake her by the fistful of hair he still held.

'Sit still.' He dropped his head to her breasts and nuzzled each in turn, none too gently, before clamping his teeth onto first one nipple and then the other.

'Oh God,' moaned Sarah. Was her boyfriend raping her? She was incredibly turned on by his behaviour, but he wasn't acting, he was really pissed off. So why was she suddenly so hot for him? It was sick, sick but true. 'Kiss me, David,' she murmured.

'Shut up,' he said again. It thrilled her.

David lifted his hand. Sarah rose with it. He marched her to the bed. If she was going to put a stop to this she'd have to do so right now. No way. Sarah wanted to give him her best, not some dewy-eyed virginal fuck but a real roll in the hay. She wanted David's best in return. His anger was making him wild. She wanted that wildness inside her.

When they got to the bed he released her hair. 'Drop your pants, whore,' he said.

Sarah did so.

'Now get down on your hands and knees on the bed, head down and ass up.'

She did.

'Now beg for it.'

Sarah turned her head to see him. He was unbuckling his belt. Dear God. 'Please fuck me, David, please, I need you so badly.'

'. . . because I am a dirty slut who likes it up the bum.'

'Because . . . I am a dirty slut who likes it up the bum.'

'A cunt who comes for money.'

'I'm a cunt who comes for money.'

He unzipped his fly. 'A horny bitch who fucks for nickels.'

She'd never been so excited. Christ, how deep did her depravity go? This was not a safe game, not at all, but she could no more rein it in than woo him back. This was no make-up sex, this was goodbye, and if she let him go without taking this scene to its climax she feared she'd never forgive herself.

David climbed onto the bed behind her and spread her knees with his. He put his hands to the cheeks of her thankfully no longer bruised ass and split them as casually as one might split a peach. He spit on his thumb and used it to open her bum hole.

'David, I –'

'Dammit, slut, if you're not going to stick to the lines I give you then just shut up!' He smacked her ass with his free hand, a resounding slap, and then another.

There was a tearing sound, then fumbling. David was putting on a condom, likely for his own protection, not hers. She felt his jeans-clad legs up against her bare ones, his cock replaced his thumb at the entrance to her back tunnel, and then he was thrusting, hard, steadily deeper.

Sarah struggled not to cry out. She sensed that David had reached the very edge of sanity when he'd ordered her to be silent. She'd best comply. But the brutish way he was taking her made her want to scream for mercy. Instead, she screamed for more.

He grabbed her hips with both hands and fucked her ass hard and fast. 'Hold still!'

Instead, she bucked up against him. The zipper of his fly bit her inner thighs. In response he forced his full weight onto her. 'Still!'

Sarah fell forwards with David on top. When she caught her breath she mumbled into the bedclothes. 'You're the best.' She meant it. She managed to slip her hand between her body and the bed and rub her frantic clit. Otherwise, she stayed motionless beneath him, for once doing exactly what David wanted.

He grunted, pulled up and thrust again.

Sarah begged for more and got it.

David panted and cussed and fucked her harder. Faster.

Sarah's climax tore through her.

'That's it,' David groaned as he emptied himself of his seed and his rage and his terrible, useless need.

They were very still. No kisses, no words, just panting, which slowed and quieted until the room was perfectly silent. Sarah was sorry when her heartbeat returned to normal. She didn't want normal. She'd rather die than have to face her shame and his pain again.

David made it easy for her. 'I won't make trouble,' he said. He freed himself from her and struggled to his feet. 'But I never want to feel like this again. I never want to touch you again.'

'How did you find out?'

'I promised I wouldn't tell.' He tugged his pants up, zipped and belted them. 'But it makes no difference to me. Her name is Nancy. She came to my place, told me what was going on and sucked me off. I wore a rubber to protect my perfect cock from her filthy mouth.'

'I see.'

'I hope you do. I hope the image of me fucking her face stays with you for ever.'

'Did you like it?'

'No, I felt guilty.' He barked a bitter laugh. 'And confused. 'Cause I didn't know if I felt guilty for cheating on a whore, or guilty for cheating on a whore's sister.'

'My sister?'

David reached for his wallet. 'Which reminds me, whore, how much do I owe you?'

'Don't be silly.'

'Two hundred? Three?'

Sarah almost laughed. Instead she shook her head. 'Nothing.'

'I don't want a freebie, goddam it.' His voice cracked. 'Goddam it, Sarah.'

'David, come to my grad. I promised my parents –'

'Sure. I'll come. I've got my ticket. Just make sure you do not touch me.'

He walked out.

Sarah was stunned. David had blown into her room like a tornado and departed just as suddenly, leaving her dishevelled and confused. He was gone, really gone, out of her life at last.

She walked to her desk, picked up the open bottle of whiskey and gulped a mouthful. It burnt her throat. Jesus. He'd been a monster, a cruel, rude monster. She'd loved it.

What hope was there for her now? She might never have a boyfriend again, only clients who paid for her favours. Shouldn't she care? She picked up the ring box he'd left on her desk and flipped it open. The diamond was small but sparkly, surrounded by tiny glinting diamond chips. Tasteful, not terribly modern. She tried it on. It fitted.

David knew her. He'd done nothing wrong, aside from making the mistake of caring for her. She sat down at her desk. Shouldn't she cry or collapse or at least ache a little? She felt nothing. She was as removed from emotion as those people on the farthest end of the Asperger's syndrome scale, the ones whose case studies she'd examined as she prepared her paper.

The paper that was still due tomorrow. She glanced at the clock. Today now. Sarah went back to work.

25

Sarah slouched in the back seat of the car, glumly watching rain pelt the streets of Toledo.

Nancy sat beside her, methodically applying and blotting coats of red lipstick.

Sarah stifled a sob.

'Something wrong Sarah?'

'My boyfriend dumped me.' Sarah turned to watch Nancy's reaction.

Nancy paused mid-blot. 'Oh no! Why?'

'He wouldn't say. He just said we were finished. God, how I loved him.' Sarah choked out another sob.

'Poor thing.' Nancy tucked her lipstick into her purse and patted Sarah's arm. 'There's plenty of fish in the sea.'

'Not like him. I thought he was The One. My heart is broken.'

'It'll mend. You'll see. Anyway tonight should take your mind off it for a while. That Jason Pettifer is a doll. I wonder what he's into.'

'Veronica said he likes gags and blindfolds. I brought mine. Dunno what the wife likes though.'

'I don't do chicks.'

'I know. You keep him happy and leave the missus to me.'

'Right. Here we are. Get your mojo working, girl.'

The Pettifers' home seemed even bigger without a crowd inside it. Jason and Caroline were as gracious and gorgeous as ever. Dinner was a formal affair, with delicious dishes served by a silent staff, fine wine and clever conversation. Afterwards, the staff departed and the foursome ascended the Scarlett O'Hara staircase. The master bedroom, as massive as Sarah remembered it, had clearly been prepared for a night of debauchery. She needn't have bothered bringing a gag and blindfold, as the Pettifers had several of each.

Jason sat on a love seat by the bay window and pulled his wife onto his lap. They kissed and watched Sarah and Nancy examine the kinky collection spread across the black satin sheet that covered their king-sized bed.

'See anything you like?'

Nancy nodded. 'Plenty.' She picked up an oversized silicone dildo and tried to fit her mouth over the head. She shook her head. 'I can't even get this thing into my mouth!'

'Don't worry, dear,' said Caroline, 'that's not where we're planning to put it.' She and Jason laughed as Nancy's eyes widened. 'What about you, Sarah?'

'I like the look of this,' said Sarah, holding up a black leather harness equipped with a black rubber dildo.

'As the giver or the taker?' Caroline's cheeks were flushed.

Sarah shrugged. 'Whatever,' she said. Everyone laughed. She picked up the ball gag. 'Here's something for Nancy,' she said.

Nancy caught her cue. 'Oh yes, I just love being gagged,' she said, batting her lashes at Jason.

Jason jiggled Caroline off his lap. 'Take care of it, pet,' he said.

Caroline stripped Nancy and Sarah down to their gauzy bras, panties, stockings and heels. First she helped Sarah into the harness. Then she gagged Nancy and pushed her down on all fours.

'Come here,' ordered Jason.

Nancy crawled to him, swinging her hips and bouncing her boobs all the way. When she reached him she sat up and thrust out her breasts in a seductive pose.

Jason patted his lap. 'Up you get,' he said. 'I feel like giving Nancy a good spanking.'

Nancy shook her head vehemently.

'That's the way she likes it best,' said Sarah. She approached, exaggerating the swing of her hips so her fake cock wagged. She held a crop, the thickest, nastiest-looking spanking implement of the bunch. 'She's a real pain slut,' said Sarah. She brought the crop down across Nancy's bum.

Nancy squeaked. She glanced around wildly, as if looking for an escape. Sarah blocked her.

'She likes to pretend to resist,' said Sarah. She drew back her arm and delivered another stinging blow.

Nancy leapt into Jason's lap. She tried to wrap her arms around his neck but he grabbed her hands and flipped her over so she was face down. She started kicking wildly.

'Are you sure?' Jason glanced at Sarah.

Sarah nodded. 'Positive,' she said.

'Great!' Jason rubbed his hands with glee.

Nancy thrashed her legs. He caught them under one of his. She tried to cover her ass with her hands but Jason grabbed both her wrists with his left hand. He gave her defenceless bum a dozen staccato slaps, raising a pink blush on the pale cheeks.

'She really loves the crop, don't you, baby?' Sarah used the leather tip of the crop to raise Nancy's chin a tad so she could look in the furious girl's eyes.

Nancy glared at her. She shook her head violently.

'That means "yes",' said Sarah. She gave Nancy a big friendly grin. 'Oh yes! She's a whore for the crop.'

Jason held out his hand. Sarah had hoped to get in a few more strokes of her own first, but she complied, handing over the crop.

Jason eagerly began laying a good beating on Nancy, taking her moaning and tears as evidence of arousal.

Wasting no time, Sarah lubed her fake cock and mounted Jason's wife on the bed. Caroline's moans mingled with Nancy's muffled protests. Sarah channelled the exultance of revenge into her fucking. When Jason seemed about to stop cropping Nancy, Sarah urged him on. 'Caroline's close, Jason,' she cried. 'Don't stop now!'

Jason complied. Caroline's groans rose in volume, her voice mingling with Nancy's high-pitched whine.

Sarah slid her cock all the way inside Caroline and stayed there. She curved her body to fit Caroline's back and used her hands on Caroline's clit to drag the other woman to the edge of ecstasy and then topple her over. She wanted Caroline to have at least one orgasm and she suspected it wasn't going to be a long night.

'What were you thinking?'

Sarah and Nancy were back in Veronica's office. Craig was nowhere to be seen. Sarah didn't know if that was a good sign, or a bad sign.

'This time the Pettifers have made it very clear they'll not be using the services of Classique again. The two of you have cost me a very lucrative account.'

'She didn't have to scream bloody murder when he took off the gag. Nancy should've played along,' said Sarah.

Nancy piped up. 'I couldn't! I was in too much pain.'

Sarah shrugged. 'It's just a few marks.'

'Stand up, Nancy. Show Sarah what you showed me.'

Nancy did as Veronica bid, lifting her skirt to display a set of marks that would make the Marquis de Sade wince.

'They'll fade,' said Sarah.

Veronica threw up her hands. 'You leave me no choice, Sarah. We never betray each other like this. I'm afraid I'm going to have to let you go.'

'Nancy betrayed me. To my boyfriend.'

'Nancy?' Veronica turned her formidable frown on the other girl.

Nancy's cheeks flushed to match the colour of her bum. 'She said she didn't know why he dumped her. You lied!' Nancy glared at Sarah.

'Yep. I lied. He told me all right. He said you came over and said I was a whore and sucked him off. She sucked off my man.' Sarah gave Veronica a level look. 'And then he dumped me. So I arranged for her to be punished. Now, once again, we're even.' She rose. 'So let's get back to work.'

'I make the decisions here!' Veronica stood, pressing both palms to the surface of her desk. 'I say who gets disciplined, for what, and how. Not you.' She pointed at Sarah. 'I make the rules at Classique.' She pointed at Nancy. 'We never, *never* betray each other to loved ones. The penalty is instant dismissal. Nancy, you're finished at Classique. Get out.'

'No! Please, Veronica, don't fire me. I'm sorry!'

'I've made my decision. Go.'

Sarah sat back smugly. She'd half-expected the incident would result in Nancy's dismissal and she was glad. She'd had more than enough of the other girl's venom.

Nancy burst into tears. 'What will I do? I don't have any skills.' She turned on Sarah. 'You! You with your university education and your boyfriend and your sister and family and la-di-da look-at-me life! What do you know about anything? You steal my clients and you . . . you trick me at parties and . . . and get Jason to crop me till I'm practically passing out. Why? Why did you have to come here? Bitch!'

Veronica spoke into her intercom. 'Debra, call security, please.'

'No. No!' Nancy was on the verge of hysteria. 'What about my kids. Veronica!' She wrung her hands. 'I'm all they've got.'

'You should've thought of that earlier, Nancy. I've tried to be lenient, to take into account your . . . background . . . but you've tied my hands here.'

'Kids?' Sarah's mouth hung open in shock. Nancy couldn't be more than twenty-two or twenty-three years old. 'How many?'

'Two. Two kids with no daddy, no grandparents, nobody but me. Please, Veronica!' Tears coursed down Nancy's cheeks. She seemed about to throw herself to the floor and wrap herself around Veronica's legs.

Sarah stood abruptly. 'I didn't know Nancy had children,' she said. 'She's right, I really have no idea about anything. I'll leave instead.'

Veronica cocked her head at Sarah. 'Are you sure?'

Sarah nodded. 'I won't be the one to make children go hungry.'

Veronica shrugged. 'Fine. I'm sorry to see you go, Sarah. You had a promising future with us.'

'But I'm not a team player. I'm sorry too, Veronica.' Sarah opened the door.

Nancy put her hand on Sarah's arm. She was still shaking like a leaf. 'Thank you,' she said. She swiped at her tears with her free hand. 'I'm sorry about your boyfriend.'

'Just be careful out there, Nancy,' said Sarah. 'Use your head.'

Nancy nodded. 'I'll try.'

Sarah stood in the waiting room for a moment. Debra, the cool receptionist, held out her hand. Sarah took the time to erase the little movie she and Jon had made the weekend he'd been her client, then handed over the BlackBerry.

'By the way,' said Debra, 'don't get any ideas about striking out on your own. It's dangerous and won't be taken well by any of the agencies, including Classique. Got it?'

Sarah nodded. She didn't trust herself to speak.

The phone rang. Debra picked up. Sarah hesitated, reluctant to leave. Debra waved her away with one hand.

Sarah left. Her life at Classique was over as abruptly as it had begun.

26

'Are you sure of this amount?' Sarah stared at the slip of paper the bank teller had just handed her. 'Would you mind checking again? I deposited two thousand dollars a week ago.'

'It was two weeks ago,' said the teller, an attractive young woman in a business suit. 'And three cheques have been cashed against it since.' She pointed to the cheque numbers on the statement. Ah yes, Christopher's April allowance and the rent cheques for not just her room in the communal house, but Donna's as well. 'Also a few large payments made by debit.'

'Right.' Sarah glanced guiltily at her new purse, a little L.A.M.B. bag in bright spring colours. 'Thanks.'

She drove home. The Volvo purred like an old cat. Sure, it was in decent condition now, but how long would it be before something started rattling again? Why the hell hadn't she at least bought herself a new car when she had the money?

Now that she was no longer going to university, her huge student loan would come due. She wouldn't be eligible for her page job either. And she'd have to move out of the communal house as it was designated student housing. Her landlady had happily made a concession when she took Donna in mid-school year, but now both sisters would have to go. Where?

In a few days she'd have a Bachelor of Arts degree, Honours in Philosophy. What skill set did that suggest? She could think. And, thanks to her months as a Classique escort, she could fuck. She imagined herself in a job interview, wearing something similar to the suit worn by the professional woman who'd given her the bad news about her bank balance. Jesus, that girl had been no older than she. Sarah could think and she could fuck, and right now she thought she was fucked.

She had to park a ways from the house as Grad. was only a few days off and everyone was in party mode. The frat houses were practically hopping on the spot to the beat of the music pounding their insides. Kids with plastic mugs of beer hung out on the lawns and porches and patios, soaking up spring sun and yelling at passers-by. She was invited to have a beer with more than one drunken yahoo but Sarah declined, heading doggedly for home. These guys, most of them at least her age and older, seemed like children to her. Barely pubescent.

So her heart lifted when she saw Christopher sitting on the steps of her house. She hadn't seen much of him since he'd confronted Jon about her marked bum. That night, Sarah had stopped at the pub just long enough to tell Christopher that his debt to her was paid in full, so he needn't come by on Wednesday nights for 'tutoring'. Since then, they'd barely spoken.

He held a plastic cup of beer, sipping it absent-mindedly, his eyes glazed with the familiar fuzziness of the contemplative philosopher, but when he saw her the fog lifted and he grinned his familiar gorgeous smile. She smiled right back. Now that he was here in person Sarah realised how much she'd missed him. It was impossible to stay mad at someone as charismatic and loveable as he was, especially when that someone's mistake had occurred because he cared.

'Hey,' she said, plopping down beside him on the steps. 'Shares?'

He handed her the cup. She sipped and made a face. 'That's not lager.'

'It's keg swill,' he said. 'But it'll do.' He took a swig. 'I'll be drinking the good stuff soon.'

'I'm going to miss you, Christopher,' she said. She hugged him.

'I'm really sorry –' he began.

Sarah cut him short. 'Forget it. I really forgive you.' She squeezed harder. 'You were being a friend.'

'Too bad Perfesser T. isn't as magnanimous as you. My final mark was a B. You?'

'A.'

'But you didn't even show up for your tête-à-tête with Trelawney. That was worth ten percent!'

Sarah shrugged. 'My paper was perfect. Anyway, how do you know I didn't show up?'

'He said so.'

'He talked about me?'

'Yeah. He asked if you were sick or something, since you didn't keep the appointment. I said I didn't know.'

'Anything else?'

'Nothing else to do with you. We talked about my paper.' Christopher shrugged. 'Actually, I didn't deserve more than a B. He was fair.'

'Good.' Sarah took the cup from Christopher and had another sip. For a few moments they sat in silence, enjoying the familiar sights and sounds of the student body at play. 'Hard to believe it's all over. Though we still have Grad. to get through.'

'Not me. I fly out tomorrow morning.'

'You're not staying for Grad.? C'mon, Christopher! It won't be the same without you.'

'Time to get my ass back to the island and get to work.'

'Where?'

'One of my uncle's hotels. I get to pick my job because I'm family. Maybe bartender or maître d', maybe work in the casinos. You'd like that, I think. Dealing blackjack or baccarat. Big spenders, even in the low season.'

'I probably would.'

'So come with me. We can spend the summer together, really getting to know each other. In the fall you could go with me if you wanted or keep working for my uncle.'

'It's tempting,' she said.

'So do it! I think we have something, Sarah.'

'Me too. We have a great time in bed. And we're good friends. But . . .'

'I know. You think I'm too vanilla. I wish I'd known you liked it rough. I would've accommodated you.'

Sarah laughed. 'Thanks.'

'I never pegged the historian as a kinky brute.'

'It wasn't David. We broke up.'

Christopher's face brightened. 'Great! I mean, I'm sorry if you're sad but he wasn't right for you. So who –'

'Forget about it!'

'OK. Then just tell me why.'

'Why what?'

'Why do you like to be – you know – beaten?'

'I don't know.'

'Really. No idea?' Christopher frowned. 'Big-time thinker like yourself has no clue?'

'Not really. It's not about dealing with an abusive childhood. I know that much. It's not about low self-esteem. If anything, my self-esteem is a bit too high.'

'Maybe it's a relief to be debased.'

'Yeah. It's different, you know? I've been told I'm good and smart all my life. And I've believed it.'

'Well, it's true.'

'So fine. I think I just like to play that I'm bad and dumb. I think all the time, as you do. But when one is subjected to that kind of pain, and perhaps called a few degrading names as well, believe me, there's no cognitive thought going on. Just sensation.' She shrugged. 'How to explain what turns a person on? There's a lot of ways to express sexuality and I'm OK with it, whether I understand it or not. You know, as long as it's consensual, between adults. After that, I'm pretty much of a mind to say, "Whatever floats your boat," and leave it at that.'

Christopher stood. Though it was spring, he wore a sweater and jeans. He stretched long and slipped his hand into the front pocket of his pants. 'If you like it rough, I'm willing to give it a try. I looked it up online. I think it'd be fun to give you a spanking. Seriously. We can start right now.'

The term 'long drink of water' occurred to Sarah. What a doll

Christopher was! She could just imagine him in his home environment, wearing nothing but a pair of cut-offs. Yum.

Christopher produced a pocket knife and made a show of inspecting the trees on the property. When he found what he was looking for he started sawing at a thin branch. 'I'll give you a good switching, you little, um, bad girl,' he said.

Sarah smiled. It was sexy, watching him strip the leaves from the branch. And it would make a fine percussion instrument. She could practically feel it now. Maybe . . .

Christopher began switching the tree. 'Take that! And that! I'm Luke Skywalker and I say the Empire must die!'

'Christopher . . .'

'Who's your daddy now, Darth Vader! What's that? You're *my* daddy? Argh!' Christopher pretended to impale himself on the branch. It broke. 'Damn.'

Sarah went to him and stopped him before he could desecrate any more foliage. 'Your debt to me has been paid, Christopher.'

'I know. And thank you again for the loan.'

'It wasn't a loan.'

'Well, I intend to pay you back after I become a celebrity.'

'And as we all know there are so many celebrity philosophers around.'

'I'll be a first. Catch me on the talk-show circuit.' Christopher grinned. 'Come with me!'

'I can't. Thank you for the offer but I can't. Right now I have to take a break from relationships. I need to, I dunno –'

'Think?'

'Yeah.'

They laughed. Both knew that no matter what they did in the future, whether it be waiting tables in a diner or lecturing in an ivory tower, they would be puzzling over theories and concepts that most people never gave a first thought, never mind a second.

'Then this is goodbye for now, sweet Sarah Meadows.' Christopher gathered her into his arms.

His full lips covered hers. Rowdy kids began to spur them on with lewd comments and unnecessary advice. They broke apart, laughing.

'Amateurs!' Christopher taunted the hooting kids. 'Watch and learn!'

'Hey you,' said Sarah. 'Keep in touch.'

'E – me, baby.'

Christopher pulled her into another goodbye kiss. Again, it became something much more, a prelude rather than an epilogue. Again, the jeering students egged them on. But this time the kiss ended when Donna's scandalised voice snapped Sarah back to reality.

'What the fuck are you doing?'

Donna stuck her key in the door and opened it. 'Slut,' she hissed at Sarah. The door slammed shut behind her.

'Oops,' said Sarah. 'Donna!' Sarah chased her sister up the stairs, but Donna had had a head start.

'Go away!' Donna fumbled to unlock the door to her room. 'Leave me alone!'

The door opened, but not before Sarah reached her. Sarah pushed her way into the room behind her sister. Donna turned on her in a fury. 'Just because you pay my rent doesn't mean I'm not entitled to privacy.'

'I agree. But I want to explain.'

'There's nothing to explain. You weren't tutoring that guy, you were fucking him. Cheating on David when David's such a nice guy. Shame on you!'

'David and I broke up.'

'Oh. He found out? Not from me.'

'No, he doesn't know about Christopher. It was something else.'

'You're an idiot.' Donna flopped down on her bed. 'Mom was right about him. He *is* a keeper. You didn't deserve him.'

'That's true.' Sarah sat down beside her sister. 'We have to talk, kiddo. I lost my job.'

'Hmm.'

'You know we have to be out of here by the end of the month, right?'

'Yes.'

'Well, I don't know where we're going. Even if we find a place to rent, I don't know how we'd pay for it.'

'Mom and Dad will be here in a few days.'

'I don't want to ask them for money.' Sarah paled at the thought.

'That's not what I meant.'

It lay unspoken between them, like a curse that must not be uttered lest it come to be. Go home? All of them, back in St Paul?

'Fuck.' Sarah felt like crying. 'Oh fuck, fuck, fuck.' She gave her little sister a push and stretched out beside her.

'I should've got a job. I tried but there's nothing I want to do.' Donna pouted.

'What do you want to be?'

'When I grow up?' Donna grimaced. 'You'll laugh your guts out.'

'I promise I won't.' Sarah took her sister's hand and rubbed her cheek with it. 'Tell.'

'I want to be a housewife and mother who volunteers for worthy efforts in her spare time.'

'You want to be Mom?' Sarah giggled.

'Don't tell her. And don't laugh!' Donna snatched her hand back.

'But she'd be thrilled. She wants grandchildren.'

'From you. She expects everything from you – the career, the marriage, the kids. Because she thinks I'm good for nothing.'

'Yeah, well, I've got news for her. I'm good for nothing, too.'

'What do you want to be, Sarah?'

'Now that I'm all grown up?'

Donna nodded. This time, she took her sister's hand. 'What are your plans?'

'I plan to graduate,' said Sarah. 'After that, I have no freakin' idea.'

This seemed hilarious to both of them. They laughed till they cried. Then they simply cried, nose to nose, as sisters sometimes do, until they fell asleep.

27

'To present the philosophy department's Bachelor of Arts degrees, we're honoured to have with us Professor Jonathon Trelawney.'

Sarah wasn't surprised. There was a stir of pleasure among the black-robed students she sat among. He'd been a popular prof.

Jon approached the podium. He'd traded his customary tweedy look for a black suit, white shirt and striped tie. A few of the women in the crowd sighed audibly.

The MC continued his introduction. 'Seneca University has had the pleasure of Professor Trelawney's presence for a mere semester, but in that time he's become one of the most popular philosophy professors in the department. So it is with regret that we bid farewell to him and wish him good luck in his future endeavours.'

Applause. Jon smiling at the crowd. Jon shooting his cuffs and beginning to speak.

It was hot in the auditorium, but that wasn't why Sarah suddenly felt faint.

He was leaving.

'We'll start with the graduating students in the Bachelor of Arts in Philosophy, Honours programme . . .'

There was no time to faint or cry. She'd be up there in a moment, shaking his hand, taking her diploma from him. He must not see how shaken she was by this news.

Sarah watched the first student ascend the stage, stride to the podium, shake Jon's right hand with his, take the diploma with the left hand, and exit the stage on the other side. It looked impossible. She was growing huge, she could feel it, her bulk filling the chair in which she sat. She'd be stuck, unable to rise when her turn came.

Sarah fanned herself with her programme. Penny glanced at her as she rose from her seat in the front row. Sarah flashed her a thumbs-up sign. Penny ascended the stage.

Good. No need to infect Penny with her blight. Penny's last name was Dickson. From D to M – how much time did she have? God what was happening? OK. Talk it through. Quick. Maybe somewhere in her subconscious she'd harboured the hope that once she wasn't a student or an escort, she could date Professor Trelawney. Now he was leaving, so that hope, if she'd harboured it, had set sail. Deal with it. Now.

Penny raised her diploma high and shook it triumphantly as she crossed the stage. The crowd laughed. The next name was called. Greenwood. There weren't a lot of honours students. She'd be up there in a moment. Parents in the crowd. Sister. Make them proud. Just one more time, Sarah. Make them proud.

So the sadistic prick was leaving town. So what. There were others. She'd find someone else. Unless, like David, no decent man would want her now. She'd set up shop, maybe in New York. Make the bastards pay to punish her and call her filthy names. Do that until she was too broken to go on.

Sarah stifled a moan. Fucked. Sarah Meadows, fucked. OK, so Sarah Meadows Fucked, make 'em proud.

'Sarah Meadows,' said Jon.

She rose, ordering herself not to be huge. It worked! Sarah miraculously made it to the stage without tripping on her robe. Jon waited, degree in hand. Take it. Shake his hand. Down the stairs. Done.

Black-robed figures descended on the quad like a murder of crows. Mortar boards flew. The noise of hundreds of young people, free from the formal graduation ceremony and clutching, at last, their hard-earned degrees, was deafening.

Sarah joined her family. David was with them, of course,

playing his part. He stood stiffly as her parents and sister hugged and kissed her. Picture time! Sarah posed with her dad, with her mom, with both parents, with her family. She smiled and smiled for the camera. She posed with David, keeping her promise, not touching him. Penny joined them and a new round of photos began.

'Are you OK?' Penny patted Sarah's flushed cheeks with her palms. 'You look weird.'

'I am weird.'

'Aren't we all?' Penny hugged her. 'Keep in touch. I'm not kidding. If I email you and you don't – Oh my God, here comes Trelawney.'

'No!' Sarah clapped her hand over her mouth. 'Don't leave me.'

'Got to, babe. The future's calling!' Penny was swept away by the crowd, leaving Sarah alone to face Jon.

'Sarah,' he said. He touched her elbow. 'I need to talk to you.'

'Mom, Dad, this is Professor Trelawney.'

Her dad piped up. 'You're the one who took over when the existentialist went cuckoo, correct?' He circled his temple with an index finger.

Sarah willed herself not to be embarrassed by her family in front of Jon. Who was he, after all, but her ex-client and ex-professor?

Her mother sashayed closer, extending her hand to Jon. 'Thank you for everything you've done for my daughter. She worked terribly hard for years and years to get this degree.' She practically swooned as Jon took her hand for a moment. Who could blame her? Jon was a very handsome man. 'I'm her mother, this is our younger daughter, Donna, and Sarah's fiancé, David.'

'Mo-ther!' It came out sounding like the whiny complaint of an adolescent. Damn.

'Oh dear, have I let the cat out of the bag? Fine, they are as good as engaged. David is a teaching assistant here at Seneca.'

David left Donna long enough to shake hands with Jon, then retreated to Donna's side again.

'I didn't get a chance to talk to you about your paper, Sarah. Have you a few moments?' Jon tried to draw her away with his hand on her elbow.

'No.' Sarah shrugged him off.

'Ah. Well, I'd be happy to give you a recommendation for graduate school.'

'I'm not going to grad. school. I've left my job with the catering agency, too. I'm footloose and fancy free.' She gave him a bright smile. 'A will o' the wisp.'

'I'm surprised. About grad. school. Your paper was remarkable, as much because of your style as your ideas, although the concept, that this, um, Asperger's syndrome might have affected many of the great philosophers throughout history, well, it's – interesting.'

Mr Meadows interjected. 'Donna has Asperger's syndrome,' he said proudly.

'No I don't, Dad,' said Donna. 'It's too complicated. I think I just have allergies, like David.' She smiled up at David. 'We're allergic to pollen and lactose intolerant.'

'Let me get a picture of you with your professor,' said Mr Meadows.

'No, Dad. No thanks.' Sarah knew if a photo of the two of them existed she'd never get past the mixed-up way Jon Trelawney made her feel. 'But Professor Trelawney, would you mind taking a photo of us?'

Jon was visibly taken aback, but, as everyone gathered around Sarah, he gamely framed and snapped the photo.

'Thanks.' Sarah took the camera from him. Their fingers touched. Tears sprung into her eyes.

'I'm scheduled to fly out tonight,' said Jon. 'I'm going to –'

'Good luck, Professor,' she said, purposely cutting him off. The less she knew about his future plans, the better.

Jon looked as if he'd like to linger but there was no legitimate reason for him to do so. 'I guess this is goodbye then.'

'I guess it is. Goodbye, Professor Trelawney. It was nice knowing you.'

28

Sarah played her final line over and over in her head in the days following. 'Nice knowing you.' It gave her shivers of pleasure. She'd been cool, even arrogant and if her eyes had been a bit wet, well, it'd probably made them sparkle. She'd shown him!

She stood in the room that had been her quarters for most of the four years she'd been attending Seneca University. The furniture was still there, but without her things in it the room was already impersonal. She trailed her hand along the desk. He'd said her paper was remarkable and her ideas interesting. Ha!

It shocked her how much she hated Jon Trelawney. Rationally speaking, he'd done nothing wrong but her belly screamed betrayal. She didn't want food, couldn't handle it. She wanted revenge. Someday she'd stop hating him and then she'd be on the glorious road to recovery, but for now hate throbbed inside her with every beat of her heart.

Sarah checked the cupboard above the desk for liquor but she and Donna had cleaned that out days ago. Donna had made the move from the room across the hall to a modern one-room apartment. 'I got my Bachelor's too,' she'd said. Sarah smiled. David had helped Donna get settled and find a job. Sarah had managed to slip the diamond ring he'd left with her into the pocket of his raincoat. She had a feeling he'd be needing it soon enough.

She closed the cupboard. Too bad. She could use a good belt to get her through the rest of the day. Sarah noticed something odd lodged in the corner. She picked it up. A mouldy old crab claw. Not thrown away, after all, just lost. She shuddered.

She'd been a girl when she'd had sex with Jack. Nine months seemed like nine years. One night with Jack and she'd created a love affair from what was clearly a simple transaction, goods, her goods, for money. She'd made that mistake at the beginning of her call-girl career and she'd made it again at the end. Idiot. Sarah tossed the claw into the plastic bag hanging on the doorknob, grabbed the bag and left.

She descended the stairs slowly, glancing around at each level to see if one of her housemates was still around. After years of not particularly paying attention to who they were she was belatedly ready to chat. But she was the last one out.

No surprise that. She was probably the only one of the bunch who had nowhere to go. She'd shipped her stuff to St Paul but she had no intention of following it there. She was all grown up now. She'd go to the bus depot, pick a destination she could afford and climb aboard. Rumble off into her future. At least she had plenty to wear.

Sarah tossed her garbage into the trash. Her luggage waited for her at the front door. She grabbed the handle and started rolling it out to the porch. The communal phone rang.

For a moment she considered simply continuing on her way. Instead, she left her luggage halfway out the door and returned to pick up.

'Sarah.' The unmistakable sound of Veronica's sultry voice purred in Sarah's ear. 'I've received a special request for you. Triple your usual fee. Interested?'

29

Sarah looked right at home in the elevator of the posh Plaza Hotel. She was one of a few chic women with luggage, on their way up to their rooms. No one could guess that the room she was travelling to wasn't hers. It was Jack's.

It had to be. Veronica had refused to divulge the name but she'd clearly been pleased for Sarah. It had to be him. Besides, at that kind of fee she'd expected the client would want her dressed as an alien or something, but Veronica had said to dress for the surroundings, not the scene. 'Anything nice will do,' she'd said. It had to be him.

Had she conjured him up with that putrefied crab claw? She giggled but turned it into a cough. Giggling wasn't sophisticated. But why had he come for her now, when it was too late? Still, if the thought of him didn't make her heart sing the way it once had at least her pussy was purring. Jack was a lot of fun. Hopefully all he wanted was to exchange a wad of cash for a good fuck. Anything more than that would be difficult now. About as difficult as it was unlikely.

In response to her knock the door opened; the man on the other side was not Jack. It was Jon.

Sarah froze. He pulled her into the hotel room and shut the door.

'I hate you,' she whispered as he propelled her past the sumptuous living room and into the study.

'I know,' he said. He pushed her into the chair on one side of the desk and took the big chair behind it. 'But I don't know why. It doesn't matter anyway because we're here to discuss your paper.'

'My paper?' Sarah's voice squeaked. 'You're kidding.' She half-rose from her chair.

'Sit.' His voice was low but emphatic.

She sat.

'I shouldn't have given you an A in Ethics when you failed to appear for our appointment. I'll rectify that now.

'I found your paper interesting and the presentation fresh. Your ideas were clear, although some seemed a bit unsubstantiated. Nonetheless the topic is fascinating and some of the questions you propose in the conclusion, particularly the ethical question of *in utero* brain surgery potentially ridding the world not only of its greatest thinkers but of its most enlightened beings – well, these are good issues that bear further study.'

Sarah shrugged. 'So, study them. Feel free to crib from my paper all you like.'

His brows knit in a frown so fierce it was funny. 'That's not what I'm suggesting. I'm suggesting you continue your course of studies. Abroad.'

'Why abroad?'

'Because that's where I'll be. I've joined a think tank in Switzerland. The local university has an excellent philosophy department. Come with me.'

'I thought ... Didn't you already leave?'

'I came back for you.'

Hate drained from her body so quickly her limbs felt weak. She couldn't have left then if she'd wanted to. Which she didn't.

'Come with me, Sarah.'

'As your mistress?'

'As my wife.'

Jon was on the move now, coming around the desk to sit on it, close to her. Close enough to touch.

'You're kidding.'

'Nope.'

'What if I'm autistic?'

'So?' He laughed. 'That's your biggest concern? I don't think we should worry about it.'

'I don't relate well to people.' Even as she said it she recalled her Classique clients. Not the regular guys, but George in his wheelchair, Peter and his mink glove, the smoking fetishist, the swinging couples and Bengie, the infantalist. She saw their faces, knew their names. She cared.

'Not true. Anyway, you like me. Or you did.' Jon held out his hand. In it was a ring: three big diamonds marching along a gold band. 'I wanted to give you this when you came for our assigned meeting. Once you were no longer my student. But you didn't come.'

Sarah groaned. She plucked the ring from his hand.

'I tried to convince myself you were better off with your young fiancé, but –'

'David?' It was Sarah's turn to laugh. 'He's history.'

Jon grinned with obvious relief. 'I knew you didn't love him. But, do you love me?'

'What is love?'

Jon groaned. 'You're not going to make this easy for me are you?'

She shook her head.

'I have an answer.'

'I expect you do. What is it?'

'Plato talked about the three levels of pleasure, as I'm sure you know.'

'Of course.' Sarah spun the ring around the baby finger on her left hand, watching the diamonds sparkle. '*Eros, philia* and *agape.*'

'I spent my youth looking for the one woman who embodied all three levels. The first, sensual, or physical pleasure.'

'Sex.' She cut him a glance from beneath lowered lids.

'Right. The second, aesthetic pleasure.'

'Beauty.' She flashed him her sweetest smile.

'And relationship. Marriage.'

'Mmm.' Sarah stopped playing with the ring. She tilted her head. 'Level three?'

'Surprisingly, this is actually the toughest level. Also the highest. Intellectual pleasure.'

'Unsullied, if I'm not wrong, by physical interaction.'

'According to Plato, but I don't think it has to be the case.' He grinned sheepishly.

'What has this to do with me?'

Jon growled. 'I stopped hunting for her because I didn't think she existed. I rested. You came and lay your head in my lap. I love you.'

'How can you love me, knowing I'm a whore?' Sarah whispered it, but she said it.

He shrugged. 'I find I don't care. After all, I was your john. I'm as depraved as you. The question now is, do you love me?'

'Equally depraved. Level one.' She was spinning the ring on her baby finger again, watching the dazzling diamonds fly by.

Jon nodded.

'Equally attractive, level two.'

'I think you're being generous but yes, fine.' He nodded again.

'Equally intelligent?'

'Well. Potentially. I mean I am older than you and I do have a PhD –'

Sarah stopped spinning the ring. She frowned.

'Yes, yes. Equally intelligent. Level three.'

'Equals?'

'Absolutely. Except when I give commands to which you respond with slavish obedience because you need debasement and pain.'

She grinned. 'Yes.'

'Yes?'

'Yes, Jon, I love you. Yes, I'll marry you.' She slid the ring off her pinkie and onto her ring finger. It fitted.

He pointed at the floor. 'On your knees, bitch.'

She knelt.

'Suck my cock. And do a good job, or I might be forced to beat you with my belt.'

A pleasurable frisson of fear shivered through her body. It was starting. Her mind dumbed down as her hot spots ignited.

Sarah unbuckled his belt with trembling hands. She glanced up once, just to reassure herself that the emotion she'd seen in his eyes was still there. It was. Love.

Sarah's lips made a round, red, obedient 'O'. She set about delivering the last and the best blow job of her short, sweet career as a call girl.

Visit the Black Lace website at
www.blacklace.co.uk

LOOK OUT FOR THE ALL-NEW BLACK LACE BOOKS – AVAILABLE NOW!

All books priced £7.99 in the UK. Please note publication dates apply to the UK only. For other territories, please contact your retailer.

To be published in July 2009

GOING TOO FAR
Laura Hamilton
ISBN 978 0 352 33657 6

Spirited adventurer Bliss Van Bon sets off on a three-month tour of South America. Along the way there's no shortage of company. From flirting on the plane to being tied up in Peru; from sex on snowy mountain peaks to finding herself out of her depth with local crooks, Bliss hardly has time to draw breath. And when brawny Australians Red and Robbie are happy to share their tent and their gorgeous bodies with her, she's spoilt for choice. But Bliss soon finds herself caught between her lovers' agendas. Will she help Red and Robbie save the planet, or will she stick with Carlos, whose wealthy lifestyle has dubious origins?

THE SEVEN YEAR LIST

Zoe Le Verdier

ISBN 978 0 352 33254 7

Newspaper photographer Julia Sargent should be happy and fulfilled. But flattering minor celebrities is not her idea of a challenge, and she's also having doubts about her impending marriage to heart-throb actor David Tindall. In the midst of her uncertainty comes an invitation to a school reunion. When the group meet up, adolescent passions are rekindled – and so are bitter rivalries – as Julia flirts with old flames Nick and Steve. Julia cannot resist one last fling with Steve, but he will not let her go – not until he has achieved the final goal on his seven-year list.

To be published in August 2009

SEXY LITTLE NUMBERS

Various

ISBN 978 0 352 34538 7

Sexy Little Numbers is a choice cut of all new and original erotic stories and the latest addition to Black Lace's immensely popular series of erotica collections. This longer collection will contain even more variety and a greater range of female sexual desire than ever before. It will be the first of an annual collection of the best erotica stories written by women. Fun, irreverent and deliciously decadent, *Sexy Little Numbers* will combine humour and attitude with wildly imaginative writing from all over the world.

UP TO NO GOOD
Karen S. Smith
ISBN 978 0 352 34528 8

Emma is resigned to attending her cousin's wedding, expecting the usual excruciating round of polite conversation and bad dancing. Instead it's the scene of a horny encounter which encourages her to behave even more scandalously than usual. When she meets motorbike fanatic Kit, it's lust at first sight, and they waste no time in getting each other off behind the marquee. They don't get the chance to say goodbye, however, and Emma resigns herself to the fact that she'll never see her spontaneous lover again. Then fate intervenes as Emma and Kit are reunited at another wedding – and so begins a year of outrageous sex, wild behaviour, and lots of getting up to no good.

THE CAPTIVE FLESH
Cleo Cordell
ISBN 978 0352 34529 5

A tale of decadent orgies amidst the sumptuous splendour of a North African mansion. Nineteenth-century French convent girls, Marietta and Claudine, learn their invitation to stay in the exotic palace of their handsome host requires something in return – the ecstasy of pleasure in pain.

To be published in September 2009

MISBEHAVIOUR
Various
ISBN 978 0352 34518 9

Fun, irreverent and deliciously decadent, this arousing anthology of erotica is a showcase of the diversity of modern women's erotic fantasies. Lively and entertaining, seductive and daring, *Misbehaviour* combines humour and attitude with wildly imaginative writing on the theme of women behaving badly.

NO RESERVATIONS
Megan Hart and Lauren Dane
ISBN 978 0352 34519 6

Kate and Leah are heading for Vegas with no reservations. Both on the run from their new boyfriends and the baggage these guys have brought with them from other women. And the biggest playground in the West has many sensual thrills to offer two women with an appetite for fun. Meanwhile, the boyfriends, Dix and Brandon, realise you don't know what you've got 'til it's gone, and pursue the girls to the city of sin to launch the most arduous methods of seduction to win the girls back. Non-stop action with a twist of romance from two of the most exciting writers in American erotica today.

TAKING LIBERTIES
Susie Raymond
ISBN 978 0352 34530 1

When attractive, thirty-something Beth Bradley takes a job as PA to Simon Henderson, a highly successful financier, she is well aware of his philandering reputation and determined to turn the tables on his fortune. Her initial attempt backfires, and she begins to look for a more subtle and erotic form of retribution. However, Beth keeps getting sidetracked by her libido, and finds herself caught up in the dilemma of craving sex with the dominant men she wants to teach a lesson.

ALSO LOOK OUT FOR

THE BLACK LACE BOOK OF WOMEN'S SEXUAL FANTASIES
Kerri Sharp

ISBN 978 0 352 33793 1

The Black Lace Book of Women's Sexual Fantasies reveals the most private thoughts of hundreds of women. Here are sexual fantasies which on first sight appear shocking or bizarre – such as the bank clerk who wants to be a vampire and the nanny with a passion for Darth Vader. Kerri Sharp investigates the recurrent themes in female fantasies and the cultural influences that have determined them: from fairy stories to cult TV; from fetish fashion to historical novels. Sharp argues that sexual archetypes – such as the 'dark man of the psyche' – play an important role in arousal, allowing us to find gratification safely through personal narratives of adventure and sexual abandon.

THE NEW BLACK LACE BOOK OF WOMEN'S SEXUAL FANTASIES
Edited and compiled by Mitzi Szereto

ISBN 978 0 352 34172 3

The second anthology of detailed sexual fantasies contributed by women from all over the world. The book is a result of a year's research by an expert on erotic writing and gives a fascinating insight into the rich diversity of the female sexual imagination.

Black Lace Booklist

Information is correct at time of printing. To avoid disappointment, check availability before ordering. Go to www.blacklace.co.uk.
All books are priced £7.99 unless another price is given.

BLACK LACE BOOKS WITH A CONTEMPORARY SETTING

❏ AMANDA'S YOUNG MEN Madeline Moore   ISBN 978 0 352 34191 4
❏ THE ANGELS' SHARE Maya Hess   ISBN 978 0 352 34043 6
❏ THE APPRENTICE Carrie Williams   ISBN 978 0 352 34514 1
❏ ASKING FOR TROUBLE Kristina Lloyd   ISBN 978 0 352 33362 9
❏ BLACK ORCHID Roxanne Carr   ISBN 978 0 352 34188 4
❏ THE BLUE GUIDE Carrie Williams   ISBN 978 0 352 34132 7
❏ THE BOSS Monica Belle   ISBN 978 0 352 34088 7
❏ BOUND IN BLUE Monica Belle   ISBN 978 0 352 34012 2
❏ CAMPAIGN HEAT Gabrielle Marcola   ISBN 978 0 352 33941 6
❏ CASSANDRA'S CONFLICT Fredrica Alleyn   ISBN 978 0 352 34186 0
❏ CASSANDRA'S CHATEAU Fredrica Alleyn   ISBN 978 0 352 34523 3
❏ CAT SCRATCH FEVER Sophie Mouette   ISBN 978 0 352 34021 4
❏ CHILLI HEAT Carrie Williams   ISBN 978 0 352 34178 5
❏ THE CHOICE Monica Belle   ISBN 978 0 352 34512 7
❏ CIRCUS EXCITE Nikki Magennis   ISBN 978 0 352 34033 7
❏ CLUB CRÈME Primula Bond   ISBN 978 0 352 33907 2   £6.99
❏ CONTINUUM Portia Da Costa   ISBN 978 0 352 33120 5
❏ COOKING UP A STORM Emma Holly   ISBN 978 0 352 34114 3
❏ DANGEROUS CONSEQUENCES Pamela Rochford   ISBN 978 0 352 33185 4
❏ DARK DESIGNS Madelynne Ellis   ISBN 978 0 352 34075 7
❏ DARK OBSESSIONS Fredrica Alleyn   ISBN 978 0 352 34524 0
❏ THE DEVIL AND THE DEEP BLUE SEA Cheryl Mildenhall   ISBN 978 0 352 34200 3
❏ EDEN'S FLESH Robyn Russell   ISBN 978 0 352 32923 3
❏ EQUAL OPPORTUNITIES Mathilde Madden   ISBN 978 0 352 34070 2
❏ FIRE AND ICE Laura Hamilton   ISBN 978 0 352 33486 2
❏ FORBIDDEN FRUIT Susie Raymond   ISBN 978 0 352 34189 1
❏ GEMINI HEAT Portia Da Costa   ISBN 978 0 352 34187 7
❏ THE GIFT OF SHAME Sarah Hope-Walker   ISBN 978 0 352 34202 7
❏ GONE WILD Maria Eppie   ISBN 978 0 352 33670 5

BLACK LACE BOOKS WITH AN HISTORICAL SETTING

- [ ] A GENTLEMAN'S WAGER Madelynne Ellis — ISBN 978 0 352 34173 0
- [ ] THE BARBARIAN GEISHA Charlotte Royal — ISBN 978 0 352 33267 7
- [ ] BARBARIAN PRIZE Deanna Ashford — ISBN 978 0 352 34017 7
- [ ] THE CAPTIVATION Natasha Rostova — ISBN 978 0 352 33234 9
- [ ] DARKER THAN LOVE Kristina Lloyd — ISBN 978 0 352 33279 0
- [ ] WILD KINGDOM Deanna Ashford — ISBN 978 0 352 33549 4
- [ ] DIVINE TORMENT Janine Ashbless — ISBN 978 0 352 33719 1
- [ ] FRENCH MANNERS Olivia Christie — ISBN 978 0 352 33214 1
- [ ] NICOLE'S REVENGE Lisette Allen — ISBN 978 0 352 32984 4
- [ ] THE SENSES BEJEWELLED Cleo Cordell — ISBN 978 0 352 32904 2 £6.99
- [ ] THE SOCIETY OF SIN Sian Lacey Taylder — ISBN 978 0 352 34080 1
- [ ] TEMPLAR PRIZE Deanna Ashford — ISBN 978 0 352 34137 2

BLACK LACE BOOKS WITH A PARANORMAL THEME

- [ ] BRIGHT FIRE Maya Hess — ISBN 978 0 352 34104 4
- [ ] BURNING BRIGHT Janine Ashbless — ISBN 978 0 352 34085 6
- [ ] CRUEL ENCHANTMENT Janine Ashbless — ISBN 978 0 352 33483 1
- [ ] DARK ENCHANTMENT Janine Ashbless — ISBN 978 0 352 34513 4
- [ ] ENCHANTED Various — ISBN 978 0 352 34195 2
- [ ] FLOOD Anna Clare — ISBN 978 0 352 34094 8
- [ ] GOTHIC BLUE Portia Da Costa — ISBN 978 0 352 33075 8
- [ ] GOTHIC HEAT — ISBN 978 0 352 34170 9
- [ ] THE PASSION OF ISIS Madelynne Ellis — ISBN 978 0 352 33993 4
- [ ] PHANTASMAGORIA Madelynne Ellis — ISBN 978 0 352 34168 6
- [ ] THE PRIDE Edie Bingham — ISBN 978 0 352 33997 3
- [ ] THE SILVER CAGE Mathilde Madden — ISBN 978 0 352 34164 8
- [ ] THE SILVER COLLAR Mathilde Madden — ISBN 978 0 352 34141 9
- [ ] THE SILVER CROWN Mathilde Madden — ISBN 978 0 352 34157 0
- [ ] SOUTHERN SPIRITS Edie Bingham — ISBN 978 0 352 34180 8
- [ ] THE TEN VISIONS Olivia Knight — ISBN 978 0 352 34119 8
- [ ] WILD KINGDOM Deana Ashford — ISBN 978 0 352 34152 5
- [ ] WILDWOOD Janine Ashbless — ISBN 978 0 352 34194 5

BLACK LACE ANTHOLOGIES

- [ ] BLACK LACE QUICKIES 1 Various — ISBN 978 0 352 34126 6 £2.99
- [ ] BLACK LACE QUICKIES 2 Various — ISBN 978 0 352 34127 3 £2.99
- [ ] BLACK LACE QUICKIES 3 Various — ISBN 978 0 352 34128 0 £2.99
- [ ] BLACK LACE QUICKIES 4 Various — ISBN 978 0 352 34129 7 £2.99

BLACK LACE NON-FICTION

☐ THE BLACK LACE BOOK OF WOMEN'S SEXUAL FANTASIES ISBN 978 0 352 33793 1   £6.99
  Edited by Kerri Sharp
☐ THE NEW BLACK LACE BOOK OF WOMEN'S SEXUAL
  FANTASIES   ISBN 978 0 352 34172 3
  Edited by Mitzi Szereto

To find out the latest information about Black Lace titles, check out the website: www.black-lace-books.com or send for a booklist with complete synopses by writing to:

Black Lace Booklist, Virgin Books Ltd
Virgin Books
Random House
20 Vauxhall Bridge Road
London SW1V 2SA

Please include an SAE of decent size. Please note only British stamps are valid.

Our privacy policy
We will not disclose information you supply us to any other parties. We will not disclose any information which identifies you personally to any person without your express consent.

From time to time we may send out information about Black Lace books and special offers. Please tick here if you do not wish to receive Black Lace information. ❏

Please send me the books I have ticked above.

Name ....

Address ....

....

....

....

Post Code ....

Send to: Virgin Books Cash Sales, Random House,
20 Vauxhall Bridge Road, London SW1V 2SA.

US customers: for prices and details of how to order
books for delivery by mail, call 888-330-8477.

Please enclose a cheque or postal order, made payable
to Virgin Books Ltd, to the value of the books you have
ordered plus postage and packing costs as follows:

UK and BFPO – £1.00 for the first book, 50p for each
subsequent book.

Overseas (including Republic of Ireland) – £2.00 for
the first book, £1.00 for each subsequent book.

If you woulnd prefer to pay by VISA, ACCESS/MASTERCARD,
DINERS CLUB, AMEX or SWITCH, please write your card
number and expiry date here: ....

....

Signature ....

Please allow up to 28 days for delivery.